Rune sat the hard bench [...] those of lesser ranking performed. This time it was a little easier to bear; it was obvious from a great many of these performances that few, if any, of the boys had the Gift to create. By the time it was Rune's turn to perform, she judged that, counting herself and the first-place holder, there could only be five real contestants for the three open Bardic apprentice slots. The rest would be suitable only as Minstrels, singing someone else's songs, unable to compose their own.

She took her place before the critical eyes of the judges, and began. By the last chorus, they were actually nodding and smiling, and one of them was tapping a finger in time to the tune. She finished with a flourish worth of a Master and waited, breathlessly. And they *applauded*. Dropped their dignity and *applauded*

None of the contestants left the tent since the last trial began. Instead of a list, the final results would be announced, and they waited in breathless anticipation to hear what they would be. Several of the boys had already approached Rune, offering smiling congratulations on her presumed first-place slot. A hush fell over them all as the chief of the judges took the platform, a list in his hand.

"First place, and first apprenticeship as Bard—Rune, son of Lista Jesaril of Karthar—"

"Pardon, my lord—" Rune called out clearly, bubbling over with happiness and unable to hold back the secret any longer. "—but it's not son—it's *daughter*." She had only a split second to take in the rage on their faces before the first staff descended on her head.

—from "Fiddler Fair"

BAEN BOOKS by MERCEDES LACKEY

BARDIC VOICES
The Lark & the Wren
The Robin & the Kestrel
The Eagle & the Nightingales
The Free Bards
Four & Twenty Blackbirds
Bardic Choices: A Cast of Corbies
(with Josepha Sherman)

URBAN FANTASIES
Bedlam's Bard
(with Ellen Guon)
The SERRAted Edge:
Born to Run (with Larry Dixon)
Wheels of Fire (with Mark Shepherd)
When the Bough Breaks (with Holly Lisle)
Chrome Circle (with Larry Dixon)

THE BARD'S TALE NOVELS
Castle of Deception (with Josepha Sherman)
Fortress of Frost & Fire (with Ru Emerson)
Prison of Souls (with Mark Shepherd)

Fiddler Fair
The Fire Rose
The Ship Who Searched
(with Anne McCaffrey)
Wing Commander: Freedom Flight
(with Ellen Guon)
If I Pay Thee Not in Gold
(with Piers Anthony)

Fiddler Fair

Mercedes Lackey

Copyright © 1998 by Mercedes Lackey

"Fiddler Fair," in *Magic in Ithkar 3* (Tor 1989) "Balance" and "Dragon's Teeth," in *Bardic Voices One* (Hypatia Press 1988) (HC), in *Spellsingers* (DAW 1988) (PB); "Dance Track," in *Alternate Heroes*, Mike Resnick, ed. (Bantam Spectra 1989); "Last Rights," in *Dinosaur Fantastic*, Martin Greenberg, ed. (DAW 1993); "Jihad," in *Alternate Warriors*, Mike Resnick, ed. (Tor 1993); "Dumb Feast," in *Christmas Ghosts*, Mike Resnick, ed. (DAW 1993); "Small Print" in *Deals with the Devil*, Mike Resnick, ed. (DAW 1994); "The Cup and the Caldron," in *Grails, Visitations, and Other Occurrences* (Unnameable Press 1992); "Once and Future," in *Excalibur!*, Martin Greenberg, ed. (Warner Aspect 1995); "Enemy of My Enemy," *Friends of the Horseclans*, Robert Adams, ed. (NAL 1989)

A Baen Books Original

Baen Publishing Enterprises
P.O. Box 1403
Riverdale, NY 10471

ISBN: 0-671-87866-2

Cover art by Clyde Caldwell

First printing, April 1998

Distributed by Simon & Schuster
1230 Avenue of the Americas
New York, NY 10020

Typeset by Windhaven Press, Auburn, NH
Printed in the United States of America

Contents

How I Spent My
Summer Vacation

And every other free minute
for five straight years

After any number of requests to put all our short stories together in one place, the idea began to take on some merit.

When Larry and I looked into the idea we discovered that we had a lot of other short fiction; about ten years' worth.

Ten years? Unbelievable as it seemed at the time, I found the very first story I ever had published (I had sold one story before that, but it wasn't published until the following month). *Fantasy Book* magazine, September 1985. The story was "Turnabout" which was a Tarma and Kethry story, which is going into another collection. For the record, the first story I ever *sold* was for Marion Zimmer Bradley's *Free Amazons of Darkover* "Friends of Darkover" anthology, which was published in December of that year. The story was "A Different Kind of Courage."

Some of these stories are a little grey around the edges, but I include them as a kind of object lesson in writing. Some of the things in them I winced at when I read again—I had no idea of how to write a well-viewpointed story, for instance, and someone should have locked my thesaurus away and not given it back to me for a while! And insofar as the march of technology goes—the earliest were written on my very first computer, which had *no* hard-drive, a whopping four kilobytes—(that's *kilo*bytes, not megabytes)—of RAM, and had two *single* sided *single* density disk drives. I wrote five whole books and many short stories on that machine, which did not have a spell-check function, either. On the other hand, if ewe sea watt effect modern spell-checkers halve on righting, perhaps it that was knot a bad thing. It's just as well; if it had, it would have taken half a day to spell-check twenty pages. So for those of you who are wailing that you can't *possibly* try to write because you only have an ancient 286 with a 40-meg hard-drive . . . forgive me if I raise a sardonic eyebrow. Feh, I say! Feh!

I held down a job as a computer programmer for American Airlines during seven of those ten years, and every minute that I wasn't working, I was writing. I gave up hobbies, I stopped going to movies, I didn't watch television; I wrote. Not less than five hours every day, all day on Saturday and Sunday. I wanted to be able to write for a living, and the only way to get better at writing is to do it. I managed to slow down a bit after being able to quit that job, but I still generally write every day, not less than ten pages a day. And that is the answer to the often-asked question, "How do you become a writer?" You *write.* You write a great deal. You give up everything else so that you can concentrate on writing.

There are many fine books out there (the title usually begins with "How to Write . . .") to teach you the mechanics of writing. Ray Bradbury has also written an excellent book on the subject. You only learn the soul of writing with practice. Practice will make you better—or it will convince you that maybe what you really want to do is go into furniture restoration and get your own television show on The Learning Channel.

Here are the answers to a few more frequently asked questions:

How do you develop an idea?

Mostly what we do is to look at what we have done in the past and try to do something different. As for finding ideas, I can only say that finding them is easy; they come all the time. Deciding which ones are worth developing is the difficult part. To find an idea, you simply never accept that there are absolute answers for anything, and as Theodore Sturgeon said, "You ask the next question" continuously. For example: one story evolved from seeing a piece of paper blowing across the highway in an uncannily lifelike manner, and asking myself, "What if that was a real, living creature *disguised* as a piece of paper?" The next questions were, "Why would it be in disguise?" and "What would it be?" and "What would happen if someone found out what it really was ?"

Do you ever get "writer's block" and what do you do about it?

When I get stalled on something, I do one of two things. I either work on another project (I always have one book in the outline stage and two in the writing stage, and I will also work on short stories at the same time) or I discuss the situation with Larry. Working with another person—sometimes even simply verbalizing a snag—always gets the book unstuck. There is a perfectly good reason for this: when you speak about something you actually move it from one side of the brain to the other, and often that alone shakes creativity loose.

How do you do revisions?

I may revise the ending of the book between outlining and actual writing, but that is only because a more logical and satisfying conclusion presents itself. I am really not thinking of anything other than that. The only other revisions are at the request of the publisher, and may vary from none to clarifying minor points or further elaborating a minor point. In the case of clarification, this amounts to less than 1,000 words in a book of 120,000 or more. In the case of elaboration this usually amounts to the addition of 5,000 words to 10,000 words, generally less.

Would you call your books "character driven?"

I think that is quite correct, my books are character-driven. To me. How people react to a given situation is what makes a story interesting. History is nothing more than a series of people's reactions, after all, and many "alternate history" stories have been written about "what would have happened if." The idea—the situation—is only half the story. What the characters do about it is the other.

Do you base your characters on people you know?

With very rare exceptions I don't base my characters on anyone I know—those exceptions are minor ones, where I'll ask permission to write a friend into a walk-on role. They do come out of my observation of people in general.

When did you know you wanted to write?

I knew I wanted to tell stories from a very early age—in fact, I told them to the kids I babysat for, then wrote them in letters to friends and pen-pals. It was only when I "graduated" from amateur fiction to being paid for what I wrote that I realized I did have a talent for writing—and I had the will to pursue it. That was some thirty years later.

Where do you start?

Plotting is usually done with Larry, and one of the first things we do is determine what the characters will be like, then what the major conflict of the book will be. Then we figure out the minor conflicts, the ways that those characters will deal with those conflicts, and ways we can make their lives even more complicated. The resolution generally comes at that point, but not always; sometimes it doesn't come to us until we are actually writing the book, and we change the way it ended in the outline.

When did you start reading science fiction?

I started reading sf/f when I was about eight or nine. As I recall, it was the "Space Cat" books, followed by something called *The City Under the Back Steps*, a kind of ant-version of "Honey, I Shrunk The Kids," followed immediately by a leap into Andre Norton, Heinlein, and my father's adult sf. *Daybreak 2250 AD* by Norton was one of the first things I read, James Schmidt's *Agent of Vega* was another. Mostly I read Norton, all the Norton I could get my hands on, saving my allowance to order them directly from Ace. Little did I guess I would one day be working for Andre's editor (Donald A. Wollheim)!

Who were your influences?

In order of influence: Andre Norton, J.R.R. Tolkien, Robert Heinlein, Theodore Sturgeon, Thomas Burnett Swann, Anne McCaffrey, C.J. Cherryh, Marion Zimmer Bradley. As for editors, I learn something from every editor I have. My three main editors, Elizabeth Wollheim, Melissa Singer, and Jim Baen, have been incredibly helpful.

What do you choose to write?

I write what I would like to read, with a caveat—after thirteen years in the marketplace, I am beginning to get a feeling for things that will sell, so obviously I do tailor what I would like to write to the marketplace. I never wrote intentionally for any particular audience, but I seem to have hit on a number of things that are archetypal in nature, which may account for the appeal. The other possibility is that I tend to write about people who are misunderstood, outsiders . . . people who read tend to think of themselves that way, particularly sf/f readers, so they can identify with the characters.

Do you answer fan-mail?

When possible, we do. We *always* read it. When mail comes without a self-addressed stamped envelope for a reply, we assume the writer doesn't want a reply; it is only courteous not to waste the time of someone you supposedly like by including a self-addressed, stamped envelope if you want an answer. We don't answer abusive mail, but it does get filed in a special file for future reference. We return manuscripts unread; after some trouble Marion Zimmer Bradley had with a fan-writer, our agent has advised both of us that we can't read unsolicited manuscripts anymore. This is an awful pity, but life is complicated enough without going out and finding ways to add trouble!

How do you work with a collaborator?

Working with collaborators depends on the collaborator. If possible, we work on the outline together until we're both happy with it, then one of us starts, passes it off to the other when s/he gets stuck, and gets it passed back under the same circumstances. It goes incredibly fast that way, and it is the way Larry and I always work, even though he is not always on the cover as a co-writer.

Have you ever encountered any censorship?

I haven't encountered any censorship at the publisher/editor level on any of my books. I have heard rumors of fundamentalist groups causing problems with the Herald Mage series because of the gay characters, but I have never had any of those rumors substantiated. There are always going to be people who have trouble with characters who don't fit their narrow ideas of what is appropriate: I have perfectly good advice for them. Don't read the books. Nobody is forcing you to march into the bookstore and buy it. Actually, I have been considering borrowing the disclaimer from the game *Stalking the Night Fantastic* by Richard Tucholka—"If anything in this book offends you, please feel free to buy and burn as many copies as you like. Volume discounts are available."

What's Larry like?
I'll let him answer for himself!

Misty and I met on a television interview just before a convention in Mississippi; we were both Guests of Honor there. By the end of that weekend, we had plotted our first book together (*Ties Never Binding*, which later became *Winds of Fate*), and have been together ever since.

I am an alumnus of the North Carolina School of the Arts, and while there I made some fairly respectable inroads into the world of Fine Arts. However, my basic trouble with galleries was that regardless of the content of my work, it would only reach that segment of the population that went to galleries. I was "preaching to the converted." Couple that distressing truth with an irrepressible irreverence, and my days of wearing black and being morose for my art were limited. I needed giggles, I needed money, and I needed to *accomplish* something. I had been an sf and fantasy fan for years. When I saw the other people who were also fans, I knew that here was a place to be welcomed, serve an audience, and make a difference through entertainment. Ever since, it has been a matter of matching the message to the medium. Some lend themselves well to text, others to paintings, others to satire or dialogues.

I have been introduced to folks as "The other half of Mercedes Lackey," and there's a bit to that. I've been working with Misty on prose since and including *Magic's Price,* which I co-plotted and alpha-edited. Incidentally, it was accepted by DAW exactly as it is printed; there were no revisions or mispe . . . misspel.., uhm.., words spelled wrong. Since then I've worked on them all, with heavier co-writing on the subsequent trilogies. I'm not about to steal any of Misty's thunder, though—she is a mighty fine writer without me! Our styles, skills, and areas of knowledge happen to complement each others'. I also get a kick out of hearing old-fogy writers grousing about female fantasy writers, when I've been one for years now. *The Black Gryphon* was about my fourth or fifth co-written book (silently, with Misty), but was one of the first with a cover credit. Go figure. My future is inextricably linked to Misty, and I would want it no other way. High Flight Arts and Letters is flying strongly, and the best is yet to come.

You may have noticed that there is not a lot of really personal information in all of this, and that's on purpose.

Larry and I tend to be very private, and frankly, we find all the self-aggrandizing, highly personal "I love this" and "I hate that" in some Author's Notes kind of distasteful. We've included some historical notes on the various stories, and while I will be the last person to claim I'm not opinionated (see the note to "Last Rights" for instance) just because *I* think something, that doesn't mean you should. Go out, read and experience everything you can, and form your own opinions; don't get life second-hand from a curmudgeon like me!

I thought it might be fun to start this off on a lighter note.

This is an entirely new story, never before seen, and was supposed to be in Esther Friesner's anthology, Alien Pregnant By Elvis *(Hey, don't blame me, this is the same lady who brought you the title of* Chicks In Chainmail *by Another Company). For some reason it never got printed, and none of us understand why. Must have dropped into the same black hole that eats alternate socks and the pair of scissors you're looking for at the time the anthology was put together.*

Anyway, here it is now. Any resemblance to the writer is purely coincidental.

Aliens Ate My Pickup

Yes'm, I'm serious. Aliens ate my pickup. Only it weren't really aliens, jest one, even though it was my Chevy four-ton, and he was a little bitty feller, not like some Japanese giant thing . . . an' he didn't really *eat* it, he just kinda chewed it up a little, look, you can see the teeth-marks on the bumper here an' . . .

Oh, start at the beginin'? Well, all right, I guess.

My name? It's Jed, Jed Pryor. I was born an' raised on this farm outsida Claremore, been here all my life. Well, 'cept for when I went t' OU.

What? Well, heck fire, sure I graduated!

What? Well, what makes you thank Okies tawk funny?

Degree? You bet I gotta degree! I gotta Batchler

11

in Land Management right there on the wall of m'livingroom and—

Oh, the alien. Yeah, well, it was dark of the moon, middle of this June, when I was out doin' some night-fishin' on m'pond. Stocked it about five years ago with black an' stripy bass, just let 'em be, started fishin' it this year. I'm tellin' you, I got a five pounder on m'third cast this spring an'—

Right, the alien. Well, I was out there drownin' a coupla lures about midnight, makin' the fish laugh, when *wham!* all of a sudden the sky lights up like Riverparks on Fourth of July. I mean t'tell you, I haven't seen nothin' like that in all my born days! I 'bout thought them scifi writers lives over on the next farm had gone an' bought out one'a them fireworks factories in Tennessee again, like they did just before New Years. Boy howdy, that was a night! I swan, it looked like the sky over ol' Baghdad, let me tell you! Good thing they warned us they was gonna set off some doozies, or—

Right, the night'a them aliens. Well, anyway, the sky lit up, but it was all over in lessn' a minute, so I figgered it couldn't be them writers. Now, we get us some weird stuff ev'ry now an' again, y'know, what with MacDac—that's MacDonald-Douglas t'you—bein' right over the county line an' all, well I just figgered they was testin' somethin' that I wasn't supposed t' know about an' I went back t' drownin' worms.

What? Why didn' I think it was a UFO? Ma'am, what makes you thank Okies got hayseeds in their haids? I got a satylite dish on m'front lawn, I watch NASA channel an' PBS an' science shows all the *time*, an' I got me a subscription t' *Skeptical* Inquirer, an' I ain't never seen nothin' t'make me think there was such a thang as UFOs. Nope, I purely don't believe in 'em. Or I didn't, anyway.

So, like I was sayin' I went back t' murderin' worms an' makin' the bass laugh, an' finally got tired'a bein' the main course fer the skeeters an' chiggers an' headed back home. I fell inta bed an' didn' think nothin' about it till I walked out next mornin'.

An' *dang* if there ain't a big ol' mess in the middle'a my best hayfield! What? Oh heckfire, ma'am, it was one'a them crop circle things, like on the cover'a that Led Zeppelin record. Purely ruint m'hay. You cain't let hay get flattened down like that, spoils it right quick 'round here if they's been any dew, an' it was plenty damp that mornin'.

How'd I feel? Ma'am, I was *hot*. I figgered it was them scifi writers, foolin' with me; them city folk, they dunno you cain't do that t'hay. But they didn' have no cause t'fool with me like that, we bin pretty good neighbors so far, I even bought their books an' liked 'em pretty much too, 'cept for the stuff 'bout the horses. Ev'body knows a white horse's deaf as a post, like as not, less'n' it's one'a them Lippyzaners. Ain't no horse gonna go read yer mind, or go ridin' through fire an' all like that an'—

Oh, yeah. Well, I got on th' phone, gonna give 'em what for, an' turns out they're gone! One'a them scifi *con*ventions. So it cain't be them.

Well, shoot, now I dunno what t'think. That's when I heerd it, under th' porch. Somethin' whimperin', like.

Now y'know what happens when you live out in the country. People dump their dang-blasted strays all th' time, thinkin' some farmer'll take care of 'em. Then like as not they hook up with one'a the dog packs an' go wild an' start runnin' stock. Well, I guess I gotta soft heart t'match my soft head, I take 'em in, most times. Get 'em fixed, let 'em run th' rabbits outa my garden. Coyotes get 'em sooner or later, but I figger while they're with me, they at least got t'eat and gotta place t'sleep. So I figgered it was 'nother dang stray, an' I better get 'im out from under th' porch 'fore he messes under there an' it starts t'smell.

So I got down on m'hands an' knees like a pure
durn fool, an' I whistled an' coaxed, an' carried on like
some kinda dim bulb, an' finally that stray come out.
But ma'am, what come outa that porch weren't no dog.

It *was* about the ugliest thing on six legs I ever
seen in my life. Ma'am, that critter looked like somebody done beat out a fire on its face with a ugly stick.
Looked like five miles 'a bad road. Like the reason
first cousins hadn't ought t'get married. Two liddle,
squinchy eyes that wuz all pupil, nose like a burnt
pancake, jaws like a bear-trap. Hide all mangy and
patchy, part scales and part fur, an' all of it putrid
green. No ears that I could see. Six legs, like I said,
an' three tails, two of 'em whippy and ratty, an' one
sorta like a club. It drooled, an' its nose ran. Id'a been
afraid of it, 'cept it crawled outa there with its three
tails 'tween its legs, whimperin' an' wheezin' an'
lookin' up at me like it was 'fraid I was gonna beat
it. I figgered, hell, poor critter's scarder of me than
I am of it—an' if *it* looks ugly *t'me,* reckon I must
look just's ugly right back.

So I petted it, an' it rolled over on its back an'
stuck all six legs in th'air, an' just acted about like
any other pup. I went off t' the barn an' got Thang—
I ended up callin' it Thang fer's long as I had it—
I got Thang a big ol' bowl'a dog food, didn' know
what else t'give it. Well, he looked pretty pleased, an'
he ate it right up—but then he sicked it right back
up too. I shoulda figgered, I guess, he bein' from
someplace else an' all, but it was worth a try.

But 'fore I could try somethin' else, he started off
fer m'bushes. I figgered he was gonna use 'em fer
the usual—

But heckfire if he didn't munch down m' junipers,
an' then sick *them* up! Boy howdy, was *that* a mess!
Look, you can see the place right there—

Yes'm, I know. I got th' stuff tested later, after it
was all over. Chemist said th' closest thang he'd ever

seen to't was somethin' he called *Aquia Reqa* or somethin' like—kind've a mix a' all kinda acids together, real nasty stuff, etches glass an' everthang.

Anyhow, I reckon gettin' fed an' then sickin' it all back up agin jest made the poor critter 'bout half crazy bein' hungry. But next I know, Thang's took off like a shot, a headin' fer one'a my chickens!

Well, he caught it, an he ate it down, beak an' feathers, an' he sicked it right back up agin' 'fore I could stop 'im.

That made me hot all over agin'. Some dang idjut makes a mess'a my hayfield, then this Thang makes messes all over m'yard, an' then it eats one'a my chickens. Now I'm a soft man, but there's one thing I don't stand for, an' that's critters messin' with the stock. I won't have no dog that runs cows, sucks eggs, or kills chickens. So I just grabbed me the first thang that I could and I went after that Thang t'lay inta him good. Happens it was a shovel, an' I whanged him a *good* one right upside th' haid 'fore he'd even finished bein' sick. Well, it seemed t'hurt him 'bout as much as a rolled-up paper'll hurt a pup, so I kept whangin' him an' he kept cowerin' an' whimperin' an' then he grabbed the shovel, the metal end.

An' he ate it.

He didn't sick that up, neither.

Well, we looked at each other, an' he kinda wagged his tails, an' I kinda forgave 'im, an' we went lookin' fer some more stuff he could eat.

I tell you, I was a pretty happy man 'fore the day was over. I reckoned I had me th' answer to one of m'bills. See, I c'n compost 'bout ev'thang organic, an' I can turn them aluminum cans in, but the rest of th' trash I gotta pay for pickup, an' on a farm, they's a lot of it what they call hazardous, an' thats extra. What? Oh, you know, barrels what had chemicals in 'em, bug-killer, weed-killer, fertilizer. That an' there's just junk that kinda accumulates. An' people are always dumpin' their dang old cars out here, like they dump their dang dogs. Lotsa trash that I cain't get rid of an' gotta pay someone t'haul.

But ol' Thang, he just ate it right up. Plastic an' metal, yes'm, that was what he et. Didn' matter how nasty, neither. Fed 'im them chemical barrels, fed 'im ol' spray-paint cans, fed 'im th' cans from chargin' the air-conditioner, he just kept waggin' his tails an' lookin' fer more. That's how he come t' chew on my Chevy; I was lookin' fer somethin' else t'feed him, an' he started chawin' on the bumpers. Look, see them teethmarks? Yes'm, he had him one good set of choppers all right. Naw, I never took thought t'be afraid of him, he was just a big puppy.

Well, like I said, by sundown I was one happy man. I figgered I not only had my trash problem licked, I could purt-near take care of the whole dang county. You know how much them fellers get t'take care'a hazardous waste? Heckfire, all I had t'do was feed it t'ol' Thang, an' what came out 'tother end looked pretty much like ash. I had me a goldmine, that's how I figgered.

Yeah, I tied ol' Thang up with what was left of a couch t'chew on an' a happy grin on his ugly face, an' I went t'sleep with m'accountin' program dancin' magic numbers an m'head.

An' I woke up with a big, bright light in m'eyes, an' not able t'move. I kinda passed out, an' when I came to, Thang was gone, an' all that was left was the leash an' collar. All I can figger is that whoever messed up m'hayfield was havin' a picnic or somethin' an' left their doggie by accident. But I reckon they figger I took pretty good care of 'im, since I 'spect he weighed 'bout forty, fifty pounds more when they got 'im back.

But I 'spose it ain't all bad. I gotta friend got a plane, an' he's been chargin' a hunnert bucks t'take people over th' field, an' splittin' it with me after he pays fer the gas. And folks that comes by here, well, I tell 'em, the story, they get kinda excited an. . . .

What ma'am? Pictures? Samples? Well sure. It'll cost you fifty bucks fer a sample'a where Thang got sick, an' seventy-five fer a picture of the bumper of my Chevy.

Why ma'am, what made you thank Okies was dumb?

This story appeared in Deals With The Devil, *edited by Mike Resnick. Larry and I live near Tulsa, Oklahoma, home of Oral Roberts University and widely termed "The Buckle of the Bible Belt." We have more televangelists per square mile here in this part of the country than I really care to think about. Maybe somebody out there will figure out how to spray for them.*

Small Print

Mercedes Lackey and Larry Dixon

Lester Parker checked the lock on the door of his cheap motel room for the fifth time; once again, it held. He checked the drapes where he had clothespinned them together; there were no cracks or gaps. He couldn't afford to be careless, couldn't possibly be too careful. If anyone from any of the local churches saw him—

He'd picked this motel because he knew it, frequented it when he had "personal business," and knew that for an extra ten bucks left on the bed, the room would be cleaned *completely* with no awkward questions asked. Like, was that blood on the carpet, or, why was there black candlewax on the bureau? Although he hadn't checked in under his own name, he couldn't afford awkward questions the next time he returned. They knew his face, even if they didn't know his name.

Unless, of course, this actually worked. Then it wouldn't matter. Such little irregularities would be taken care of.

His hands trembled with excitement as he opened his briefcase on the bed and removed the two sets of papers from it. One set was handwritten, in fading pen on yellowed paper torn from an old spiral-bound notebook. These pages were encased in plastic page-protectors to preserve them. The other was a brand-new contract, carefully typed and carefully checked.

He had obtained—been given—the first set of papers less than a week ago, here in this very motel.

He'd just completed a little "soul-searching" with Honey Butter, one of the strippers down at Lady G's and a girl he'd "counseled" plenty of times before. He'd been making sure that he had left nothing incriminating behind—it had become habit—when there was a knock on the door.

Reflexively he'd opened it, only realizing when he had it partly open just where he was, and that it could have been the cops.

But it hadn't been. It was one of Honey's coworkers with whom he also had an arrangement; she knew who and what he really was and she could be counted on to keep her mouth shut. Little Star DeLite looked at him from under her fringe of thick, coarse per-oxide-blonde hair, a look of absolute panic on her face, her heavily made-up eyes blank with fear. Without a word, she had seized his hand and dragged him into the room next door.

On the bed, gasping in pain and clutching his chest, was a man he recognized; anyone who watched religious broadcasting would have recognized that used-car-salesman profile. Brother Lee Willford, a fellow preacher, but a man who was to Lester what a whale is to a sardine. Brother Lee was a televangelist,

with his own studio, his own TV shows, and a take
of easily a quarter million a month. Lester had known
that Brother Lee had come to town for a televised
revival, of course; that was why he himself had taken
the night off. No one would be coming to his little
storefront church as long as Brother Lee was in town,
filling the football stadium with his followers.

He had not expected to see the preacher here—
although he wasn't particularly surprised to see him
with Star. She had a weakness for men of the cloth,
and practically begged to be "ministered to." Besides,
rumor said that Brother Lee had a weakness for
blonds.

Lester had taken in the situation in a glance, and
acted accordingly.

He knew enough to recognize a heart attack when
he saw one, and he had also known what would
happen if Brother Lee was taken to a hospital from
this particular motel. People would put two and two
together—and come up with an answer that would
leave Brother Lee in the same shape as Jim Bakker.
Ruined and disgraced, and certainly not fluid enough
to pay blackmail.

First things first; Brother Lee's wallet had been
lying on the stand beside the bed. Lester grabbed
it, pulled some bills out of it and shoved them at
Star. The little blond grabbed them and fled without a word.

Now one complication had been dealt with. Star
wouldn't say anything to anyone; a hooker whose
clients died didn't get much business.

Then, he had helped Brother Lee back into his
pants; shoved the wallet into his coat-pocket (a small
part of his mind writhing with envy to see that the
suit was Armani and the fabric was silk) and draped
the coat over Brother Lee's shoulders. He could not
be found here; he had to be found somewhere neutral and safe.

There were car keys on the nightstand too; Lester had assumed they were for the vehicle outside. He had hoped there was a car-phone in it, but even if there hadn't been he could still have worked something out.

But there had been a phone, a portable; Lester dialed the emergency number, returned to the motel room, got Brother Lee into the car and got the car down into the street moments before the ambulance arrived. There was, after all, no harm in being rescued from the street—only in being taken from a motel room in a state of undress. He had followed the ambulance in Brother Lee's car, and claiming to be a relative, set himself up in the waiting room.

The reporters came before the doctors did. He had told them a carefully constructed but simple story; that he had met Brother Lee just that day, that the great man had offered his advice and help out of the kindness of his heart, and that they had been driving to Lester's little storefront church when Brother Lee began complaining of chest pains, and then had collapsed. Smiling modestly, Lester credited the Lord with helping him get the car safely to the side of the road. He'd also spewed buckets of buzzwords about God calling the man home and how abundant life was to believers. The reporters accepted the story without a qualm.

He had made certain that Brother Lee found out exactly what he had told the reporters.

He bided his time, checking with the hospital twice a day, until Lee was receiving visitors. Finally Brother Lee asked to see him.

He had gone up to the private room to be greeted effusively and thanked for his "quick thinking." Lester had expected more than thanks, however.

He was already framing his discreet demand, when Brother Lee startled him by offering to give him his heart's desire.

"I'm going to give you the secret of my success," the preacher had said, in a confidential whisper. "I used to be a Man of God; now I just run a nice scam. You just watch that spot there."

Lester had been skeptical, expecting some kind of stunt; but when the quiet, darkly handsome man in the blue business suit appeared in a ring of fire at the foot of Brother Lee's hospital bed, he had nearly had a heart-attack himself. It wasn't until Brother Lee introduced the—being—as "My colleague, Mister Lightman" that Lester began to understand what was going on.

Brother Lee had made a compact with the Devil. The "number one saver of souls" on the airwaves was dealing with the Unholy Adversary.

And yet—it made sense. How else could Brother Lee's career have skyrocketed the way it had without some kind of supernatural help? Lester had assumed it was because of Mafia connections, or even help from—Him—but it had never occurred to him that Brother Lee had gone over to the Other Side for aid. And Brother Lee and his "colleague" had made it very clear to Lester that such aid was available to him as well.

Still, there was such a thing as high-tech trickery. But Mr. Lightman was ready for that suspicion.

"I will give you three requests," the creature said. "They must be small—but they should be things that would have *no* chance of occurring otherwise." He had smiled, and when Lester had a glimpse of those strange, savagely pointed teeth, he had not thought "trickery," he had shuddered. "When all three of those requests have been fulfilled, you may call upon me for a more complete contract, if you are convinced."

Lester had nodded, and had made his requests. First, that the transmission of his car, which he had already had inspected and knew was about to go, be "healed."

Lightman had agreed to that one, readily enough.

Second, that his rather tiresome wife should be removed permanently from his life.

Lightman had frowned. "No deaths," he had said. "That is not within the scope of a 'small' request."

Lester had shrugged. "Just get her out. You can make me look stupid," he said. "Just make me sympathetic." Lightman agreed.

And third, that the sum of ten thousand, two hundred and fifty three dollars end up in Lester's bank account. Why that sum, Lester had no idea; it was picked arbitrarily, and Lightman agreed to that, as well.

He had vanished the same way he had arrived, in a ring of fire that left no marks on the hospital linoleum. That was when Brother Lee had given him the battered pages, encased in plastic sleeves.

"This is yours, now," Brother Lee had said. "When you want Lightman to bring you a contract, you follow these directions." He grimaced a little. "I know they're kind of unpleasant, but Lightman says they prove that you are sincere."

Lester had snorted at the idea of the Devil relying on sincerity, but he had taken the sheets anyway, and had returned to his car to wait out the fulfillment of the requests.

The very first thing that he noticed was that the transmission, which had been grinding and becoming harder to shift, was now as smooth as if it was brand new. Now, it might have been possible for Lightman to know that Lester's tranny was about to go—certainly it was no secret down at the garage—but for him to have gotten a mechanic and a new transmission into the parking lot at the hospital, performed the switch, and gotten out before Lester came down from the hospital—well, that was practically impossible.

But there were other explanations. The men at the garage might have been lying. They might have doctored his transmission the last time he was in, to make him think it needed work that it didn't. Something could have been "fixed" with, he didn't know, a turn of a screw.

Then two days later, he came home to find a process-server waiting for him. The papers were faxed from his wife, who was filing for divorce in Mexico. He found out from a neighbor that she had left that morning, with no explanations. He found out from a sniggering "friend" that she had run off with a male stripper. As he had himself specified; she was gone, he had been made to look stupid, but among his followers, he also was garnering sympathy for having been chained to "that kind" of woman for so long.

She had cleaned out the savings account, but had left the checking account alone.

But that left him in some very dire straits; there were bills to pay, and her secretarial job had been the steady income in the household. With that gone—well, he was going to *need* that ten grand. If it came through.

Late that Wednesday night, as he was driving back from the storefront church and contemplating a collection of less than twenty dollars, the back of an armored car in front of him had popped open and a bag had fallen out. The armored car rolled on, the door swinging shut again under its own momentum as the car turned a corner. There was no one else on the street. No witnesses, either walking or driving by.

He stopped, and picked up the bag.

It was full of money; old worn bills of varying denominations; exactly the kind of bills people put into the collection plate at a church. There were several thousand bills in the bag.

They totaled exactly ten thousand, two hundred, and fifty three dollars. Not a copper penny more.

He drove straight to the bank, and deposited it all in his savings account. Then he drove straight home, took out the papers Brother Lee had given him and began to read.

Before he was finished, his mind was made up.

The ritual called for some nasty things—not impossible to obtain or perform, but unpleasant for a squeamish man to handle and do. Dancing around in the nude was embarrassing, even if there was no one there to see him. And although he was certain that this motel room had seen worse perversions than the ones he was performing, he felt indescribably filthy when he was through.

Still; if this really worked, it would be worth it all. If. . . .

"Now how could you possibly doubt me?" asked a genteel voice from behind him.

Lester jumped a foot, and whirled. Mr. Lightman sat comfortably at his ease in the uncomfortable green plastic chair beneath the swag-lamp at the window. Lester thought absently that only a demonic fiend could have been comfortable in that torture-device disguised as a chair.

He was flushing red with acute shame, and terribly aware of his own physical inadequacies. Mr. Lightman cocked his head to one side, and frowned.

"Shame?" he said. "I think not. We'll have none of that here."

He gestured—not with his index finger, but with the second. Suddenly Lester's shame vanished, as if the emotion had been surgically removed. And as he looked down bemusedly at himself, he realized that his physical endowments had grown to remarkable adequacy.

"A taste of things to come," Lightman said easily.

"You must be a perfect specimen, you know. People trust those who are handsome; those who are sexy. Think how many criminals are convicted who are plain, or even ugly—and how few who are handsome. People want to believe in the beautiful. They want to believe in the powerful. Above all, they want to believe."

Lester nodded, and lowered himself down onto the scratchy bedspread. "As you can see, I'm ready to deal," he told the fiend calmly.

"So I do see." Lightman snapped his fingers, and the neatly-typed pages of Lester's contract appeared in his hand. He leafed through them, his mouth pursed. "Yes," he murmured, and, "Interesting." Then he looked up. "You seem to have thought this through very carefully. Brother Lee was not quite so—thorough. The late Brother Lee."

Lester nodded; then took in the rest of the sentence. "The—late?"

Lightman nodded. "His contract ran out," the fiend said, simply. "Perhaps he had been planning to gain some extra years by bringing you into the flock, but he had not written any such provision into his contract—and a bargain is a bargain, after all. The usual limit for a contract is seven years. I rarely make exceptions to that rule."

Lester thought back frantically, and could recall no such provision in his own contract.

But then he calmed himself with the remembrance of his loophole. The very worst that would happen would be that he would live a fabulous life and then die. That prospect no longer held such terror for him with the hard evidence of an afterlife before him. With the Devil so real, God was just as real, right?

That beautiful loophole; so long as he repented, merciful God would forgive his sins. The Adversary would not have him. And he would repent, most truly and sincerely, every sin he committed as *soon as* he committed them. It was all there in the Bible, in unambiguous terms. If you repented, you were forgiven. That was the mistake everyone else who made these bargains seemed to make; they waited until the last minute, and before they could repent, *wham*. He wouldn't be so stupid.

But Mr. Lightman seemed blithely unconcerned by any of this. "I'd like to make a slight change in this contract, if I might," he said instead. "Since Brother Lee's empire is going begging, I would like to install you in his place. Conservation of effort, don't you know, and it will make his flock so much more comfortable."

Lester nodded cautiously; the fiend waved his hand and the change appeared in fiery letters that glowed for a moment.

"And now, for my articles." Lightman handed the contract back, and there was an additional page among the rest. He scanned them carefully, including all the fine print. He had expected trouble there, but to his surprise, it seemed to be mostly verses from the Bible itself, including the Lord's Prayer, with commentaries. It looked, in fact, like a page from a Bible-studies course. He looked up from his perusal to see Lightman gazing at him sardonically.

"What, have you never heard that the Devil can quote Scripture?" The fiend chuckled. "It's simply the usual stuff. So that you know that I know all the things people usually count on for loopholes."

That gave him pause for a moment, but he dismissed his doubts. "I'm ready to sign," he said firmly.

Lightman nodded, and handed him a pen filled with thick, red fluid. He doubted it was ink.

He was the most popular televangelist ever to grace the home screen; surpassing Brother Lee's popularity and eclipsing it. His message was a simple one, although he never phrased it bluntly: *buy your way into heaven, and into heaven on earth.* Send Lester Parker money, and Lester will not only see that God puts a "reserved" placard on your seat in the heavenly choir, he'll see to it that God makes your life on earth a comfortable and happy one. He told people what they wanted to hear, no uncomfortable truths. And there were always plenty of letters he could show, which told stories of how the loyal sheep of his flock had found Jesus, peace of mind, and material prosperity as soon as they sent Lester their check.

Of course, some of those same people would have been happy to ascribe a miraculous reversal of fortune to their "personal psychic" if they'd called the Psychic Hotline number instead of Lester's. Above all else, people wanted to believe—wasn't that what both sides said?

He had a computerized answering service for all his mail; no dumping letters into the trash at the bank for him, no sir! He had a fanatically loyal bunch of part-time housewives read the things, enter the letter's key words into the computer, and have an answer full of homey, sensible advice and religious homilies tailored to the individual run up by the machine in about the time it took to enter the address. Every letter came out a little different; every letter sounded like one of his sermons. Every letter looked like a personal answer from Lester. The computer was a wonderful thing.

They could have gotten the same advice from Dear Abby—in fact, a good part of the advice tendered *was* gleaned from the back issues of Dear Abby's compiled columns. But Abby didn't claim to speak for God, and Lester did.

He also preached another sort of comfort—that hatred was no sin. It was no accident that his viewers were nearly one hundred percent white; white people had money, and black, yellow, and red ones didn't, or if they did, they generally weren't going to part with it. That's what his Daddy had taught him. He sprinkled his sermons with Bible quotations *proving* that it was no sin to hate unbelievers—or to act on that hatred. After all, *those* people had placed themselves beyond the pale of God's forgiveness. They had not and would not repent. They should be purged from the body of mankind. "If thine eye offends thee, pluck it out!" he stormed, and his legions of followers went out looking for offending eyes, their own blind to mirrors.

Most of his prosperity he owed to his own cleverness, but there were times when he needed that little helping hand—just as he had thought he might. Like the time when his network of informers let him know that *Newsweek* had found his ex-wife, and she was going to spill some embarrassing things about him. Or that one of his many ex-mistresses was going to write a tell-all biography. Or that the IRS was planning an audit.

All he had to do was whisper Lightman's name, and his request, and by midnight, it was taken care of.

By twelve-oh-one, he was truly, sincerely, repenting that he had ordered his wife's murder—or whatever other little thing he had requested. Truly, sincerely, and deeply, confessing himself to God and showing that repentance in concrete sacrifices of tears and cash. From the beginning, he had told himself that he *was* acting on God's behalf, spitting in the face of Satan by tricking the Great Trickster. He told himself every time he prayed that he *was* working for God.

It was a foolproof scheme, and the seven years flew by. During the last year, he was cautious, but resigned. He knew that Lightman would arrange for his death, so there was no point in trying to avoid it. And, indeed, on the very instant of the seventh-year anniversary of the contract, he had a heart attack. As he prayed before his video-congregation. Just like Brother Lee.

✧   ✧   ✧

Lester stood beside the body in the expensive hospital bed and stared down at it. The monitors were mostly flatlined; the only ones showing any activity were those reporting functions that had been taken over by machines. *Strange,* he thought. The man in the bed looked so healthy.

"Ah, Lester, you're right on time," Lightman said genially, stepping around from behind a curtain.

Lester shrugged. "Is there any reason why I shouldn't be?" he asked, just as genially. He could afford to be genial; after all, he wasn't going to be leaving with Lightman.

"What, no screaming, no crying, no begging?" Lightman seemed genuinely surprised. "Normally your kind are the worst—"

Lester only chuckled. "Why should I be worried?" he replied. "You only *think* you have me. But I repented of every single one of those crimes I asked you to commit. Every death, every blackmail scheme, every disgrace—I even repented the small things, repented every time I accepted someone's Social Security check—every time I arranged a special-effects miracle or convinced someone to leave me everything in their will—"

But he stopped as Lightman began laughing. "Oh yes, you did," Lightman told him merrily. "And my Opponent has forgiven you for those sins. But *you* didn't read the fine print." He handed Lester the copy of his contract, and pointed to the last page. "Read the commentary, dear boy. Carefully, this time."

The words leapt off the page at him.

Sins repented will be forgiven by the Opposition, but forgiveness does not imply repayment. All sins committed by the party of the first part must be repaid to the party of the second part regardless of whether or not forgiveness has been obtained.

"These are the sins you'll be repaying, my boy," Lightman said pleasantly, waving his hand. A stack of computer forms as tall as Lester appeared beside him. "But that is not why I am truly pleased to have you among us—"

Another stack of computer forms appeared, impossibly high, reaching up as far as Lester could see, millions of them.

"This stack—" Lightman placed his hand on the first pile "—represents all the sins you committed directly. But *this* pile represents all those you encouraged others to commit, with your doctrine of salvation through donation and hate-thy-neighbor. And those, dear boy, you did not repent of. You are a credit to our side! And we will be so happy to have you with us!"

The floor opened up, and Lightman stood in midair. "Learn to enjoy it, dear Lester," he chuckled, as the demons drew the false prophet down among them. "You'll reach your depth soon enough."

Lightman smiled as the mountain of sin forms buried Lester Parker. "So I believe."

*Larry and I are members of the North American Fal-
conry Association and federally licensed raptor (bird of
prey) rehabilitators. We have to be pragmatic and scien-
tific—when you take care of predatory birds, they eat
meat, and when you teach them to hunt so that they can
be released, they have to learn how to make kills on their
own. There is no shortcut for that process, and no way to
"fake" making a kill. Needless to say, we Do Not Do
Politically Correct, although we have not (yet) suffered
harassment at the hands of people with Way Too Much
Spare Time On Their Hands that some other rehabbers and
fellow falconers have. Nevertheless, we've gotten very tired
of seeing people who have never lived next to a field of
cattle claim that cows are gentle, harmless, and intelligent—
or try to raise their dogs on a vegetarian diet. So when
Mike Resnick asked us for a story for* Dinosaur Fantastic,
we knew immediately what we were going to write for him.

Last Rights

Mercedes Lackey and Larry Dixon

Two men and a woman huddled in the wet bushes
surrounding the GenTech Engineering facility in Los
Lobos, California. Across the darkened expanse of
expensive GenTech Grasite lay their goal; the
GenTech Large Animal Development Project. It was
"Grasite," not "grass"; this first product of GenTech's

researches was a plant that was drought-resistant, seldom needed mowing, and remained green even when dry; perfect for Southern California. Sadly, it also attracted grasshoppers who seemed to be fooled by its verdant appearance; they would remain on a Grasite lawn, hordes of them, trying valiantly to extract nourishment from something the texture and consistency of Astroturf, all during the worst droughts. Anyone holding a garden party in Hollywood had better plan on scheduling CritterVac to come in and sweep the premises clean or his guests would find every step they took crunching into a dozen insects, lending the soiree all the elegance of the wrath of Moses.

But Grasite was not the target tonight; these three had no argument with gene-tailored plantlife. In fact, they strongly supported many of GenTech's products— RealSkin, which reacted to allergens and irritants exactly the way human skin did, or Steak'N'Taters, a tuber with the consistency and taste of a cross between beef and baked potato. But all three of them were outraged by this assault upon helpless animals that GenTech was perpetrating in their new development lab—

Mary Lang, Howard Emory, and Ken Jacobs were self-styled "guerrillas" in defense of helpless beasties everywhere, charter members of Persons In Defense of Animo-beings; P.I.D.A. for short. There was nothing they would not do to secure the rights of exploited and abused animals. This year alone they, personally, had already chalked up the release of several hundred prisoner-rats from a lab in Lisle, Illinois. It was too bad about the mutated bubonic plague spreading through Chicago afterwards, but as Ken said, people had choices, the rats didn't. Tonight, they were after bigger game.

DinoSaurians. Patent Pending.

Real, living, breathing dinosaurs—slated to become

P.O.Z.s (Prisoners of Zoos) the world over. And all because some corporate MBA on the Board of the San Diego Zoo had seen the attendance numbers soar when the Dunn traveling animated dinosaur exhibit had been booked there for a month. He had put that together with the discovery that common chickens and other creatures could be regressed to their saurian ancestors—the pioneering work had already been done on the eohippus and aurochs— and had seen a goldmine waiting for both the zoos and GenTech.

"How could they do this to me?" Mary whined. "They had such a promising record! I was going to ask them for a corporate donation! And now—this—"

"Money," Ken hissed. "They're all money-grubbing bastards, who don't care if they sell poor animals into a life of penal servitude. Just wait; next thing you'll be seeing is DinoBurgers."

Howard winced, and pulled the collar of his unbleached cotton jacket higher. "So, what have we got?" he asked. "What's the plan?"

Ken consulted the layout of the facility and the outdoor pens. It had been ridiculously easy to get them; for all the furor over the DinoSaurians, there was remarkably little security on this facility. Only signs, hundreds of them, warning of "DANGEROUS ANIMALS." Ridiculous. As if members of P.I.D.A. would be taken in by such blatant nonsense! There was no such thing as a dangerous animal; only an animal forced to act outside of its peaceful nature. "There are only three dino-animopersons at the moment, and if we can release all three of them, it will represent such a huge loss to GenTech that I doubt they'll ever want to create more. There's a BrontoSaurian here—" He pointed at a tiny pen on the far northern corner of the map. "It's inside a special pen with heavy-duty electric fences and alarms around it, so that will be your target, Howard. You're the alarms expert."

Howard looked over Ken's shoulder, and winced again. "That pen isn't even big enough for a horse to move around in!" he exclaimed. "This is inhuman! It's veal calves all over again!"

Ken tilted the map towards Mary. "There's something here called a 'Dinonychus' that's supposed to be going to the San Diego Zoo. It looks like they've put it in some kind of a bare corral. You worked with turning loose the rodeo horses and bulls last year, so you take this one, Mary."

Mary Lang nodded, and tried not to show her relief. The corral didn't look too difficult to get into, and from the plans, all she'd have to do would be to open the corral gate and the animal would run for freedom. "Very active" was the note photocopied along with the map. That was fine; the rodeo horses hadn't wanted to leave their pens, and it had taken *forever* to get them to move. And she'd gotten horsecrap all over her expensive synthetic suede pants.

"That leaves the Tricerotops in the big pasture to me." Ken folded the map once they had all memorized the way in. "Meet you here in an hour. Those poor exploited victims of corporate humanocentrism are already halfway to freedom. We'll show the corporate fat cats that they can't live off the misery of tortured, helpless animals!"

Howard had never seen so many alarms and electric shock devices in his life. He thought at first that they were meant to keep people out—but all the detectors pointed inward, not outward, so they had all been intended to keep this pathetic BrontoSaurian trapped inside his little box.

Howard's blood pressure rose by at least ten points when he saw the victim; they were keeping it inside a bare concrete pen, with no educational toys, nothing to look at, no variation in its environment at all. It looked like the way they used to pen "killer" elephants in the bad old days; the only difference was that this BrontoSaurian wasn't chained by one ankle. There was barely enough room for the creature to turn around; no room at all for it to lie down. There was nothing else in the pen but a huge pile of green vegetation at one end and an equally large pile of droppings at the other.

Good God, he thought, appalled, *Don't they even clean the cage?*

As he watched, the BrontoSaurian dropped its tiny head, curved its long, flexible neck, and helped itself to a mouthful of greenery. As the head rose, jaws chewing placidly, another barrel of droppings added itself to the pile from the other end of the beast.

The BrontoSaurian seemed to be perfect for making fertilizer, if nothing else.

Well, soon he would be fertilizing the acreage of the Los Lobos National Park, free and happy, and the memory of this dank, cramped prison would be a thing of the past.

Howard disabled the last of the alarms and shock fences, pulled open the gates, and stepped aside, proudly waiting for the magnificent creature to take its first steps into freedom.

The magnificent creature dropped its head, curved its neck, and helped itself to another mouthful of greenery. As the head rose, jaws chewing placidly, it took no note of the open gates just past its nose.

"Come on, big boy!" Howard shouted, waving at it.

It ignored him.

He dared to venture into the pen.

It continued to ignore him. Periodically it would take another mouthful and drop a pile, but except for that, it could just as well have been one of the mechanical dinosaurs it was supposed to replace.

Howard spent the next half hour trying, with diminishing patience, to get the BrontoSaurian to leave. It didn't even *look* at him, or the open door, or anything at all except the pile of juicy banana leaves and green hay in front of it. Finally, Howard couldn't take it any longer.

His blood-pressure rising, he seized the electric cattle prod on the back wall, and let the stupid beast have a good one, right in the backside.

As soon as he jolted the poor thing, his conscience struck him a blow that was nearly as hard. He dropped the prod as if it had shocked *him,* and wrapped his arms around the beast's huge leg, babbling apologies.

Approximately one minute later, while Howard was still crying into the leathery skin of the Bronto's leg, it noticed that it had been stung. Irritating, but irritation was easy to avoid. It shifted its weight, as it had been taught, and stepped a single pace sideways.

Its left hind foot met a little resistance, and something made a shrieking sound—but there had been something shrieking for some time, and it ignored the sound as it had all the rest. After all, the food was still here.

Presently, it finished the pile of food before it and waited patiently. There was a buzzing noise, and a hole opened in the wall a little to its right. That was the signal to shift around, which it did.

A new load of fresh vegetation dropped down with a rattle and a dull thud, as the automatic cleaning system flushed the pile of droppings and the rather flat mortal remains of her savior Howard down into the sewage system.

Mary approached the corral carefully, on the alert for guards and prepared to act like a stupid, lost bimbo if she were sighted. But there were no guards; only a high metal fence of welded slats, centered with a similar gate. There was something stirring restlessly inside the corral; she couldn't see what it was, for the slats were set too closely together. But as she neared the gate, she heard it pacing back and forth in a way that made her heart ache.

Poor thing—it needed to run loose! How could these monsters keep a wild, noble creature like this penned up in such an unnaturally barren environment?

There were alarms on the gate and on the fence; she didn't have Howard's expertise in dealing with such things, but these were easy, even a child could have taken them off-line. As she worked, she talked to the poor beast trapped on the other side of the gate, and it paused in its pacing at the sound of her voice.

"Hang in there, baby," she crooned to it. "There's a whole big National Park on the other side of the lab fence—as soon as we get you loose, we'll take that big BrontoSaurian through it, and that will leave a hole big enough for a hundred animopersons to run through! Then you'll be free! You'll be able to play in the sunshine, and roll in the grass—eat all the flowers you want—we'll make sure they never catch you, don't you worry."

The beast drew nearer, until she felt the warmth of its breath on her coat sleeve as she worked. It snuffled a little, and she wrinkled her nose at the smell.

Poor thing! What were they feeding it, anyway? Didn't they ever give it a chance to bathe? Her resentment grew as it sniffed at the gap between the metal slats. Why, it was lonely! The poor thing was as lonely as some of those rodeo horses had been! Didn't anyone ever come to pet and play with it?

Finally she disabled the last of the alarms. The creature inside the corral seemed to sense her excitement and anticipation as she worked at the lock on the gate. She heard it shifting its weight from foot to foot in a kind of dance that reminded her of her pet parakeet when he wanted out of his cage, before she'd grown wiser and freed it into the abundant outdoors.

"Don't worry little fellow," she crooned at it. "I'll have you out of here in no time—"

With a feeling of complete triumph, she popped the lock, flipped open the hasp on the gate, and swung it wide, eager for the first sight of her newly freed friend.

The first thing she saw was a huge-headed lizard, about six feet tall, that stood on two legs, balancing itself with its tail. It was poised to leap through the gate. The last thing she saw was a grinning mouth like a bear-trap, full of sharp, carnivorous teeth, closing over her head.

Hank threw his rope over a chair in the employee lounge and sank into the one next to it, feeling sweat cool all over his body. He pulled his hat down over his eyes. This had not been the most disastrous morning of his life, but it was right up there. Somehow the Dino had gotten into Gertie's pen—and whoever had left the gate open last night was going to catch hell. The little carnivore couldn't hurt the Bronto, but he had already eaten all the Dobermans that were supposed to be guarding the complex, and he was perfectly ready to add a lab tech or lab hand to the menu. You couldn't trank the Saurians; their metabolism was too weird. You couldn't drive a Dino; there wasn't anything he was afraid of. The only safe way to handle the little bastard was to get two ropes on him and haul him along, a technique Hank had learned roping rhinos in Africa. It had taken him and Buford half the morning to get the Dino roped and hauled back to his corral. They'd had to work on foot since none of the horses would come anywhere near the Dino. All he needed was one more thing—

"Hank!" someone yelled from the door.

"What, dammit?" Hank Sayer snapped. "I'm tired!

Unless you've got the chowderhead that left Dino and Gertie's pens open"

"They weren't *left* open, they were opened last night," said the tech, his voice betraying both anger and excitement. "Some animal-rights yoyos got in last night, the security guys found them on one of the tapes. *And* the cleanup crews found what was left of two of them in the pit under Gertie's pen and just inside Dino's doghouse!"

That was more than enough to make Hank sit up and push his hat back. "What the hell—how come—"

The tech sighed. "These bozos think every animal is just like the bunny-wunnies they had as kids. I don't think one of them has been closer to a real bull than videotape. They sure as hell didn't research the Saurians, else they'd have known the Dino's a land-shark, and it takes Gertie a full minute to process any sensation and act on it. We found what was left of the cattle-prod in the pit."

Hank pushed his hat back on his head and scratched his chin. "Holy shit. So the bozos just got in the way of Gertie after they shocked her, and opened Dino's pen to let him out?"

"After disabling the alarms and popping the locks," the tech agreed. "Shoot, Dino must have had fifteen or twenty minutes to get a good whiff and recognize fresh meat. . . ."

"He must've thought the pizza truck had arrived—" Suddenly another thought occurred to him. "Man, we've got three Saurians in here—did anybody think to check Tricky's pen?"

Alarm filled the tech's face. "I don't think so—"

"Well, come *on* then," Hank yelled, grabbing his lariat and shooting for the door like Dino leaping for a side of beef. "Call it in and meet me there!"

Tricky's pen was the largest, more of an enclosure than a pen; it had been the home of their herd of aurochs before the St. Louis zoo had taken delivery. Tricky was perfectly placid, so long as you stayed on your side of the fence. Triceratops, it seemed, had a very strong territorial instinct. Or at least, the GenTech reproductions did. It was completely safe to come within three feet of the fence. Just don't come any closer. . . .

Hank saw with a glance that the alarms and cameras had been disabled here, too. And the gate stood closed—but it was not locked anymore.

Tricky was nowhere in sight.

"He wouldn't go outside the fence," Hank muttered to himself, scanning the pasture with his brow furrowed with worry. "Not unless someone dragged him—"

"Listen!" the tech panted. Hank held his breath, and strained his ears.

"Help!" came a thin, faint voice, from beyond the start of the trees shading the back half of Tricky's enclosure. *"Help!"*

"Oh boy." Hank grinned, and peered in the direction of the shouts. "This time we got one."

Sure enough, just through the trees, he could make out the huge brown bulk of the Tricerotops standing in what Hank recognized as a belligerent aggression-pose. The limbs of the tree moved a little, shaking beneath the weight of whoever Tricky had treed.

"Help!" came the faint, pathetic cry.

"Reckon he didn't read the sign," said Buford, ambling up with both their horses, and indicating the sign posted on the fence that read, "If you cross this field, do it in 9.9 seconds; Tricky the Triceratops does it in 10."

"Reckon not," Hank agreed, taking the reins of Smoky from his old pal and swinging into the saddle. He looked over at the tech, who hastened to hold open the gate for both of them. "You'd better go get

Security, the cops, the medics and the lawyers in that order," he said, and the tech nodded.

Hank looked back into the enclosure. Tricky hadn't moved.

"Reckon that'un's the lucky'un," Buford said, sending Pete through the gate at a sedate walk.

"Oh, I dunno," Hank replied, as Smoky followed, just as eager for a good roping and riding session as Hank wasn't. Smoky was an overachiever; best horse Hank had ever partnered, but a definite workaholic.

"Why you say that?" Buford asked.

Hank shook his head. "Simple enough. Gettin' treed by Tricky's gonna be the best part of his day. By the time the lawyers get done with 'im—well, I reckon he's likely to wish Gertie'd stepped on him, too. They ain't gonna leave him anything but shredded underwear. If he thought Tricky was bad—"

"*Uh-huh,*" Buford agreed, his weathered face splitting with a malicious grin. Both of them had been top rodeo riders before the animal-rights activists succeeded in truncating the rodeo-circuit. They'd been lucky to get this job. "You know, I reckon we had oughta take our time about this. Exercise'd do Tricky some good."

Hank laughed, and held Smoky to a walk. "Buford, old pal, I reckon you're readin' my mind. You don't suppose the damn fools hurt Tricky, do ya?"

Faint and far, came a snort; Hank could just barely make out Tricky as he backed up a little and charged the tree. A thud carried across the enclosure, and the tree shook. "Naw, I think Tricky's healthy as always."

"*Help!*" came the wail from the leaves. Hank pulled Smoky up just a little more.

And grinned fit to split his face.

This wasn't the best day of his life, but damn if it wasn't right up there.

Mike Resnick is one of my favorite anthology editors, and he got us to do a number of stories at the same time; when he first said the book this story was slated for was to be called Christmas Ghosts, *the concept was so weird I knew I had to contribute!*

Warning: this is not a nice story, but then I'm not always a nice person.

Dumb Feast

Aaron Brubaker considered himself a rational man, a logical man, a modern man of the enlightened nineteenth century. He was a prosperous lawyer in the City, he had a new house in the suburbs, and he cultivated other men like himself, including a few friends in Parliament. He believed in the modern; he had gas laid on in his house, had indoor bathrooms with the best flushing toilets (not that a polite man would discuss such things in polite company), and had a library filled with the writings of the best minds of his time. Superstition and old wives' tales had no place in his cosmos. So what he was about to do was all the more extraordinary.

If his friends could see him, he would have died of shame. And yet—and yet he would have gone right on with his plans.

Nevertheless, he had made certain that there was no chance he might be seen; the servants had been dismissed after dinner, and would not return until tomorrow after church services. They were grateful for the half-day off, to spend Christmas Eve and morning with their own families, and as a consequence had not questioned their employer's generosity. Aaron's daughter, Rebecca, was at a properly chaperoned party for young people which would end in midnight services at the Presbyterian Church, and she would not return home until well after one in the morning. And by then, Aaron's work would be done, whether it bore fruit, or not.

The oak-paneled dining room with its ornately carved table and chairs was strangely silent, without the sounds of servants or conversation. And he had not lit the gaslights of which he was so proud; there must only be two candles tonight to light the proceedings, one for him, one for Elizabeth. Carefully, he laid out the plates, the silver; arranged Elizabeth's favorite winter flowers in the centerpiece. One setting for himself, one for his wife. His dear, and very dead, wife.

His marriage had not precisely been an *arranged* affair, but it had been made in accordance with Aaron's nature. He had met Elizabeth in church; had approved of what he saw. He had courted her, in proper fashion; gained consent of her parents, and married her. He had seen to it that she made the proper friends for his position; had joined the appropriate societies, supported the correct charities. She had cared for his home, entertained his friends in the expected manner, and produced his child. In that, she had been something of a disappointment, since it should have been "children," including at least one son. There was only Rebecca, a daughter rather than a son, but he had forgiven her for her inability to do better. Romance did not precisely enter into the equation. He had expected to feel a certain amount of modest grief when Elizabeth died—

But not the depth of loss he had uncovered. He had mourned unceasingly, confounding himself as well as his friends. There simply was no way of replacing her, the little things she did. There had been an artistry about the house that was gone now; a life that was no longer there. His house was a home no longer, and his life a barren, empty thing.

In the months since her death, the need to see her again became an obsession. Visits to the cemetery were not satisfactory, and his desultory attempt to interest himself in the young widows of the parish came to nothing. And that was when the old tales from his childhood, and the stories his grandmother told, came back to—literally—haunt him.

He surveyed the table; everything was precisely in place, just as it had been when he and Elizabeth dined alone together. The two candles flickered in a draft; they were in no way as satisfactory as the gaslights, but his grandmother, and the old lady he had consulted from the Spiritualist Society, had been adamant about that—there must be two candles, and only two. No gaslights, no candelabra.

From a chafing dish on the sideboard he took the first course: Elizabeth's favorite soup. Tomato. A pedestrian dish, almost lower-class, and not the clear consummes or lobster bisques that one would serve to impress—but he was not impressing anyone tonight. These must be *Elizabeth's* favorites, and not his own choices. A row of chafing dishes held his choices ready: tomato soup, spinach salad, green peas, mashed potatoes, fried chicken, apple cobbler. No wine, only coffee. All depressingly middle-class . . .

That was not the point. The point was that they were the bait that would bring Elizabeth back to him, for an hour, at least.

He tossed the packet of herbs and what-not on the fire, a packet that the old woman from the Spiritualists had given him for just that purpose. He was

not certain what was in it; only that she had asked
for some of Elizabeth's hair. He'd had to abstract it
from the lock Rebecca kept, along with the picture
of her mother, in a little shrine-like arrangement on
her dresser. When Rebecca had first created it, he
had been tempted to order her to put it all away, for
the display seemed very pagan. Now, however, he
thought he understood her motivations.

This little drama he was creating was something that
his grandmother—who had been born in Devonshire—
called a "dumb feast." By creating a setting in which
all of the deceased's favorite foods and drink were
presented, and a place laid for her—by the burning of
certain substances—and by doing all this at a certain
time of the year—the spirit of the loved one could be
lured back for an hour or two.

The times this might be accomplished were four.
May Eve, Midsummer, Halloween, and Christmas
Eve.

By the time his need for Elizabeth had become
an obsession, the Spring Equinox and Midsummer had
already passed. Halloween seemed far too pagan for
Aaron's taste—and besides, he had not yet screwed
his courage up to the point where he was willing to
deal with his own embarrassment that he was resort-
ing to such humbug.

What did all four of these nights have in common?
According to the Spiritualist woman, it was that they
were nights when the "vibrations of the earth-plane
were in harmony with the Higher Planes." According to his grandmother, those were the nights when
the boundary between the spirit world and this world
thinned, and many kinds of creatures, both good and
evil, could manifest. According to her, that was why
Jesus had been born on that night—

Well, that was superstitious drivel. But the Spiritualist had an explanation that made sense at the time;
something about vibrations and currents, magnetic

attractions. Setting up the meal, with himself, and all of Elizabeth's favorite things, was supposed to set up a magnetic attraction between him and her. The packet she had given him to burn was supposed to increase that magnetic attraction, and set up an electrical current that would strengthen the spirit. Then, because of the alignment of the planets on this evening, the two Planes came into close contact, or conjunction, or—something.

It didn't matter. All that mattered was that he see Elizabeth again. It had become a hunger that nothing else could satisfy. No one he knew could ever understand such a hunger, such an overpowering desire.

The hunger carried him through the otherwise unpalatable meal, a meal he had timed carefully to end at the stroke of midnight, a meal that must be carried out in absolute silence. There must be no conversation, no clinking of silverware. Then, at midnight, it must end. There again, both the Spiritualist and his grandmother had agreed. The "dumb feast" should end at midnight, and then the spirit would appear.

He spooned up the last bite of too-sweet, sticky cobbler just as the bells from every church in town rang out, calling the faithful to Christmas services. Perhaps he would have taken time to feel gratitude for the Nickleson's party, and the fact that Rebecca was well out of the way—

Except that, as the last bell ceased to peal, *she* appeared. There was no fanfare, no clamoring chorus of ectoplasmic trumpets—one moment there was no one in the room except himself, and the next, Elizabeth sat across from him in her accustomed chair. She looked exactly as she had when they had laid her to rest; every auburn hair in place in a neat and modest French Braid, her body swathed from chin to toe in an exquisite lace gown.

A wild exultation filled his heart. He leapt to his feet, words of welcome on his lips—

Tried to, rather. But he found himself bound to his chair, his voice, his lips paralyzed, unable to move or to speak.

The same paralysis did not hold Elizabeth, however. She smiled, but not the smile he loved, the polite, welcoming smile—no, it was another smile altogether, one he did not recognize, and did not understand.

"So, Aaron," she said, her voice no more than a whisper.

"At last our positions are reversed. You, silent and submissive; and myself the master of the table."

He almost did not understand the words, so bizarre were they. Was this Elizabeth, his dear wife? Had he somehow conjured a vindictive demon in her place?

She seemed to read his thoughts, and laughed. Wildly, he thought. She reached behind her neck and let down her hair; brushed her hand over her gown and it turned to some kind of medievalist costume, such as the artists wore. The ones calling themselves "Pre-Raphelites," or some such idiocy. He gaped to see her attired so, or would have, if he had been in control of his body.

"I am no demon, Aaron," she replied, narrowing her green eyes. "I am still Elizabeth. But I am no longer 'your' Elizabeth, you see. Death freed me from you, from the narrow constraints you placed on me. If I had known this was what would happen, I would have died years ago!"

He stared, his mind reeled. What did she mean? How could she say those things?

"Easily, Aaron," Elizabeth replied, reclining a little in the chair, one elbow on the armrest, hand supporting her chin. "I can say them very, very easily. Or don't you remember all those broken promises?"

Broken—

"Broken promises, Aaron," she continued, her tone even, but filled with bitterness. "They began when you courted me. You promised me that you did not want me to change—yet the moment the ring was on my finger, you broke that promise, and began forcing me into the mold *you* chose. You promised me that I could continue my art—but you gave me no place to work, no money for materials, and no time to paint or draw."

But that was simply a childish fancy—

"It was my *life*, Aaron!" she cried passionately. "It was my life, and you took it from me! And I believed all those promises, that in a year you would give me time and space—after the child was born—after she began school. I believed it right up until the moment when the promise was 'after she finishes school.' Then I knew that it would become 'after she is married,' and then there would be some other, distant time—" Again she laughed, a wild peal of laughter than held no humor at all. "Cakes yesterday, cakes tomorrow, but never cakes today! Did you think I would never see through that?"

But why did she have to paint? Why could she not have turned her artistic sensibilities to proper lady's—

"What? Embroidery? Knitting? Lace-making? I was a *painter*, Aaron, and I was a good one! Burne-Jones himself said so! Do you know how rare that is, that someone would tell a girl that she must paint, must be an artist?" She tossed her head, and her wild mane of red hair—now as bright as it had been when he had first met her—flew over her shoulder in a tumbled tangle. And now he remembered where he had seen that dress before. She had been wearing it as she painted, for she had been—

"Painting a self-portrait of myself as the Lady of Shallot," she said, with an expression that he could not read. "Both you and my father conspired together to break me of my nasty artistic habits. 'Take me out of my dream-world,' I believe he said. Oh, I can hear you both—" her voice took on a pompous tone, and it took him a moment to realize that she was imitating him, " 'don't worry, sir, once she has a child she'll have no time for that nonsense—' And you saw to it that I had no time for it, didn't you? Scheduling ladies' teas and endless dinner parties, with women who bored me to death and men who wouldn't know a Rembrandt from an El Greco! Enrolling me without my knowledge or consent in group after group of other useless women, doing utterly useless things! And when I _wanted_ to do something—anything!—that might serve a useful purpose, you forbade it! Forbade me to work with the Salvation Army, forbade be to help with the Wayward Girls—oh no, _your_ wife couldn't do that, it wasn't _suitable!_ Do you know how much I came to hate that word, 'suitable'? Almost as much as the words 'my good wife.' "

But I gave you everything—

"You gave me nothing!" she cried, rising now to her feet. "You gave me jewelry, gowns ordered by _you_ to _your_ specifications, furniture, useless trinkets! You gave me nothing that mattered! No freedom, no authority, no responsibility!"

Authority? He flushed with guilt when he recalled how he had forbidden the servants to obey her orders without first asking him—how he had ordered her maid to report any out-of-the-ordinary thing she might do. How he had given the cook the monthly budget money, so that she could not buy a cheaper cut of roast and use the savings to buy paint and brushes.

"Did you think I didn't know?" she snarled, her eyes ablaze with anger as she leaned over the table. "Did you think I wasn't aware that I was a prisoner in my own home? And the law supported _you_, Aaron! I was well aware of that, thanks to the little amount

of work I did before you forbade it on the grounds
of 'suitability.' One woman told me I should be grateful that you didn't beat me, for the law permits that
as well!"

He was only doing it for her own good. . . .

"You were only doing it to be the master, Aaron,"
she spat. "What I wanted did not matter. You proved
that by your lovemaking, such as it was."

Now he flushed so fiercely that he felt as if he had
just stuck his head in a fire. How could she be so—

"Indelicate? Oh I was more than indelicate, Aaron,
I was passionate! And you killed that passion, just as
you broke my spirit, with your cruelty, your indifference to me. What should have been joyful was shameful, and you made it that way. You hurt me, constantly,
and never once apologized. Sometimes I wondered
if you made me wear those damned gowns just to
hide the bruises from the world!"

All at once, her fury ran out, and she sagged back
down into her chair. She pulled the hair back from
her temples with both hands, and gathered it in a
thick bunch behind her head for a moment. Aaron
was still flushing from the last onslaught. He hadn't
known—

"You didn't care," she said, bluntly. "You knew; you
knew it every time you saw my face fall when you
broke another promise, every time you forbade me
to dispose my leisure time where it would do some
good. You knew. But all of that, I could have forgiven,
if you had simply let Rebecca alone."

This time, indignation overcame every other feeling. How could she say something like that? When
he had given the child everything a girl could want?

"Because you gave her nothing that *she* wanted,
Aaron. You never forgave her for not being a boy.
Every time she brought something to you—a good
grade, a school prize, a picture she had done—you
belittled her instead of giving her the praise her soul

thirsted for!" Elizabeth's eyes darkened, and the expression on her face was positively demonic.

"Nothing she did was good enough—or was as good as a boy would have done."

But children needed correction—

"Children need *direction*. But that wasn't all, oh no. You played the same trick on her that you did on me. She wanted a pony, and riding lessons. But that wasn't suitable; she got a piano and piano lessons. Then, when her teacher told you she had real talent, and could become a concert artist, you took both away, and substituted *French* lessons!" Again, she stood up, her magnificent hair flowing free, looking like some kind of ancient Celtic goddess from one of her old paintings, paintings that had been filled with such pagan images that he had been proud to have weaned her away from art and back to the path of a true Christian woman. She stood over him with the firelight gleaming on her face, and her lips twisted with disgust. "You still don't see, do you? Or rather, you are so *sure*, so *certain* that you could know better than any foolish woman what is best for her, that you still think you were right in crushing my soul, and trying to do the same to my daughter!"

He expected her to launch into another diatribe, but instead, she smiled. And for some reason, that smile sent cold chills down his back.

"You didn't even guess that all this was my idea, did you?" she asked, silkily. "You had no idea that I had been touching your mind, prodding you toward this moment. You forgot what your grandmother told you, because I made you forget—that the dumb feast puts the living in the power of the dead."

She moved around the end of the table, and stood beside him. He would have shrunk away from her if he could have—but he still could not move a single muscle. "There is a gas leak in this room, Aaron," she said, in the sweet, conversational tone he remembered so well. "You never could smell it, because you have no sense of smell. What those awful cigars of yours didn't ruin, the port you drank after dinner killed. I must have told you about the leak a hundred times, but you never listened. I was only a woman, how could I know about such things?"

But why hadn't someone else noticed it?

"It was right at the lamp, so it never mattered as long as you kept the gaslights lit; since you wouldn't believe me and I didn't want the house to explode, I kept them lit day and night, all winter long. Remember? I told you I was afraid of the dark, and you laughed, and permitted me my little indulgence. And of course, in the summer, the windows were open. But you turned the lights off for this dumb feast, didn't you, Aaron. You sealed the room, just as the old woman told you. And the room has been filling with gas, slowly, all night."

Was she joking? No, one look into her eyes convinced him that she was not. Frantic now, he tried to break the hold she had over his body, and found that he still could not move.

"In a few minutes, there will be enough gas in this room for the candles to set it off—or perhaps the chafing dish—or even the fire. There will be a terrible explosion. And Rebecca will be free—free to follow her dream and become a concert pianist. Oh, Aaron, I managed to thwart you in that much. The French teacher and the piano teacher are very dear friends. The lessons continued, even though you tried to stop them. And you never guessed." She looked up, as if at an unseen signal, and smiled. And now he smelled the gas.

"It will be a terrible tragedy—but I expect Rebecca will get over her grief in a remarkably short time. The young are so resilient." The smell of gas was stronger now.

She wiggled her fingers at him, like a child. "Goodbye, Aaron," she said, cheerfully. "Merry Christmas. See you soon—"

This story was for one of Mike Resnick's "Alternate" anthologies, Alternate Celebrities, I believe. The wonderful thing about the alternate-history books is that you can take someone in history that you really like but who may not have . . . made some of the wisest choices in the world . . . and make him (or her) into something a little better.

Since Larry and I decided to do this one together, we combined our two passions—his for cars and mine for dance. Although . . . I am coming to share that passion for cars, and even took a High-Performance Racing school at Stevens Racing at Hallet Raceway (enjoying it very much, thank you). That, by the way, is the same track Mark Shepherd and I set Wheels of Fire at. We're currently thinking about getting a Catterham Seven, which is a new old Lotus Seven, and doing vintage racing and autocross— but I digress.

In this case, we took the Mother of Modern Dance, Isadora Duncan, and gave her a little more common sense. We also had her born about 25 years later than she actually was, so that she participated in World War Two rather than World War One. But yes, in WWI, she did drive an ambulance for the Allies. As for her protégé Jimmy, well, we made his fate a lot kinder, too.

Dance Track

Mercedes Lackey and Larry Dixon

Dora blew her hair out of her eyes with an impatient snort and wiped sweat off her forehead. And simultaneously adjusted the timing on the engine, yelled a correction on tire selection to her tire man, and took a quick look out of the corner of her eye for her driver.

He wasn't late—yet. He liked to give her these little heart attacks by showing up literally at the last possible moment. She would, of course, give him hell, trying to sound like the crew chief that she was, and not like his mother, which she was old enough to be—

—And most certainly not like an aging lover, which half the Bugatti team and every other team assumed she was.

The fact that they *weren't* had no bearing on the situation. Dora had been well aware from the moment she joined Bugatti at the end of the war that her position in this part of Man's World would always be difficult. That was all right; when had she ever had an easy life?

"All right!" She pulled clear of the engine compartment, hands up and in plain sight, as she had taught all her mechanics to do. Too many men in Grand Prix racing had missing fingers from being caught in the wrong place when an engine started— but not on her team. The powerful Bugatti engine roared to life; she nodded to the mechanic in Jimmy's seat, and he floored the pedal.

She cocked her head to one side, frowning a little; then grinned and gave the mech a thumbs-up. He killed the engine, answering her grin, and popped out of the cockpit—just as Jimmy himself came swaggering up through the chaotic tangle of men and machines in the pits.

She knew he was there by the way the men's eyes suddenly moved to a point just behind and to one side of her. They never learned—or else, they never guessed how they gave themselves away. Probably the latter; they *were* mostly Italian, steeped in generations of presumed male superiority, and they would never even think that a woman could be more observant than they, no matter how often she proved it to them.

She pivoted before Jimmy could slap her butt, and gave him The Look. She didn't even have to say anything, it was all there in The Look.

He stopped, standing hip-shot as if he were posing for one of his famous publicity shots, his born-charmer grin countering her Look. The blue eyes that made millions of teenage girls suffer heart-palpitations peered cheerfully at Dora through his unruly blond hair. He'd grown a thatch over his eyes for his last movie, and hadn't cut it yet. He probably wouldn't, Dora reflected. His image as a rebel wasn't just an image, it was the real Jimmy.

She pulled her eyes away from his, and The Look turned to a real frown as she took in the dark ankle-length trenchcoat and the flamboyant, long silk scarf he wore.

"Out," she ordered, and watched his grin fade in surprise. "You heard me," she said when he hesitated. "You know the pit-rules. *Nothing* that can get caught in machinery! God help us, that scarf could get your neck broken! I told you once, and I meant it; I don't care how many movies you've made, in here you're the Bugatti rookie-driver, you're here on probation, even if you *are* the best damn driver I've ever seen, and you toe the line and act like a professional. And if you think you're going to make me break my promise not to compete again by getting yourself strangled, you can think again! Now get out of here and come back when you're dressed like a driver and not some Hollywood gigolo."

She turned her back on him, and went back to the crew changing the tires, but she did not miss his surprised—and suddenly respectful—"*Yes ma'am!*" She also didn't miss the surprised and respectful looks on the faces of her mechanics and pit-crew. *So, they didn't expect me to chew him out in public.* She couldn't help but see the little nods, and the satisfaction on the men's faces. And she hid a grin of her own, as she realized what that meant. The last rumors of her protege being her lover had just gone up in smoke. No lovelorn, aging female would lay into her young lover that way in public. And no young stud would put up with that kind of treatment from a woman, young or old, unless the only position she held in his life was as respected mentor.

She raised her chin aggressively, and raked her crew with her stern gaze. "Come on, come on, pick it up," she said, echoing every other crew chief here in the pits. "We're running a race here, not an ice cream social! *Move it!*"

"Ready, Miz Duncan," said a sober voice at her shoulder. She turned to see Jimmy was back already, having ditched the coat and scarf for the racing suit of her own design. His helmet tucked under one arm, he waited while she looked him over critically. "Nothing binding?" she asked, inspecting every visible seam and wrinkle. It was as fireproof as modern technology could make it, asbestos fabric over cotton, covering the driver from neck to ankle. Thick asbestos boots covered his feet, which would be under the engine compartment. It would be hotter than all the fires of hell in there, but Jimmy would be cooler than most of the other drivers, who shunned her innovations in favor of jerseys and heavy canvas pants.

And he would be safer than she had been, who'd won the French Grand Prix in '48 in a leotard and tights.

And if she could have put an air-conditioner in there, she would have. Temperatures in the cockpit ran over 120 Fahrenheit while the car was moving—worse when it idled. In the summer, and at those temperatures, strange things started to happen to a driver's brain. Heat exhaustion and the dangerous state leading up to it had probably caused more crashes than anyone wanted to admit.

She finished her inspection and gave him the nod; he clapped his helmet on—a full head helmet, not just an elaborate leather cap, but one with a face-plate—and strolled over to his car, beginning his own inspection.

Just as she had taught him.

While the mechanics briefed him on the Bugatti's latest quirks—and Grand Prix racers always developed new quirks, at least a dozen for each race, not counting intended modifications—she took a moment to survey the nearest crews. To her right, Ferrari and Lola; to her left, Porsche and Mercedes.

Nothing to show that this was Wisconsin and not Italy or Monte Carlo. Nothing here at the track, that is. She had to admit that it was a relief being back in the U.S.; not even the passing of a decade had erased all the scars the War had put on the face of Europe. And there were those who thought that reviving the Grand Prix circuit in '46 had been both frivolous and ill-considered in light of all that Europe had suffered.

Well, those people didn't have to invest their money, their time, or their expertise in racing. The announcement that the Indianapolis 500 would be held in 1946 had given those behind the project the incentive they needed to get the plans off the drawing board and into action. The Prince in Monaco had helped immeasurably by offering to host the first race. Monte Carlo had not suffered as much damage as some of the other capitals, and it was a neutral enough spot to lure even the Germans there.

She shook herself mentally. Woolgathering again; it was a good thing she was out of the cockpit and on the sidelines, if she was going to let her thoughts drift like that.

Jimmy nodded understanding as the steering-specialist made little wiggling motions with his hand. Dora cast another glance up and down pit row, then looked down at the hands of her watch. Time.

She signaled to the crew, who began to push the car into its appointed slot in line. This would be a true Le Mans start; drivers sprinting to their cars on foot and bullying through the pack, jockeying for position right from the beginning. In a way, she would miss it if they went to an Indy-type start; with so little momentum, crashes at the beginning of the race were seldom serious—but when they were, they were devastating. And there were plenty of promising contenders taken out right there in the first four or five hundred yards.

She trotted alongside Jimmy as they made their way to the starting line. "All right, now listen to me: save the engine, save the tires. You have a long race ahead of you. We've got a double whammy on us," she warned. "Remember, a lot of drivers have it in for Bugatti because of me—and the Europeans aren't really thrilled with the Bugatti preference for Yankee drivers. The other thing: this is Ford country; Ford is fielding six cars in the factory team alone. None of the other chiefs I've talked to know any of the drivers personally, which tells me they're in Ford's back pocket."

"Which means they might drive as a team instead of solo?" Jimmy hazarded shrewdly. "Huh. That could be trouble. Three cars could run a rolling roadblock."

"We've worked on the engine since the trials, and there's another twenty horse there," she added. "It's just the way you like it: light, fast, and all the power you need. If I were you, I'd use that moxie early, get yourself placed up in the pack, then lay off and see what the rest do."

She slowed as they neared driver-only territory; he waved acknowledgment that he had heard her, and trotted on alone. She went back to the pits; the beginning of the race really mattered only in that he made it through the crush at the beginning, and got in a little ahead of the pack. That was one reason why she had given over the cockpit to a younger driver; she was getting too old for those sprints and leaps. Places where she'd hurt herself as a dancer were starting to remind her that she was forty-five years old now. Let Jimmy race to the car and fling himself into it, he was only twenty-five.

The view from her end of pit-row wasn't very good, but she *could* see the start if she stood on the concrete fire-wall. One of the men steadied her; Tonio, who had been with her since *she* was the driver. She handed her clipboard down to him, then noticed a stranger in their pit, wearing the appropriate pass around his neck. She was going to say something, but just then the drivers on the line crouched in preparation for the starting gun, and her attention went back to them.

The gun went off; Jimmy leapt for his car like an Olympic racer, vaulting into it in a way that made her simultaneously sigh with envy and wince. The Bugatti kicked over like a champ; Jimmy used every horse under that hood to bully his way through the exhaust-choked air to the front of the pack, taking an outside position. Just like she'd taught him.

The cars pulled out of sight, and she jumped down off the wall. The stranger was still there—and the pits were for the first time today, quiet. They would not be that way for long, as damaged or empty cars staggered into the hands of their keepers, but they were for the moment, and the silence impacted the ears as the silence between incoming artillery barrages had—

She headed for the stranger—but he was heading for her. "Miss Duncan?" he said quickly. "Jim got me this pit pass—he came over to see us do *Death of a*

Salesman last night and when he came back-stage and found out I race too, he got me the pass and told me to check in with you."

"What kind of racing?" she asked cautiously. It would be just like Jimmy to pal around with some kid just because he was an up-and-coming actor and saddle her with someone who didn't know when to get the hell out of the way.

"Dirt-track, mostly," he said modestly, then quoted her credentials that made her raise her eyebrow. "I'll stay out of the way."

The kid had an open, handsome face, and another set of killer blue eyes—and the hand that shook hers was firm and confident. She decided in his favor.

"Do that," she told him. "Unless there's a fire—tell you what, you think you can put up with hauling one of those around for the rest of the race?" She pointed at the rack of heavy fire-bottles behind the fire-wall, and he nodded. "All right; get yourself one of those and watch our pit, Porsche, and Ferrari. That's the cost of you being in here. If there's a fire in any of 'em, deal with it." Since the crews had other things on their minds—and couldn't afford to hang extinguishers around their necks—this kid might be the first one on the spot.

"Think you can handle that—what is your name, anyway?"

"Paul," he said, diffidently. "Yeah, I can handle that. Thanks, Miss Duncan."

"Dora," she replied automatically, as she caught the whine of approaching engines. She lost all interest in the kid for a moment as she strained to see who was in front.

It was Lola, but the car was already in trouble. She heard a tell-tale rattle deep in, and winced as the leaders roared by—

Jimmy was in the first ten; that was all that

mattered, that; and his first-lap time. She glanced at Fillipe, who had the stop-watch; he gave her a thumbs-up and bent to his clipboard to make notes, as he would for almost every lap. She let out her breath in a sigh.

"Miss Duncan, how did you get into racing?"

She had forgotten the kid but he was still there—as he had promised, out of the way, but still within talking distance.

She shook her head, a rueful smile on her lips. "Glory. How fleeting fame. Retire, and no one's ever heard of you—"

"Oh, I know all about the Grand Prix wins," the kid said hastily. "I just wanted to know why you stopped dancing. Jimmy told me you were kind of a—big thing in Europe. It doesn't seem like a natural approach to racing. I mean, Josephine Baker didn't go into racing."

She chuckled at being compared to the infamous cabaret dancer, but no one had ever asked her the question in quite that way. "A couple of reasons," she replied, thoughtfully. "The biggest one is that my dingbat brother was a better dancer than I ever was. I figured that the world only needed one crazy dancing Duncan preaching Greek revival and naturalism. And really, Ruth St. Denis and Agnes de Mille were doing what I would have been doing. Agnes was doing more; she was putting decent dancing into motion pictures, where millions of little children would see it. When I think about it, I don't think Isadora Duncan would have made any earth-shaking contributions to dancing." Then she gave him her famous impish smile, the one that peeled twenty years off of her. "On the other hand, every Grand Prix driver out there does the 'Duncan dive' to hit the cockpit. And they are starting to wear the driving suits I've been working on. So I've done that much for racing."

The kid nodded; he started to ask something else, but the scream of approaching engines made him shake his head before she held up her hand.

Jimmy was still there, still within striking distance of the leaders. But there was trouble developing— because the Ford drivers were doing just what Dora had feared they would do. They were driving as a team—in two formations of three cars each. Quite enough to block. Illegal as hell, but only if the race officials caught on and they could get someone on the Ford team to spill the beans. Obvious as it might be, the worst the drivers would get would be fines, unless someone fessed up that it was premeditated— then the whole team could be disqualified.

Illegal as hell, and more than illegal—dangerous. Dora bit her lip, wondering if they really knew just how dangerous.

Halfway through the race, and already the kid had more than earned his pit-pass. Porsche was out, bullied into the wall by the Ford flying-wedge, in a crash that sent the driver to the hospital. Ferrari was out too, victim of the same crash; both their LMCs had taken shrapnel that had nicked fuel-lines. Thank God Paul'd been close to the pits when the leaking fuel caught fire. The Ferrari had come in trailing a tail of fire and smoke and the kid was right in there, the first one on the scene with his fire-bottle, foaming the driver down first then going under the car with the nozzle. He'd probably prevented a worse fire— And now the alliances in the pits had undergone an abrupt shift. It was now the Europeans and the independents against the Ford monolith. Porsche and Ferrari had just come to her—her, who Porsche had never been willing to give the time of day!— offering whatever they had left. "Somehow" the race officials were being incredibly blind to the illegal moves Ford was pulling.

Then again . . . how close was Detroit to Wisconsin?

It had happened before, and would happen again, for as long as businessmen made money on sport. All the post-race sanctions in the world weren't going to help that driver in the hospital, and no fines would change the outcome of the inevitable crashes.

The sad, charred hulk of the Ferrari had been towed, its once-proud red paint blistered and cracked; the pit crew was dejectedly cleaning up the oil and foam.

On the track, Jimmy still held his position, despite two attempts by one of the Ford wedges to shove him out of the way. That was the advantage of a vehicle like the Bugatti, as she and the engineers had designed it for him. The handling left something to be desired, at least so far as she was concerned, but it was Jimmy's kind of car. Like the 550 Porsche he drove for pleasure now, that he used to drive in races, she'd built it for speed. "Point and squirt," was how she often put it, dryly. Point it in the direction you wanted to go, and let the horses do the work.

The same thing seemed to be passing through Paul's mind, as he watched Jimmy scream by, accelerating out of another attempt by Ford to pin him behind their wedge. He shook his head, and Dora elbowed him.

"You don't approve?" she asked.

"It's not that," he said, as if carefully choosing his words. "It's just not my kind of driving. I like handling; I like to slip through the pack like—like I was a fish and they were the water. Or I was dancing on the track—"

She had to smile. "Are you quoting that, or did you not know that was how they described my French and Monte Carlo Grand Prix wins?"

His eyes widened. "I didn't know—" he stammered, blushing. "Honest! I—"

She patted his shoulder, maternally. "That's fine,

Paul. It's a natural analogy. Although I bet you don't know where I got my training."

He grinned. "Bet I do! Dodging bombs! I read you were an ambulance driver in Italy during the war. Is that when you met Ettore Bugatti?"

She nodded, absently, her attention on the cars roaring by. Was there a faint sound of strain in her engine? For a moment her nerves chilled.

But no, it was just another acceleration; a little one, just enough to blow Jimmy around the curve ahead of the Mercedes.

Her immediate reaction was annoyance; he shouldn't have had to power his way out of that, he should have been able to *drive* his way out. He was putting more stress on the engine than she was happy with.

Then she mentally slapped her own hand. *She* wasn't the driver, he was.

But now she knew how Ettore Bugatti felt when she took the wheel in that first Monte Carlo Grand Prix.

"You know, Bugatti was one of my passengers," she said, thinking aloud, without looking to see if Paul was listening. "He was with the Resistance in the Italian Alps. You had to be as much a mechanic as a driver, those ambulances were falling apart half the time, and he saw me doing both before I got him to the field hospital."

Sometimes, she woke up in the middle of the night, hearing the bombs falling, the screams of the attack-fighters strafing the road— Seeing the road disintegrate in a flash of fire and smoke behind her, in front of her; hearing the moans of the wounded in her battered converted bread-truck.

All too well, she remembered those frantic moments when getting the ambulance moving meant getting herself and her wounded passengers out of there before the fighter-planes came back. And for a moment, she heard those planes— No, it was the cars returning. She shook her head to free it of unwanted memories. She had never lost a passenger, or a truck, although it had been a near thing more times than she cared to count. Whenever the memories came between her and a quiet sleep, she told herself that—and reminded herself why she had volunteered in the first place.

Because her brother, the darling of the Metaphysical set, was hiding from the draft at home by remaining in England among the blue-haired old ladies and balletomanes who he charmed. Because, since they would not accept her as a combatant, she enlisted as a noncombatant.

Some noncombatant. She had seen more fire than most who were on the front lines.

Bugatti had been sufficiently impressed by her pluck and skill to make her an offer.

"When this is over, if you want a job, come to me."

Perhaps he had meant a secretarial job. She had shown up at the decimated Bugatti works, with its "EB" sign in front cracked down the middle, and offered herself as a mechanic. And Bugatti, faced with a dearth of men who were able-bodied, never mind experienced, had taken her on out of desperation.

"It was kind of a fluke, getting to be Bugatti's driver," she continued, noting absently that Paul was listening intently. "The driver for that first Grand Prix had broken an ankle, right at starting-lineup, and I was the only one on the team that could make the sprint for the car!"

Paul chuckled, and it had been funny. Everyone else was either too old, or had war-injuries that would slow them down. So she had grabbed the racing-helmet before anyone could think to object and had taken the man's place. In her anonymous coverall, it was entirely possible none of the officials had even noticed her sex.

She had made the first of her famous "Duncan

dives" into the cockpit; a modified *grand jeté* that
landed her on the seat, with a twist and bounce down
into the cockpit itself.

"I can still hear that fellow on the bullhorn—there
was no announcer's booth, no loudspeaker system—"
She chuckled again. *"And coming in third—Isadora
Duncan?"*

The next race, there had been no doubt at all of
her sex. She had nearly died of heat-stroke behind
that powerful engine, and she had been shocked at
what that had done to her judgment and reflexes. So
this time, she had worn one of her old dancing
costumes, a thick cotton leotard and tights—worn
inside-out, so that the seams would not rub or abrade
her.

The other drivers had been so astounded that she
had gotten nearly a two-second lead on the rest of
them in the sprint—and two seconds in a race meant
a quarter mile.

For her third race, she had been forbidden to
wear the leotard, but by then she had come up with
an alternative; almost as form-fitting, and enough
to cause a stir. And that had been in France, of
course, and the French had been amused by her
audacity. "La Belle Isadora" had her own impromptu
fanclub, who showed up at the race with noisemak-
ers and banners.

Perhaps that had been the incentive she needed,
for that had been her first win. She had routinely
placed in the first three, and had taken home to
Bugatti a fair share of first-place trophies. The other
drivers might have been displeased, but they could
not argue with success.

Bugatti had been overjoyed, and he had continuously modified his racing vehicles to Isadora's specifications: lighter, a little smaller than the norm, with
superb handling. And as a result of Isadora's win, the
Bugatti reputation had made for many, many sales of

sportscars in the speed-hungry, currency-rich American market. And it did not hurt that his prize driver was an attractive, *American* lady.

But in 1953 she had known that she would have to retire, and soon. She was slowing down—and more importantly, so were her reflexes. That was when she had begun searching for a protege, someone she could groom to take her place when she took over the retiring crew-chief's position.

She had found it in an unlikely place: Hollywood. And in an unlikely person, a teenage heartthrob, a young, hard-living actor. But she had not seen him first on the silver screen; she had seen him racing, behind the wheel of his treasured silver Porsche.

He had been torn by indecision, although he made time for her coaching and logged a fair amount of time in Bugatti racing machines. She and the retiring crew chief worked on design changes to suit his style of driving to help lure him. But it was Hollywood itself that forced his choice.

When a near-fatality on a lonely California highway left his Porsche a wreck, his studio issued an ultimatum. *Quit driving, or tear up your contract. We don't cast corpses.*

He tore up his contract, took the exec's pipe from his mouth, stuffed the scraps in the pipe, slammed it down on the desk and said "Smoke it." He bought a ticket for Italy the same day.

"Miss Duncan?" Paul broke into her thoughts. "We have company."

She turned, to see the crew-chiefs of Ferrari, Mercedes, Lola, and a dozen more approaching. Her first thought was—*What have we done now?*

But it was not what she had done, nor her crew, nor even Jimmy.

It was what Ford had done.

"Isadora," said Paul LeMond, the Ferrari crew-chief, who had evidently been appointed spokesman, "We need your help."

Ten years of fighting her way through this man's world, with no support from anyone except Bugatti and a few of her crew had left her unprepared for such a statement.

She simply stared at them, while they laid out their idea.

This would be the last pit-stop before the finish, and Dora was frankly not certain how Jimmy was going to take this. But she leaned down into the cockpit where she would not be overheard and shouted the unthinkable into his ear over the roar of his engine. How the crews of every other team still on the track were fed up with the performance of the Ford drivers—and well they should be, with ten multi-car wrecks leaving behind ruined vehicles and drivers in hospital. The fact that one of those wrecks had included one of the Ford three-car flying wedges had not been good enough.

"So if Ford is going to play footsie with the rules, so are we," she shouted. "They think you're the best driver on the track, Jimmy. The only one good enough to beat cheaters. So every other driver on the track's been given orders to block for you, or let you pass."

She couldn't see Jimmy's expression behind the faceplate, but she did see the muscles in his jaw tense. "So they're going to just give me the win?" he shouted back.

That was not how Jimmy wanted his first Grand Prix to end—and she didn't blame him.

"Jimmy—they decided you're the best out there! Not only your peers, but *mine!* Are you going to throw that kind of vote away?" It was the only way she would win this argument, she sensed it. And she sensed as his mood turned to grudging agreement. "All right," he said finally. "But you tell them this—" She rapped him on the top of the helmet. "No, you listen. They said to tell *you* that if you get by Ford early enough, they're going to do the same for Giorgio with the old Ferrari and Peter for Citroen. And as many more as they can squeeze by."

She sensed his mood lighten again, although he didn't answer. But by then the crew was done, and she stood back as he roared back out onto the track.

When he took the track, there were ten laps to go—but five went by without anyone being able to force a break for Jimmy, not even when the Ford wedge lapped slower cars. She had to admit that she had seldom seen smoother driving, but it was making her blood boil to watch Jimmy coming up behind them, and being forced to hold his place.

Three laps to go, and there were two more cars wrecked, one of them from Citroen. Two laps. One.

Flag lap.

Suddenly, on the back stretch, an opening, as one of the Ford drivers tired and backed off a little. And Jimmy went straight for it.

Dora was on the top of the fire-wall, without realizing she had jumped up there, screaming at the top of her lungs, with half the crew beside her. Ford tried to close up the wedge, but it was too late.

Now it was just Jimmy and the lead Ford, neck and neck—down the backstretch, through the chicane, then on the home run for the finish line.

Dora heard his engine howling; heard strain that hadn't been there before. Surely if she heard it, so would he. He should have saved the engine early on—if he pushed it, he'd blow the engine, he had to know that—

He pushed it. She heard him drop a gear, heard the engine scream in protest—

And watched the narrow-bodied, lithe steel Bugatt'

surge across the finish-line a bare nose ahead of the Ford, engine afire and trailing a stream of flame and smoke that looked for all the world like a victory banner.

Dora was the first to reach him, before he'd even gotten out of the car. While firefighters doused the vehicle with impartial generosity, she reached down and yanked off his helmet.

She seized both his ears and gave him the kind of kiss only the notorious Isadora Duncan, toast of two continents, could have delivered—a kiss with every year of her considerable amatory experience behind it.

"That's for the win," she said, as he sat there, breathless, mouth agape and for once completely without any kind of response.

Then she grasped his shoulders and shook him until his teeth rattled.

"And *that's* for blowing up my engine, you idiot!" she screamed into his face.

By then, the crowd was on him, hauling him bodily out of the car and hoisting him up on their shoulders to ride to the winner's circle.

Dora saw to it that young Paul was part of that privileged party, as a reward for his fire-fighting and his listening. And when the trophy had been presented and the pictures were all taken, she made sure he got up to the front.

Jimmy recognized him, as Jimmy would, being the kind of man he was. "Hey!" he said, as the Race Queen hung on his arm and people thrust champagne bottles at him, "You made it!"

Paul grinned, shyly. Dora felt pleased for him, as he shoved the pass and a pen at Jimmy. "Listen, I know it's awful being asked—"

"Awful? Hell no!" Jimmy grabbed the pen and pass. "Have you made up your mind about what you want to do yet? Acting, or whatever?"

Paul shook his head, and Dora noticed then what she should have noticed earlier—that his bright blue eyes and Jimmy's were very similar. *And if he isn't a heartbreaker yet,* she thought wryly, *he will be.*

"I still don't know," he said.

"Tell you what," Jimmy said, pausing a moment to kiss another beauty queen for the camera, "you make a pile of money in the movies, *then* go into racing. Get a good mentor like Dora."

And then he finished the autograph with a flourish—and handed it back to the young man.

To Paul Newman, who can be my driver when I take over the chief mechanic slot from Dora, best of luck.

And the familiar autograph, *James Dean.*

NOTE:

Just as a postscript—yes, Paul Newman *was* doing dinner-theater and summer-stock in the Midwest in the 1950's. He did drive dirt-track, as well as going into professional auto racing. And James Dean was considered by his peers to be an excellent race-driver with great potential in the sport.

And in case you don't happen to be a dance-buff, Isadora Duncan was killed when the long, trailing scarf she wore (about twelve feet worth of silk) was caught in the wheel-spokes of a Bugatti sports-car in which she was riding, breaking her neck.

This story was for Mike Resnick's Alternate Heroes. *While T. E. Lawrence (aka Lawrence of Arabia, another historical favorite of mine) was really a hero, I wondered what would have happened if a certain life-shattering experience he had at Deraa had come out a bit differently. . . .*

Due to the actual historical details this story is rather a stiff one at the beginning, and definitely NC-17.

Jihad

Pain was a curtain between Lawrence and the world; pain *was* his world, there was nothing else that mattered. "Take him out of here, you fools! You've spoiled him!" Lawrence heard Bey Nahi's exclamation of disgust dimly; and it took his pain-shattered mind a moment to translate it from Turkish to English.

Spoiled him; as if he was a piece of meat. Well, now he was something less than that.

He could not reply; he could only retch and sob for mercy. There was no part of him that was not in excruciating pain.

Pain. All his life, since he had been a boy, pain had been his secret terror and obsession. Now he was drugged with it, a too-great force against which he could not retain even a shred of dignity.

As he groveled and wept, conversation continued on above his head. There were remonstrations on the part of the soldiers, but the Bey was adamant—and angry. Most of the words were lost in the pain, but he caught the sense of a few. "Take him out—" and "Leave him for the jackals."

So, the Bey was not to keep him until he healed. Odd. After Nahi's pawing and fondling, and swearing of desire, Lawrence would have thought—

"You stay." That, petulantly, to the corporal, the youngest and best-looking of the lot. Coincidentally, he was the one who had been the chiefest and most inventive of the torturers. He had certainly been the one that had enjoyed his role the most. "Take that out," the Bey told the others. Lawrence assumed that Nahi meant him.

If he had been capable of appreciating anything, he would have appreciated that—the man who had wrought the worst on his flesh, should take his place in the Bey's bed.

The remaining two soldiers seized him by the arms. Waves of pain rolled up his spine and into his brain, where they crashed together, obliterating thought. He couldn't stand up; he couldn't even get his feet under him. His own limbs no longer obeyed him.

They dragged him outside; the cold air on his burning flesh made him cry out again, but this time no one laughed or struck him. Once outside, his captors were a little gentler with him; they draped his arms over their shoulders, and half-carried him, letting him rest most of his weight on them. The nightmarish journey seemed to last a lifetime, yet it was only to the edge of the town.

Deraa. The edge of Deraa. The edge of the universe. He noted, foggily, that he did not recognize the street or the buildings as they passed; they must have brought him to the opposite side of the town. There was that much more distance now between himself and his friends and allies. Distance controlled and watched by the enemy.

Assuming he wanted to reach them. Assuming he

wanted them to find him, see him—see what had been done to him, guess at the lacerations that were not visible.

No.

His captors let him down onto the muddy ground at the side of the road. Gently, which was surprising. One of them leaned over, and muttered something—Lawrence lost the sense of it in the pain. He closed his eyes and snuggled down into the mud, panting for breath. Every breath was an agony, as something, probably a broken bone, made each movement of his ribs stab him sharply.

He heard footsteps retreating, quickly, as if his erstwhile captors could not leave his presence quickly enough.

Tears of despair, shameful, shamed tears, trickled down his cheeks. The unmoved stars burned down on him, and the taste of blood and bile was bitter in his mouth.

Slowly, as the pain ebbed to something he could think through, he itemized and cataloged his injuries to regain control of his mind, as he had tried to count the blows of the whip on his back. The bones in his foot, fractured during the chaos of the last sabotage-raid, had been shattered again. The broken rib made breathing a new torture. Somewhere in the background of everything, the dull pain of his head spoke of a concussion, which had probably happened when they kicked him to the head of the stairs. The lashes that had bit into his groin had left their own burning tracks behind.

His back was one shapeless weight of pain. He had thought to feel every separate, bleeding welt, but he could only feel the accumulated agony of all of them in a mass. But as he lay in the mud, the cold of the night numbed him, leaving only that final injury still as sharp and unbearable as ever, the one that was not visible. The laceration of his soul.

Now he knew how women felt; to be the helpless plaything of others, stronger or more powerful. To be forced to give of their bodies whether or not they willed or wanted it. To be handled and used— *Like a piece of meat*— And worst of all, at one level, the certainty that he had somehow deserved it all. That he had earned his punishment. That he had asked for his own violation. After all, wasn't that what they said of women, too? It was this final blow that had cracked the shell of his will and brought down the walls of the citadel of his integrity.

How could he face them, his followers, now? They would watch him, stare at him, and murmur to one another—no matter how silent he kept, they would know, surely they would know. And knowing, how could they trust him?

They would not, of course. He no longer trusted himself. His nerve was broken, his will, his soul broken across that guardroom bench. There was nothing left but despair. He literally had nothing left to live for; the Revolt had become his life, and without it, he had no will to live. The best thing he could do for the Revolt would be to die. Perhaps Feisal would take it upon himself to avenge his strange English friend, Aurens; certainly Auda, that robber, would use Aurens' death as an excuse to further raid the Turks. And Ali, Ali ibn el Hussein; he would surely exact revenge. But could they hold the Revolt together?

Inshallah. As God wills it. Here, in his extremity, he had at last come to the fatalism of the Moslem. It was no longer his concern. Life was no longer his concern. Only death, and the best way to meet it, without further torment, to drown his shame in its dark waters where no one would guess what those waters hid.

This would not be the place to die. Not here, where his beaten and brutalized body would draw attention—where his anxious followers might even

come upon it and guess the foulness into which he
had fallen. Let him crawl away somewhere; let him
disappear into the waste and die where he would not
be found, and let his death become a mystery to be
wondered at.

Then he would be a martyr, if the Revolt could
have such a thing. It might even be thought that he
vanished, like one of the old prophets, into the desert,
to return at some vague future date. His death would
become a clean and shining thing. They would
remember him as the confident leader, not the battered, bloody rag of humanity he was now.

He lay in a sick stupor, his head and body aching
and growing slowly numb with cold. Finally a raging
thirst brought him to life—and spurred him to rise.

He struggled to his feet, and rocked in place,
moaning, his shaking hands gathering his torn clothing
about him. He might have thought that this was a
nightmare, save for the newly-wakened pain. Somewhere he heard someone laughing, and the sound
shocked him like cold water. Deraa felt inhuman with
vice and cruelty; he could not die here.

The desert. The desert was clean. The desert would
purge him, as it had so many times before.

He stopped at a trough by the wells; scooped a
little water into his hands and rubbed it over his
face, then drank. He looked up at the stars, which
would not notice if there was one half-Arab Englishman less on the earth, and set off, one stumbling
step at a time, for the clean waste beyond this vile
pit of humanity. He walked for a long time, he
thought. The sounds of humanity faded, replaced by
the howling of dogs or jackals, off in the middle
distance. Tears of pain blurred his sight; he hoped
he could find some hole to hide himself away before
dawn, a grave that he might fall into, and falling,
fall out of life.

He stumbled, jarring every injury into renewed

agony, and a white light of pain blinded him. He
thought he would die then, dropping in his tracks;
then he thought that the blackness of unconsciousness would claim him.

But the light did not fade; it grew brighter. It
burned away the pain, burned away thought, burned
away everything but a vague sense of self. It engulfed
him, conquered him, enveloped him. He floated in
a sea of light, dazzled, sure that he had dropped dead
on the road. But if that were true, where was he?
And what was this?

Even as he wondered that, he became aware of
a Presence within the light. Even as he recognized
it, it spoke.

I AM I.

On the bank of the Palestine Railway above the
huddle of Deraa they waited; Sherif Ali ibn el
Hussein, together with the two men that Aurens had
designated as his bodyguards, Halim and Faris, and
the sheik of Tafas, Talal el Hareidhin. "Tell me again,"
Ali said fiercely. "Tell me what it was you did."

Faris, old and of peasant stock, did not hesitate,
although this was the fifth time in as many hours that
Ali had asked the question. Talal hissed through his
teeth, but did not interrupt.

"We came into Deraa by the road, openly," Faris
recounted, as patient as the sand. "There was wire,
and trenches, some flying machines in the sheds; some
men about, but they took no note of us. We walked
on, into Deraa. A Syrian asked after our villages, and
whether the Turks were there; I think he meant to
desert. We left him and walked on again; someone
called after us in Turkish, which we feigned not to
understand. Then another man, in a better uniform,
ran after us. He took Aurens by the arm, saying 'The
Bey wants you.' He took Aurens away, through the
tall fence, into their compound. This was when I saw

him no more. I hung about, but there was no sign of him although I watched until well after nightfall. The Turks became restless, and looked evilly at me, so I left before they could take me too."

Talal shook his head. "This is pointless," he said. "Aurens is either dead or a prisoner, and in neither case can we help him. If the former, it is the will of Allah; if the latter, we must think of how long he will deceive them, and where we must go when he does."

"Into the desert, whence we came," Ali said glumly. "The Revolt is finished. There is no man of us who can do as he has done, for there is no man of us who has not a feud with another tribe; there is not a one of us who has no tribe to answer to. There is no one we may trust to whom the English will listen, much less give gold and guns to. We are finished."

Talal widened his eyes at that, but did not speak. Ali took a last look at Deraa, and the death of their hopes, and turned resolutely away.

"Where do we go, lord?" asked Faris, humbly, the peasant still.

"To Azrak," Ali replied. "We must collect ourselves, and then scatter ourselves. If Aurens has been taken and betrayed us, we must think to take ourselves where the Turks cannot find us."

The others nodded at this gloomy wisdom, as the rains began again, falling down impartially upon Turks and Bedouin alike.

The ride to the old fortress of Azrak, which Aurens and his followers had taken for the winter, was made longer by their gloom. There was not one among them who doubted the truth of Ali's words; and Ali thought perhaps that there was not one among them who was not trying to concoct some heroic scheme, either to rescue Aurens, or to avenge him. But a thousand unconnected raids of vengeance would not have a quarter of the power of the planned and coordinated raids Aurens had led them in. And there was still the matter of gold and guns—gold, to buy the loyalty of the wilder tribes, to make Suni fight beside Shia, half-pagan desert tribesman beside devout Meccan. Guns, because there were never enough guns, never enough ammunition, and because there were those who would fight for the promise of guns who would not be moved for anything else. Swords would not prevail against the Turkish guns, no matter how earnest the wielder. They must gather their people, each his own, and scatter. Ali would take it upon himself to bear the evil news to Feisal, who would, doubtless, take it to his father and the English.

More ill thoughts; how long would King Hussein, ever jealous of his son's popularity and inclined to mistrust him, permit Feisal even so much as a body-guard? Without Aurens to speak to the English, and the English to temper the father, the son could not rally the Revolt either.

It was truly the death of their hopes.

The fortress loomed in the distance, dark and dismal in the rain. Ali did not think he could bear to listen to the spectral wailings of the ghost-dogs of Beni Hillal about the walls tonight. He would gather his people and return to his tribe— What was that noise?

He raised his eyes from contemplating the neck of his camel, just as a shaft of golden light, as bright as the words of the Koran, broke through the clouds. Where it struck the ground, on the road between them and the fortress, there was a stark white figure, that seemed to take in the golden light and transmute it to his own brightness.

Ali squinted against the light. Who was this? Was it mounted?

Yes, as it drew nearer, strangely bringing the beam of sunlight with it, he saw that it was mounted. Not upon a camel, but upon a horse of a whiteness surpassing anything Ali had ever seen. Not even the stud reft away from the Turks was of so noble a color—

Now he saw what the noise was; behind the rider came every man of the fortress, cheering and firing into the air—

Ali goaded his mount into a loping canter, his heart in his throat. It could not be, could it?

From the canter he urged the camel into a gallop. The size was right; the shape—but whence the robes, the headcloth, even the headropes, of such dazzling whiteness? They had been mired in mud for months, he had not thought ever to see white robes until spring.

It was. His heart leapt with joy. It was! The figure was near enough to see features now; and it was not to be mistaken for any other. Aurens!

He reined his camel in beside the white stallion, and the beast did not even shy, it simply halted, though Aurens made no move to stop it. He raised his hand, and the mob at his back fell respectfully silent.

Ali looked down at his friend; Aurens looked up, and there was a strange fire in those blue eyes, a burning that made Ali rein his camel back a pace. There was something there that Ali had never seen before, something that raised the hair on the back of his neck and left him trembling between the wish to flee and the wish to fall from his camel's back and grovel at the Englishman's feet.

"Lawrence?" Ali said, using the English name, rather than the one they all called him. As if by using that name, he could drive that strangeness from Aurens' eyes. "Lawrence? How did you escape from the Turks?"

The blue eyes burned brighter, and the robes he wore seemed to glow. "Lawrence is dead," he said. "The Turks slew him. There is only Aurens. Aurens, and the will of Allah."

Ali's blood ran hot and cold by turns as he stared down into those strange, unhuman blue eyes. "And what," he whispered, as he would whisper in a mosque, "is the will of Allah?"

At last the eyes released him, leaving him shivering with reaction, and with the feeling that he had gazed into something he could not, and would never, understand.

"The will of Allah," said Aurens, gazing toward Deraa, toward Damascus, and beyond, "Is this."

Silence, in which not even the camels stirred.

"There will be *jihad*."

General Allenby swore, losing the last of his composure. "He's *where*?" the commander of the British forces in the Middle East shouted, as his aides winced and the messenger kept his upper lip appropriately stiff in the face of the general's anger.

"Outside of Damascus, sir," he repeated. "I caught up with him there." He paused for a moment, for if this much of the message had the general in a rage, the rest of it would send him through the roof. He was sweatingly grateful that it was no longer the custom to slay the bearer of bad news. "He sent me to tell you, sir, that if you wish to witness the taking of Damascus, you had best find yourself an aeroplane."

The general did, indeed, go through the roof. Fortunately, early on in the tirade, Allenby said something that the messenger could take as a dismissal, and he took himself out.

There was a mob lying in wait for him in the officers' mess.

"What did he say?" "What did he do?" "Is it true he's gone native?" "Is it—"

The messenger held up his hands. "Chaps! One at a time! Or else, let me tell it once, from the beginning."

The hubbub cooled then, and he was allowed to

take a seat, a throne, rather, while the rest of them gathered around him, as attentive as students upon a Greek philosopher.

Or as Aurens' men upon his word. The similarity did not escape him. What he wondered now, was how he had escaped that powerful personality. Or had he been *permitted* to escape, because it suited Aurens' will to have him take those words back to Jerusalem?

First must come how he had found Aurens—he could no more think of the man as "T. E. Lawrence" than he could think of the Pope as "Binky." There was nothing of Britain in the man he had spoken to, save only the perfect English, and the clipped, precise accent. Not even the blue eyes—they had held something more alien than all the mysteries of the east.

"I was told he had last been seen at Deraa, so that was where I went to look for him. He wasn't there; but his garrison was."

"His garrison! These wogs couldn't garrison a stable!" There was an avalanche of comments about that particular term; most disparaging. Kirkbride waited until the comments had subsided.

"I tell, you, it was a *garrison.*" He shook his head. "I can't explain it. As wild as you like, tribesmen riding like devils in their games outside, the Turkish headquarters wrecked and looted—but everything outside that, untouched. The Turks, prisoners, housed and fed and clean—the guards on the town, as disciplined as—" He lacked words. The contrast had been so great, he could hardly believe it. But more than that, the town had been held by men from a dozen different tribes, or more—and yet there was no serious quarreling, no feuding. When he ventured to ask questions, it had been "Aurens said," and "Aurens commanded," as though Aurens spoke for Allah.

Aurens, it appeared, was on the road to Damascus, sweeping all before him.

"They gave me a guide, and sent me off camel-back, and what was the oddest, I would have sworn that they knew I was coming and were only waiting for me." That had been totally uncanny. The moment he had appeared, he had been escorted to the head of the garrison, some Sheik or other, then sent immediately out to the waiting guide and saddled camel. And the only answer to his question of "Where are you taking me?" was "Aurens commands."

Deraa had been amazing. The situation outside Damascus was beyond imagination.

As he described it for his listeners, he could not fault them for their expressions of disbelief. He would not have believed it, if he had not seen it. Massed before Damascus was the greatest Arab army the world had ever seen. Kirkbride had been an Oxford scholar in History, and he could not imagine that such a gathering had ever occurred even at the height of the Crusades. Tribe after feuding tribe was gathered there, together, in the full strength of fighters. Boys as young as their early teens, and scarred old greybeards. There was order; there was discipline. Not the "discipline" of the British regulars, of drill and salute, of uniforms and ranks—a discipline of a peculiarly Eastern kind, in which individual and tribal differences were forgotten, submerged in favor of a goal that engaged every mind gathered here in a kind of white-hot fervor. Kirkbride had recognized Bedouins that were known to be half-pagan alongside Druses, alongside King Hussein's own devout guard from Mecca—

That had brought him up short, and in answer to his stammered question, his guide had only smiled whitely. "You shall see," he said only. "When we reach Aurens."

Reach Aurens they did, and he was brought into the tent as though into the Presence. He was announced, and the figure in the spotlessly white robes turned his eyes on the messenger.

His listeners stilled, as some of his own awe communicated itself to them. He had no doubt, at that moment, that Aurens *was* a Presence. The blue eyes were unhuman; something burned in them that Kirkbride had never seen in all of his life. The face was as still as marble, but stronger than tempered steel. There was no weakness in this man, anywhere.

Aurens would have terrified him at that moment, except that he remembered the garrison holding Deraa. The Turks there were cared for, honorably. Their wounded were getting better treatment than their own commanders gave them. Somewhere, behind the burning eyes, there was mercy as well.

It took him a moment to realize that the men clustered about Aurens, as disciples about a master, included King Hussein, side-by-side, and apparently reconciled, with his son Feisal. King Hussein, pried out of Mecca at last—

Clearly taking a subservient role to Aurens, a foreigner, a Christian.

Kirkbride had meant to stammer out his errand then—except that at that moment, there came the call to prayer. Wild and wailing, it rang out across the camp.

Someone had translated it for Kirkbride once, imperfectly, or so he said. *God alone is great; I testify that there are no Gods but God, and Mohammed is his Prophet. Come to prayer; come to security. God alone is great; there is no God but God.*

And Aurens, the Englishman, the Christian, unrolled his carpet, faced Mecca with the rest, and fell upon his face.

That kept Kirkbride open-mouthed and speechless until the moment of prayer was over, and all rose again, taking their former places.

"He did *what?*" The officers were as dumbfounded as he had been.

Once again, Kirkbride was back in that tent, under the burning, blue gaze of those eyes. "He said to tell Allenby that if he wanted to see the taking of Damascus, he should find an aeroplane, else it would happen before he got there." Kirkbride swallowed, as the mess erupted in a dozen shouted conversations at once.

Some of those involved other encounters with Aurens over the past few weeks. How he had been in a dozen places at once, always riding a white Arabian stallion or a pure white racing camel of incredible endurance. How he had rallied the men of every tribe. How he had emptied Mecca of its fighting men.

How he had appeared, impeccably uniformed, with apparently genuine requisition orders for guns, ammunition, explosives, supplies. How he had vanished into the desert with laden camels—and only later, were the orders proved forgeries so perfect that even Allenby could not be completely sure he had not signed them.

How, incredibly, all those incidents had taken place in the same day, at supply depots spread miles apart.

It was possible—barely. Such a feat could have been performed by a man with access to a high-powered motor-car. No one could prove Aurens had such access—but Hussein did; he owned several. And Hussein was now with Aurens—

It would still have taken incredible nerve and endurance. Kirkbride did not think *he* had the stamina to carry it off.

No one was paying any attention to him; he slipped out of the officers' mess with his own head spinning. There was only one thing of which he was certain now.

He wanted to be in at the kill. But to do that, he had to get himself attached to Allenby's staff within the next hour.

Impossible? Perhaps. But then again, had Aurens not said, as he took his leave, "We will meet again in Damascus"?

Kirkbride sat attentively at the general's side; they had not come by aeroplane after all, but by staff car, and so they had missed the battle.

All six hours of it.

Six hours! He could scarcely credit it. Even the Germans had fled in terror at the news of the army camped outside their strongholds; they had not even waited to destroy their own supplies. The general would not have believed it, had not French observers confirmed it. Allenby had mustered all of the General Staff of the Allied forces, and a convoy of staff cars had pushed engines to the breaking-point to convey them all to the city, but Kirkbride had the feeling that this was the mountain come to Mohammed, and not the other way around. He had been listening to the natives, and the word in their mouths, spoken cautiously, but fervently, was that Aurens *was* Mohammed, or something very like him. The victories that Allah had granted were due entirely to his holiness, and not to his strategy. Strangest of all, this was agreed upon by Suni and Shiite, by Kurd and Afghani, by purest Circassian and darkest Egyptian, by Bedouin wanderer and Lebanese shopkeeper. There had been no such accord upon a prophet since the very days of Mohammed himself.

Allenby had convinced himself somehow that Aurens was going to simply, meekly, hand over his conquests to his rightful leader.

Kirkbride had the feeling that Allenby was not going to get what he expected.

Damascus was another Deraa, writ large. Only the Turkish holdings had been looted; the rest remained unmolested. There were no fires, no riots. High-spirited young warriors gamed and sported outside the city walls; inside, a stern and austere martial order prevailed. Even the hospital holding the wounded and sick Turkish prisoners was in as good order as might be expected, for a place that had been foul when the city was in Turkish hands. There was government; there was order. It was not an English order; organization was along tribal lines, rather than rank, to each tribe, a duty, and if they failed it, another was appointed to take it, to their eternal shame. But it was an order, and at the heart of it was the new Arab Government.

Allenby had laughed to hear that, at the gates of the city. As they were ushered into that government's heart, he was no longer laughing. There were fire brigades, a police force; the destitute were being fed by the holy men from out of the looted German stores, and the sick tended by the Turkish doctors out of those same stores. There were scavenger-gangs to clear away the dead, with rights to loot the bodies to make up for the noisome work. British gold became the new currency; there was a market already, with barter encouraged. Everywhere Kirkbride looked, there was strange, yet logical, order. And Allenby's face grew more and more grave.

Aurens permitted him, and the envoys of the other foreign powers, into his office, commandeered from the former Governor. The aides remained behind. "My people will see to us, and to them," Aurens said, with quiet authority. A look about the room, at the men in a rainbow of robes, with hands on knife-hilts, dissuaded arguments.

The door closed.

Kirkbride did not join with the others, drinking coffee and making sly comments about their guardians.

He had the feeling, garnered from glances shared between dark faces, and the occasional tightening of a hand on a hilt, that all of these "barbarians" knew English quite well. Instead, he kept to himself, and simply watched and waited.

The hour of prayer came, and the call went up. All the men but one guarding them fell to praying; Kirkbride drew nearer to that one, a Circassian as blond as Aurens himself.

"You do not pray?" he asked, expecting that the man would understand.

And so he did. He shrugged. "I am Christian, for now." He cast his glance towards the closed door, and his eyes grew bright and thoughtful. "But—perhaps I shall convert."

Kirkbride blinked in surprise; not the least of the surprises of this day. "What was it that the caller added to the end of the chant?" he asked, for he had noted an extra sentence, called in a tone deeper than the rest.

The man's gaze returned to Kirkbride's face. "He said, 'God alone is good, God alone is great, and He is very good to us this day, Oh people of Damascus.'"

At that moment, the door opened, and a much subdued delegation filed out of the door. Allenby turned, as Aurens followed a little into the ante-chamber, and stopped. His white robes seemed to glow in the growing dusk, and Kirkbride was astonished to see a hint of a smile on the thin, ascetic lips.

"You can't keep this going, you know," Allenby said, more weary than angry. "This isn't natural. It's going to fall apart."

"Not while I live, I think," Aurens said, in his crisp, precise English.

"Well, when you die, then," Allenby retorted savagely. "And the moment you're dead, we'll be waiting—just like the vultures you called us in there."

If anything, the smile only grew a trifle. "Perhaps. Perhaps not. There is wealth here, and wealth can purchase educations. In a few years, there will be men of the tribes who can play the politicians' game with the best of them. Years more, and there will be men of the tribes who look farther than the next spring, into the next century. We need not change, you know— we need only adopt the tools and weapons, and turn them to our own use. I would not look to cut up the East too soon, if I were you." Now he chuckled, something that surprised Kirkbride so much that his jaw dropped. "And in any event," Aurens concluded carelessly, "I intend to live a very long time."

Allenby swore under his breath, and turned on his heel. The rest, all but Kirkbride, followed.

He could not, for Aurens had turned that luminous blue gaze upon him again.

"Oxford, I think," the rich voice said.

He nodded, unable to speak.

The gaze released him, and turned to look out one of the windows; after a moment, Kirkbride recognized the direction. East.

Baghdad.

"I shall have need of Oxford men, to train my people in the English way of deception," the voice said, carelessly. "And the French way of double-dealing, and the German way of ruthlessness. To train them so that they understand, but do not become these things."

Kirkbride found his voice. "You aren't trying to claim that 'your people' aren't double-dealing, deceitful, and ruthless, I hope?" he said, letting sarcasm color his words. "I think that would be a little much, even from you."

The eyes turned back to recapture his, and somewhere, behind the blue fire, there was a hint of humor.

"Oh, no," Aurens said, with gentle warmth. "But those are *Arab* deceptions, double-dealings, and ruthlessness. Clever, but predictable to another Arab; these things are understood all around. They have not yet learned the ways of men who call themselves civilized. I should like to see them well-armored, before Allah calls me again."

Kirkbride raised an eyebrow at that. "You haven't done anything any clever man couldn't replicate," he replied, half in accusation. "Without the help of Allah."

"Have I ever said differently?" Aurens traded him look for ironic look.

"I heard what happened before the battle." Aurens, they said, had ridden his snow-white stallion before them all. "In whose name do you ride?" he had called. "Like a trumpet," Kirkbride's informant had told him, as awed as if he had spoken of the Archangel Gabriel.

And the answer, every man joined in one roar of response. *"In the name of Allah, and of Aurens."*

Aurens only looked amused. "Ride with me to Baghdad." This had less the sound of a request than a command. "Ride with me to Yemen. Help me shape the world." Again, the touch of humor, softening it all. "Or at least, so much of it as we can. *Inshallah.* I have Stirling, I have some others, I should like you."

Kirkbride weighed the possibilities, the gains, the losses. Then weighed them against the intangible; the fire in the eyes, the look of eagles.

Then, once again, he looked Aurens full in the eyes; was caught in the blue fire of them, and felt that fire catch hold in his soul, outweighing any other thoughts or considerations.

Slowly, knowing that he wagered all on a single cast of the dice, he drew himself up to attention. Then he saluted; slowly, gravely, to the approval of every one of the robed men in that room.

"To Baghdad, and Yemen, Aurens," he said. *"Inshallah."*

This story first appeared in Fantasy Book *magazine; it was later combined with the following story, "Dragon's Teeth," and stories by Marion Zimmer Bradley and Jennifer Roberson for a volume originally called* Bardic Voices, *later published by DAW as* Spell Singers.

Martis is very close to being a soul-sister to Tarma and Kethry.

Balance

"You're my bodyguard?"

The swordsman standing in the door to Martis' cluttered quarters blinked in startled surprise. He'd been warned that the sorceress was not easy to work with, but he hadn't expected her to be quite so rude. He tried not to stare at the tall, disheveled mage who stood, hands on hips, amid the wreckage she'd made of her own quarters. The woman's square features, made harsher by nervous tension, reflected her impatience as the mercenary groped for the proper response to make.

Martis was a little embarrassed by her own ill-manners, but really, this—child—must surely be aware that his appearance was hardly likely to invoke any confidence in his fighting ability!

For one thing, he was slim and undersized; he didn't even boast the inches Martis had. For another, the way he dressed was absurd; almost is if he were

93

a dancer got up as a swordsman for some theatrical production. He was too clean, too fastidious; that costume wasn't even the least worn-looking—and silk, for Kevreth's sake! Blue-green silk at that! He carried two swords, and whoever had heard of anyone able to use two swords at once outside of a legend? His light brown hair was worn longer than any other fighter Martis had ever seen—too long, Martis thought with disapproval, and likely to get in the way despite the headband he wore to keep it out of his eyes. He even moved more like a dancer than a fighter.

This was supposed to guard her back? It looked more like she'd be guarding *him.* It was difficult to imagine anything that looked less like a warrior.

"The Guard-serjant did send this one for that purpose, Mage-lady, but since this one does not please, he shall return that another may be assigned."

Before Martis could say anything to stop him, he had whirled about and vanished from the doorway without a sound. Martis sighed in exasperation and turned back to her packing. At this moment in time she was not about to start worrying about the tender feelings of a hire-sword!

She hadn't gotten much farther along when she was interrupted again—this time by a bestial roar from the bottom of the stair.

"MARTIS!" the walls shook with each step as Trebenth, Guard-serjant to the Mage's Guild, climbed the staircase to Martis' rooms. Most floors and stairs in the Guild-hold shook when Trebenth was about. He was anything but fat—but compared to the lean mages he worked for, he was just so—massive. Outside of the Guards' quarters, most of the Guild-hold wasn't designed to cope with his bulk. Martis could hear him rumbling under his breath as he ascended; the far-off mutterings of a volcano soon to erupt. She flinched and steeled herself for the inevitable outburst.

He practically filled the doorframe; as he glared at Martis, she half expected steam to shoot from his nostrils. It didn't help that he *looked* like a volcano, dressed in Mage-hireling red, from his tunic to his boots; it matched the red of his hair and beard, and the angry flush suffusing his features. "Martis, what in the name of the Seven is your *problem?*"

"My *problem,* as you call it, is the fact that I need a bodyguard, not a temple dancer!" Martis matched him, glare for glare, her flat gray eyes mirroring his impatience. "What are you trying to push on me, Ben? Zaila's toenails, if it weren't for the fact that Guild law prevents a mage from carrying weapons, I'd take sword myself rather than trust my safety to *that* toy!"

"Dammit, Martis, you've complained about every guard I've ever assigned to you! *This* one was too sullen, *that* one was too talkative, t'other one *snored* at night—" he snorted contemptuously. "Mother of the Gods, Martis, snored?"

"You ought to know by now that a mage needs undisturbed sleep more than food—besides, anyone stalking us would have been able to locate our campsite by ear alone!" she replied, pushing a lock of blond hair—just beginning to show signs of gray—out of her eyes. The gesture showed both her annoyance and her impatience; and pulling her robe a bit straighter could not conceal the fact that her hands trembled a little.

He lost a portion of his exasperation; after all, he and Martis were old friends, and she *did* have a point. "Look, when have I ever sent you a guard that couldn't do the job? I think this time I've really found the perfect match for you—he's quiet, half the time you don't even know he's there, in fact—and Mart, the lad's *good.*"

"*Him?* Ben, have you lost what little mind you ever had? Who told you he was good?"

"Nobody," he replied, affronted. "I don't take

anyone's word on the guards I hire. I tested him myself. The boy moves so fast he doesn't *need* armor, and as for those two toy swords of his, well—he's good. He came within a hair of taking *me* down."

Martis raised an eyebrow in surprise. To her certain knowledge, it had been years since anyone could boast of taking Trebenth down—or even coming close.

"Why's he dress himself up like a friggin' faggot, then?"

"I don't know, Mart. Ask him yourself. I don't care if my guards wear battle-plate or paint themselves green, so long as they can do the job. Mart, what's bothering you? You're not usually so damn picky. You generally save your complaining till the job's over."

Martis collapsed tiredly into a chair, shoving aside a box of tagged herbs and a pile of wrinkled clothing. Trebenth saw with sudden concern the lines of worry crossing her forehead and her puffy, bruised-looking eyelids.

"It's the job. Guild business—internal problems."

"Somebody need disciplining?"

"Worse. Gone renegade—and he's raising power with blood-magic. He was very good before he started this; I've no doubt he's gotten better. If we can't do something about him now, we'll have another Sable Mage-King on our hands."

Trebenth whistled through his teeth. "A black adept in the making, eh? No wonder they're sending you."

Martis sighed. "Just when I'd begun to think the Guild would never set me to anything but teaching again. But that's not what's troubling me, old friend. I knew him—a long and close association. He was one of my best students."

Trebenth winced. To set Martis out after one of her old students was a cruel thing to do. The powers manipulated by mages gifted them with much that lesser folk could envy—but those powers took as well as gave. Use of magic for any length of time rendered the user sterile. In many ways Martis' students took the place of the children she'd never have.

They often took the place of friends, too. She'd served the Guild since she'd attained Masterclass, and her barely past what for the unTalented would have been marriageable age. There were few sorcerers among her contemporaries, male or female, that didn't secretly fear and envy the Masterclass mages. There were no mages of her own rank interested in taking a lover whose powers equaled their own. They preferred their women pliant, pretty, and not too bright. Martis's relations with her own kind were cordial, but barren.

Trebenth himself had been one of the few lovers she'd had—and she hadn't taken another since he'd toppled like a felled tree for his little Margwynwy, and she'd severed that side of their relationship herself. It was times like this one, with her loneliness standing bare in her eyes, that he pitied her with all his heart.

Martis caught his glance, and smiled thinly. "The Council did their level best to spare me this, I'll give them that much. The fact is, we don't know for certain how deeply he's gotten himself in yet; we know he's been sacrificing animals, but so far rumors of *human* deaths are just that—rumors. They want to give him every chance to get himself out of the hole he's digging for himself. Frankly, he's got too much Talent to waste. One of the factors in deciding to send me is that they hope he'll give me a chance to reason with him. If reason doesn't work, well, I'm one of the few sorcerers around with a chance of defeating him. After all, I taught him. I know all his strengths and weaknesses."

"*Knew,*" Trebenth reminded her, "Can I assign Lyran to your service, now that I've vouched for his ability, or are you still wanting someone else?"

"Who? Oh—the boy. All right, Ben, you know what

you're doing. You've been hiring guards as long as
I've been training mages. Tell him to get the horses
ready, I want to make a start before noon."

When Martis had finished ransacking her room for
what she wanted, she slung her packed saddlebags
over her shoulder and slammed the door on the entire
mess. By the time she returned—*if* she returned—
the Guild servants would have put everything back
in order again. That was one of the few benefits of
being a Masterclass sorceress. The Guild provided
comfortable, safe quarters and reliable servants who
never complained—at least not to her. Those benefits
were paid for, though; a Masterclass mage lived and
died in service to the Guild. No one with that rat-
ing was ever permitted to take service independently.

Martis had a liking for heights and a peculiar
phobia about having people living above her, so her
room was at the top of the staircase that linked all
four floors of the Masters' quarters. As she descended
the stairs, she found that a certain reluctant curiosity was beginning to emerge concerning this unlikely
swordsman, Lyran. The order she'd given Trebenth,
to have the lad ready the horses, was in itself a test.
Martis' personal saddlebeast was an irascible bay
gelding of indeterminant age and vile temper, the
possessor of a number of bad habits. He'd been the
cause of several grooms ending in the Healer's hands
before this. Martis kept him for two reasons—the first
was that his gait was as sweet as his temper was foul;
the second that he could be trusted to carry a babe
safely through Hell once it was securely in the saddle.
To Martis, as to any other mage, these traits far
outweighed any other considerations. If this Lyran
could handle old Tosspot, there was definitely hope
for him.

It was Martis' turn to blink in surprise when she
emerged into the dusty, sunlit courtyard. Waiting for

her was the swordsman, the reins of his own beast
in one hand and those of Tosspot in the other. Tosspot
was not trying to bite, kick, or otherwise mutilate
either the young man or his horse. His saddle was
in place, and Martis could tell by his disgruntled
expression that he hadn't managed to get away with
his usual trick of "blowing" so that his saddle girth
would be loose. More amazing still, the swordsman
didn't appear to be damaged in any way, didn't even
seem out of breath.

"Did he give you any trouble?" she asked, fastening
her saddlebags to Tosspot's harness, and adroitly
avoiding his attempt to step on her foot.

"He is troublesome, yes, Mage-lady, but this one
has dealt with a troublesome beast before," Lyran
replied seriously. At just that moment the swordsman's
dust-brown mare lashed out with a wicked hoof,
which the young man dodged with reflexive agility.
He reached up and seized one of the mare's ears and
twisted it once, hard. The mare immediately resumed
her good behavior. "Sometimes it would seem that
the best animals are also the vilest of temper," he
continued as though he hadn't been interrupted. "It
then is of regrettable necessity to prove, that though
they are stronger, this one has more knowledge."

Martis mounted Tosspot, and nodded with satisfaction when his girth proved to be as tight as it
looked. "I don't think this old boy will be giving you
any more trouble. From the sour look he's wearing,
I'd say he learned his lesson quite thoroughly."

The swordsman seemed to glide into his saddle and
gracefully inclined his head in thanks for the com-
pliment. "Truly he must have more intelligence than
Jesalis," he replied, reining in his mare so that the
sorceress could take the lead, "For this one must prove
the truth of the lesson to her at least once a day."

"Jesalis?" Martis asked incredulously; for the jesalis
was a fragile blossom of rare perfume, and nothing

about the ugly little mare could remind anyone of a flower.

"Balance, Mage-lady," Lyran replied, so earnestly that Martis had to hide a smile. "So foul a temper has she, that it is necessary to give her a sweet name to leaven her nature."

They rode out of the Guild hold in single file with Martis riding in the lead, since protocol demanded that the "hireling" ride behind the "mistress" while they were inside the town wall. Once they'd passed the gates, they reversed position. Lyran would lead the way as well as providing a guard, for all of Martis' attention must be taken up by her preparations to meet with her wayward former student. Tosspot would obey his training and follow wherever the rider of Jesalis led.

This was the reason that Tosspot's gait and reliability were worth more than gold pieces. Most of Martis' time in the saddle would be spent in a trance-like state as she gradually gathered power to her. It was this ability to garner and store power that made her a Master-class sorceress—for after all, the most elaborate spell is useless without the power to set it in motion.

There were many ways to accumulate power. Martis' was to gather the little aimless threads of it given off by living creatures in their daily lives. Normally this went unused, gradually dissipating, like dye poured into a river. Martis could take these little tag-ends of energy, spin them out and weave them into a fabric that was totally unlike what they had been before. This required total concentration, and there was no room in her calculations for mistake.

Martis was grateful that Lyran was neither sullen nor inclined to chatter. She was able to sink into her magic gathering-trance undistracted by babble and undisturbed by a muddy, surly aura riding in front of her. Perhaps Ben had been right after all. The boy was so unobtrusive that she might have been riding alone. She spared one scant moment to regret faintly that she would not be able to enjoy the beauties of the summer woods and meadows they were to ride through. It was so seldom that she came this way . . .

The atmosphere was so peaceful that it wasn't until she sensed—more than felt—the touch of the bodyguard's hand on her leg that she roused up again. The sun was westering, and before her was a small clearing, with Lyran's horse contentedly grazing and a small, neat camp already set up. Martis' tent was to the west of the clearing, a cluster of boulders behind it, and the tent-flap open to the cheerful fire. Lyran's bedroll lay on the opposite side. Jesalis was unsaddled, and her tack laid beside the bedroll. From what Martis could see, all of her own belongings had been placed unopened just inside the tent. And all had been accomplished without Martis being even remotely aware of it.

"Your pardon, Mage-lady," Lyran said apologetically, "But your horse must be unsaddled."

"And you can't do that with me still sitting on him," Martis finished for him, highly amused. "Why didn't you wake me earlier? I'm perfectly capable of helping make camp."

"The Guard-serjant made it plain to this one that you must be allowed to work your magics without distraction. Will you come down?"

"Just one moment—" There was something subtly wrong, but Martis couldn't pinpoint what it was. Before she could say anything, however, Lyran suddenly seized her wrist and pulled her down from her saddle, just as an arrow arced through the air where she had been. Lyran gave a shrill whistle, and Jesalis threw up her head, sniffed the breeze, and charged into the trees to their left. Martis quickly sought cover in some nearby bushes, as Lyran hit the ground and rolled up into a wary crouch.

A scream from where the mare had vanished told that the horse had removed the obstacle of the archer, but he had not been alone. From under the cover of the trees stepped not one, but three swordsmen. Lyran regained his feet in one swift motion, drew the swords he wore slung across his back, and faced them in a stance that was not of any fighting style Martis recognized. He placed himself so that they would have to pass him to reach her.

The first of the assassins—Martis was reasonably sure that this was what they were—laughed and swatted at Lyran with the flat of his blade in a careless, backhanded stroke, aiming negligently for his head.

"This little butterfly is mine—we will see if he likes to play the woman he apes—" he began.

Lyran moved, lithe as a ferret. The speaker stared stupidly at the sword blade impaling his chest. Lyran had ducked and come up inside his guard, taking him out before he'd even begun to realize what the bodyguard was about.

Lyran pulled his blade free of the new-made corpse while the assassin still stood. He whirled to face the other two before the first fell to the ground.

They moved in on him with far more caution than their companion had, circling him warily to attack him from opposite sides. He fended off their assault easily, his two swords blurring, they moved so fast, his movement dance-like. But despite his skill he could seem to find no opening to make a counter-attack. For the moment all three were deadlocked. Martis chafed angrily at her feeling of helplessness—the combative magics she'd prepared were all meant to be used against another mage. To use any of the spells she knew that would work against a fighter, she'd have to reach her supplies in her saddlebags—now rather hopelessly out of reach. She found that she was sharply aware of the incongruous scent of the crushed blossoms that lay beneath the dead man's body.

The deadlock was broken before Martis could do more than curse at her own helplessness.

Within the space of a breath, Lyran feinted at the third of the assassins, drawing the second to attack. He caught his opponent's blade in a bind, and disarmed him with practiced ease. Then the third lunged at him, and he moved aside just enough for his blade to skim past his chest. Lyran's left-hand blade licked out and cut his throat with the recovery of the stroke that had disarmed the second. Before Martis could blink, he continued the flow of movement before the third could fall to cut the second nearly in half with the sword in his right.

And behind him, the first dead man rose, sword in hand, and hacked savagely at the unsuspecting Lyran's blind side. Lyran got one blade up in time to deflect the blow, but the power behind it forced him to one knee. The Undead hammered at the bodyguard, showing sorcerous strength that far exceeded his abilities in life. Lyran was forced down and back, until the Undead managed to penetrate his defenses with an under-and-over strike at his left arm.

The slice cut Lyran's arm and shoulder nearly to the bone. The sword dropped from his fingers and he tried to fend off the liche with the right alone.

The Undead continued to press the attack, its blows coming even faster than before. Lyran was sent sprawling helplessly when it caught him across the temple with the flat of its blade.

Martis could see—almost as if time had slowed—that he would be unable to deflect the liche's next strike.

She, Lyran, and the Undead all made their moves simultaneously.

Martis destroyed the magic that animated the corpse, but not before it had made a two-handed stab at the bodyguard.

But Lyran had managed another of those

ferret-quick squirms. As the liche struck, he threw himself sideways—a move Martis would have thought impossible, and wound up avoiding impalement by inches. The Undead collapsed then, as the magic supporting it dissolved.

Freed from having to defend himself, Lyran dropped his second blade, groped for the wound, and sagged to his knees in pain.

Martis sprinted from out of hiding, reaching the swordsman's side in five long strides. Given the amount of damage done his arm, it was Lyran's good fortune that his charge was Masterclass! In her mind she was gathering up the strands of power she'd accumulated during the day, and reweaving them into a spell of healing; a spell she knew so well she needed nothing but her memory to create.

Even in that short period of time, Lyran had had the presence of mind to tear off the headband that had kept his long hair out of his eyes and tie it tightly about his upper arm, slowing the bleeding. As Martis reached for the wounded arm, Lyran tried feebly to push her away.

"There is—no need—Mage-lady," he gasped, his eyes pouring tears of pain.

Martis muttered an obscenity and cast the spell. "No guard in *my* service stays wounded," she growled, "I don't care what or who you've served before; I take care of my own."

Having said her say and worked her magics, she went to look at the bodies while the spell did its work.

What she found was very interesting indeed, so interesting that at first she didn't notice that Lyran had come to stand beside her where she knelt. When she did notice, it was with some surprise that she saw the slightly greenish cast to the guard's face, and realized that Lyran was striving valiantly not to be sick. Lyran must have seen her surprise written clear in her expression, for he said almost defensively, "This one makes his living by the sword, Mage-lady, but it does not follow that he enjoys viewing the consequences of his labor."

Martis made a noncommittal sound and rose. "Well, you needn't think your scoutcraft's at fault, young man. These men—the archer, too, I'd judge—were brought here by magic just a few moments before they attacked us. I wish you could have taken one alive. He could have told us a lot."

"It is this one's humble opinion that one need not look far for the author of the attack," Lyran said, looking askance at Martis.

"Oh, no doubt it's Kelven's work, all right. He knows what my aura looks like well enough to track me from a distance and pinpoint my location with very little trouble, and I'm sure he knows that it's me the Guild would send after him. And he knows the nearest Gatepoint, and that I'd be heading there. No, what I wish I knew were the orders he gave this bunch. Were they to kill—or to disable and capture?" She dusted her hands, aware that the sun was almost gone and the air was cooling. "Well, I'm no necromancer, so the knowledge is gone beyond my retrieval."

"Shall this one remove them?" Lyran still looked a little sick.

"No, the healing-spell I set on you isn't done yet, and I don't want you tearing that wound open again. Go take care of Tosspot and find your mare, wherever she's gotten herself to. I'll get rid of them."

Martis piled the bodies together and burned them to ash with mage-fire. It was a bit of a waste of power, but the energy liberated by the deaths of the assassins would more than make up for the loss—though Martis felt just a little guilty at using that power. Violent death always released a great deal of energy— it was a short-cut to gaining vast quantities of it— which was why blood-magic was proscribed by the Guild. Making use of what was released when you had to kill in self-defense was one thing—cold-blooded killing to gain power was something else.

When Martis returned to the campsite, she discovered that not only had Lyran located his mare and unharnessed and tethered Tosspot, but that he'd made dinner as well. Browning over the pocket-sized fire was a brace of rabbits.

"Two?" she asked quizzically. "I can't eat more than half of one. And where did you get them?"

"This one has modest skill with a sling, and there were many opportunities as we rode," Lyran replied, "And the second one is for breakfast in the morning."

Lyran had placed Tosspot's saddle on the opposite side of the fire from his own, just in front of the open tent. Martis settled herself on her saddle to enjoy her dinner. The night air was pleasantly cool, night creatures made sounds around them that were reassuring because it meant that no one was disturbing them. The insects of the daylight hours were gone, those of the night had not yet appeared. And the contradictions in her guard's appearance and behavior made a pleasant puzzle to mull over.

"I give up," she said at last, breaking the silence between them, silence that had been punctuated by the crackle of the fire. "You are the strangest guard I have ever had."

Lyran looked up, and the fire revealed his enigmatic expression. He had eaten his half of the rabbit, but had done so as if it were a duty rather than a pleasure. He still looked a bit sickly.

"Why does this one seem strange to you, Mage-lady?"

"You dress like a dancer playing at being a warrior, you fight like a friggin' guard-troop all by yourself—then you get sick afterwards because you killed someone. You wear silks that would do a harlot proud, but you ride a mare that's a damn trained killer. What *are* you, boy? What land spawned something like you?"

"This one comes from far—a great distance to the west and south. It is not likely that you have ever heard of the People, Mage-lady. The Guard-serjant had not. As for why this one is the way he is—this one follows a Way."

"*The* Way?"

"No, Mage-lady, A Way. The People believe that there are many such Ways, and ours is of no more merit than any other. Our way is the Way of Balance."

"You said something about 'balance' before—" Now Martis' curiosity was truly aroused. "Just what does this Way entail?"

"It is simplicity. One must strive to achieve Balance in all things in one's life. This one—is on a kind of pilgrimage to find such Balance, to find a place where this one may fit within the pattern of All. Because this one's nature is such that he does well to live by the sword, he must strive to counter this by using that sword in the service of peace—and to cultivate peace in other aspects of his life. And, in part, it must be admitted that this one fosters a helpless outer aspect," Lyran smiled wryly. "The Mage-lady will agree that appearing ineffectual does much to throw the opponent off his guard. So—that is the *what* of this one. As to the why—the People believe that the better one achieves Balance, the better one will be reborn."

"I certainly hope you don't include good and evil in your Balance—either that, or I'll do the cooking from now on." Lyran laughed.

"No Mage-lady, for how could one weigh 'good' and 'evil'? Assuredly, it was 'good' that this one slew your foes, but was it not 'evil' to them? Sometimes things are plainly one or the other, but too often it depends upon where one stands one's own self. A primary tenet of our Way is to do no harm when at all possible—to wound, rather than kill, subdue rather than wound, reason rather than subdue, and recall when reasoning that the other may have the right of it."

"Simple to state, but—"

"Ai, difficult to live by. It would seem that most things worth having are wrapped in difficulty. Have you not spent your life in magecraft, and yet still learn? And does this not set you farther apart from others—sacrificing knowledge for the common ties of life?"

Martis scrutinized her companion across the flames. Not so young, after all. Not nearly so young as she had thought—nor so simple. It was only the slight build, the guileless eyes, the innocence of the heart-shaped face that made you think "child." And attractive too. Damned attractive . . . "Don't be a fool," she scolded herself, "You haven't the time or energy to waste—besides, he's young enough to be your son. Well, maybe not your son. But too damned young for the likes of you! Hellfires! You have more to think about than a sweet-faced hireling! Get your mind back to business."

"Before we sleep, I'm intending to gather power as I was doing on the road," she stretched a little. "I want you to rouse me when the moon rises."

"Mage-lady—would quiet chanting disturb you?" Lyran asked anxiously. "This one would offer words for those slain."

"Whatever for? They wouldn't have mourned *you!*" Once again, Lyran had surprised her.

"That is their Way, not this one's. If one does not mourn that one has slain, the heart soon dies. Under other circumstances, might they not have been comrades?"

"I suppose you're right," Martis replied thoughtfully. "No, chanting isn't going to disturb me any. Just make sure you also keep a good watch out for any more surprises."

"Of a certainty, Mage-lady." Lyran didn't even seem annoyed at the needless admonition, a fact that made Martis even more thoughtful. Professional mercenaries she'd known in the past tended to get a bit touchy about mages giving them "orders" like she'd just given him. Nothing much seemed to ruffle that serene exterior. How long, she wondered, had it taken him to achieve that kind of mind-set? And what kind of discipline had produced it? A puzzle; truly a puzzle.

The next day brought them to a ring of standing stones—the Gate-site. The inherent magic residing in this place made it possible to use it as a kind of bridge to almost any other place on the earth's surface. Martis had been to Kelven's tower once, and with mage-habit had memorized the lay of the land surrounding it. They would be able to ride straight from *here* to *there* once the proper spell was set into motion. This would have another benefit, besides saving them a long and tiring journey; Kelven would 'lose' them if he had been tracking them, and without knowing exactly where to look for them, would not know how many of them had survived his attack. They rested undisturbed that evening, with Martis quickly regaining from the place the energy she spent in shielding their presence there.

The Gate spell took the better part of the next morning to set up. Martis had no intentions of bringing them in very near, for she had other notions as to how she wanted this confrontation to be played out. After a light noon meal, she activated the Gate.

The standing stones began to glow, not from within, but as if an unquenchable fire burned along their surfaces. The fire from each reached out to join with the fires of the stones on either side. Before an hour had passed, the ring was a near-solid thing of pulsating orange light.

Martis waited until the power-flux built to an internal drawing that was well-nigh unendurable—then led them at a gallop between two of the stones. They rode in through one side—but not out the other.

They emerged in the vicinity of Kelven's tower—and the confrontation Martis had been dreading was at hand.

She wasn't sure whether the fact that there had been no attempt to block them at the Gate was good or bad. It could be that Kelven was having second thoughts about the situation, and would be ready to be persuaded to amend his ways. It also could be that he was taking no further chances on the skills of underlings or working at a distance, and was planning to eliminate her himself in a sorcerers' duel.

They rode through country that was fairly wild and heavily wooded, but Kelven's tower lay beyond where the woods ended, at the edge of a grass-plain. Martis described the situation to Lyran, who listened attentively, then fell silent. Martis was not inclined to break that silence, lost in her own contemplations.

"Mage-lady—" Lyran broke into Martis' thoughts not long before they were to reach Kelven's stronghold. "—is it possible that the Mage-lord may not know about the continued survival of this one?"

"It's more than possible, it's likely," Martis told him. "I've been shielding our movements ever since the attack."

"But would you have gone on if this one had fallen? Would it not have been more likely that you would return to the Guild Hall to seek other guards?"

They had stopped on the crest of a ridge. Below them lay grasslands and scrub forest that stretched for furlongs in all directions but the one they had come.

Kelven's tower was easily seen from here, and about an hour's distance away. The sun beat down on their heads, and insects droned lazily. The scene seemed ridiculously incongruous as a site of imminent conflict.

Martis laughed—a sound that held no trace of humor. "Anybody else but me *would* do just that. But I'm stubborn, and I've got a rotten temper. Kelven knows that. He watched me drag myself and two pupils—he was one of them—through a stinking, bug-infested bog once, with no guides and no bodyguards. The guides had been killed and the guards were in no shape to follow us, y'see; we'd been attacked by a Nightmare. I was by-Zaila not going to let it get away back to its Lair! By the time we found it I was so mad that I fried the entire herd at the Lair by myself. If you'd been killed back there, I'd be out for blood—or at least a *damn* convincing show of repentance. And I wouldn't let a little thing like having no other guard stand in my way."

"Then let this one propose a plan, Mage-lady. The land below is much like this one's homeland. It would be possible to slip away from you and make one's way hidden in the tall grass—and this one has another weapon than a sling." From his saddlebag Lyran took a small, but obviously strong bow, unstrung, and a quiverful of short arrows. "The weapon is too powerful to use for hunting, Mage-lady, unless one were hunting larger creatures than rabbits and birds. This one could remain within bow-shot, but unknown to the Mage-lord, if you wished."

"I'm glad you thought of that, and I think it's more than a good idea," Martis said, gazing at the tower. Several new thoughts had occurred to her, none of them pleasant. It was entirely possible that Kelven wanted her here, had allowed them to walk into a trap. "If nothing else—this is an order. If Kelven takes me captive—shoot *me*. Shoot to kill. Get him too, if you can, but make sure you kill me. There's too many ways he could use me, and anyone can be broken, if the mage has time enough. I can bind my own death-energy before he can use it—I think."

Lyran nodded, and slipped off his mare. He rearranged saddle-pad and pack to make it appear that Martis was using the ill-tempered beast as a pack animal. In the time it took for Martis to gather up the mare's reins, he had vanished into the grassland without a trace.

Martis rode towards the tower as slowly as she could, giving Lyran plenty of time to keep up with the horses and still remain hidden.

She could see as she came closer to the tower that there was at least one uncertainty that was out of the way. She'd not have to call challenge to bring Kelven out of his tower—he was already waiting for her. Perhaps, she thought with a brightening of hope, this meant he *was* willing to cooperate.

When Lyran saw, after taking cover in a stand of scrub, that the mage Kelven had come out of his tower to wait for Martis, he lost no time in getting himself positioned within bowshot. He actually beat the sorceress's arrival by several moments. The spot he'd chosen, beneath a bush just at the edge of the mowed area that surrounded the tower, was ideal in all respects but one—since it was upwind of where the mage stood, he would be unable to hear them speak. He only hoped he'd be able to read the mage's intentions from his actions.

There were small things to alert a watcher to the intent of a mage to attack—provided the onlooker knew exactly what to look for. Before leaving, Trebenth had briefed him carefully on the signs to watch for warning of an attack by magic without proper challenge being issued. Lyran only hoped that his own eyes and instincts would be quick enough.

"Greetings, Martis," Kelven said evenly, his voice giving no clue as to his mindset.

Martis was a little uneasy to see that he'd taken
to dressing in stark, unrelieved black. The Kelven she
remembered had taken an innocent pleasure in dressing like a peacock. For the rest, he didn't look much
different from when he'd been her student—he'd
grown a beard and moustache, whose black hue did
not quite match his dark brown hair. His narrow face
still reminded her of a hawk's, with sharp eyes that
missed nothing. She looked closer at him, and was
alarmed to see that his pupils were dilated such that
there was very little to be seen of the brown irises.
Drugs sometimes produced that effect—particularly
the drugs associated with blood-magic.

"Greetings, Kelven. The tales we hear of you are
not good these days," she said carefully, dismount-
ing and approaching him, trying to look stern and
angry.

"Tales. Yes, those old women on the Council are
fond of tales. I gather they've sent you to bring the
erring sheep back into the fold?" he said. She couldn't
tell if he was sneering.

"Kelven, the course you're set on can do no one any
good," she faltered a little, a recollection of Kelven
seated contentedly at her feet suddenly springing to
mind. He'd been so like a son—this new Kelven *must*
be some kind of aberration! "Please—you were a good
student; one of my best. There must be a lot of good
in you still, and you have the potential to reach Masterclass if you put your mind to it." She was uncomfortably aware that she was pleading, and an odd
corner of her mind noted the buzzing drone of the
insects in the grass behind her. "I was very fond of you,
you know I was—I'll speak for you, if you want. You
can 'come back to the fold,' as you put it, with no one
to hold the past against you. But you must also know
that no matter how far you go, there's only one end
for a practitioner of blood-magic. And you must know
that if I can't persuade you, I have to stop you."

There was a coldness about him that made her recoil a little from him—the ice of one who had divorced himself from humankind. She found herself longing to see just a hint of the old Kelven; one tiny glimpse to prove he wasn't as far gone as she feared he must be. But it seemed no such remnant existed.

"Really?" he smiled. "I never would have guessed."

Any weapon of magic she would have been prepared for. The last thing she ever would have expected was the dagger in his hand. She stared at the flash of light off the steel as he lifted it, too dumbfounded to do more than raise her hands against it in an ineffectual attempt at defense.

His attack was completed before she'd done more than register the fact that he was making it.

"First you have to beat me, *teacher*," he said viciously, as he took the single step between them and plunged it into her breast.

She staggered back from the shock and pain, all breath and thought driven from her.

"I'm no match for you in a sorcerer's duel—" he said, a cruel smile curving his lips as his hands moved in the spell to steal her dying power from her. "—not yet—but I'll be the match of *any* of you with all I shall gain from your death!"

Incredibly, he had moved like a striking snake, his every movement preplanned—all this had taken place in the space of a few eyeblinks. She crumpled to the ground with a gasp of agony, both hands clutching ineffectually at the hilt. The pain and shock ripped away her ability to think, even to set into motion the spell she'd set to lock her dying energy away from his use. Blood trickled hotly between her fingers, as her throat closed against the words she had meant to speak to set a death-binding against him. She could only endure the hot agony, and the knowledge that she had failed—and then looked up in time to see three arrows strike him almost simultaneously, two in the chest, the third in the throat. Her hands clenched on the dagger hilt as he collapsed on top of her with a strangling gurgle. Agony drove her down into darkness.

Her last conscious thought was of gratitude to Lyran.

There were frogs and insects singing, which seemed odd to Martis. No one mentioned frogs or insects in any version of the afterlife that she'd ever heard. As her hearing improved, she could hear nightbirds in the distance, and close at hand, the sound of a fire and the stirring of nearby horses. That definitely did not fit in with the afterlife—unless one counted Hellfires, and this certainly didn't sound big enough to be one of those. Her eyes opened slowly, gritty and sore, and not focusing well.

Lyran sat by her side, anxiety lining his brow and exhaustion graying his face.

"Either I'm alive," Martis coughed, "or you're dead—and I don't remember you being dead."

"You live, Mage-lady—but it was a very near thing. Almost, I did not reach you in time. You are fortunate that sorcerers are not weapons-trained—no swordsman would have missed your heart as he did."

"Martis. My name is Martis—you've earned the right to use it." Martis coughed again, amazed that there was so little pain—that the worst she felt was a vague ache in her lungs, a dreamy lassitude and profound weakness. "Why am I still alive? Even if he missed the heart, that blow was enough to kill. You're no Healer—" she paused, all that Lyran had told her about his "Way" running through her mind. "—are you?"

"As my hands deal death, so they must also preserve life," Lyran replied. "Yes, among my people, all who live by weapons are also trained as Healers, even as Healers must learn to use weapons, if only to defend themselves and the wounded upon the field of battle."

He rubbed eyes that looked as red and sore as her own felt. "Since I am not Healer-born, it was hard, very hard. I am nearly as weak as you as a consequence. It will be many days before I regain my former competence, my energy, or my strength. It is well you have no more enemies that I must face, for I would do so, I fear, on my hands and knees!"

Martis frowned. "You aren't talking the way you used to."

Lyran chuckled. "It is said that even when at the point of death the Mage will observe and record— and question. Yes, I use familiar speech with you, my Mage-lady. The Healing for one not born to the Gift is not like yours—I sent my soul into your body to heal it; for a time we were one. That is why I am so wearied. You are part of myself as a consequence— and I now speak to you as one of my People."

"Thank the gods. I was getting very tired of your everlasting 'this one's.'" They laughed weakly together, before Martis broke off with another fit of coughing.

"What happens to you when we get back to the Guild-hold?" Martis asked presently.

"My continued employment by the Guild was dependent on your satisfaction with my performance," Lyran replied. "Since I assume that you are satisfied—"

"I'm alive, aren't I? The mission succeeded. I'm a good bit more than merely 'satisfied' with the outcome."

"Then I believe I am to become part of the regular staff, to be assigned to whatever mage happens to need a guard. And—I think here I have found what I sought; the place where my sword may serve peace, the place the Way has designed for me." Despite his contented words, his eyes looked wistful.

Martis was feeling unwontedly sensitive to the nuances in his expression. There was something behind those words she had not expected—hope—longing? And—directed at *her?*

And—under the weariness, was there actually *desire?*

"Would that I could continue in your service, Mage—Martis. I think perhaps we deal well together."

"Hmm," Martis began tentatively, not sure she was reading him correctly; not daring to believe what she thought she saw. "I'm entitled to a permanent hireling as a Master, I just never exercised the privilege. Would you be interested?"

"As a hireling—alone? Or, could I hope you would have more of me than bought-service?"

Dear gods, was he asking what she *thought* he was asking? "Lyran, you surely can't be seriously propositioning me?"

"We have been one," he sighed, touching her cheek lightly. "As you have felt a tie to me, so have I felt drawn to you. There is that in each of us that satisfies a need in the other, I think. I—care for you. I would gladly be a friend; more than friend, if you choose."

"But I'm old enough to be your mother!"

"Ah, lady," he smiled, his eyes old in his young face, "What are years? Illusion. Do each of us not know the folly of illusion?" And he cupped one hand gently beneath her cheek to touch his lips to hers. As her mouth opened beneath his, she was amazed at the stirring of passion—it was impossible, but it was plainly there, despite years, wounds, and weariness. Maybe—maybe there was something to this after all.

"I—" she began, then chuckled.

"So?" he cocked his head to one side, and waited for enlightenment.

"Well—my friends will think I'm insane, but this certainly fits your Way of Balance—my grey hairs against your youth."

"So—" the smile warmed his eyes in a way Martis found fascinating, and totally delightful, "—then we shall confound your friends, who lack your clear sight. We shall seek Balance together. Yes?"

She stretched out her hand a little to touch his, already feeling some of her years dissolving before that smile. "Oh, yes."

Dragon's Teeth

Trebenth, broad of shoulder and red of hair and beard, was Guard-serjant to the Mage Guild. Not to put too fine a point on it, he was Guard-serjant at High Ridings, *the* chief citadel of the Mage Guild, and site of the Academe Arcanum, *the* institution of Highest Magicks. As such, *he* was the warrior responsible for the safety and well-being of the Mages he served.

This was hardly the soft post that the uninformed thought it to be. Mages had many enemies—and were terribly vulnerable to physical attack. It only took one knife in the dark to kill a mage—Trebenth's concern was to circumvent that vulnerability; by overseeing their collective safety in High Ridings, or their individual safety by means of the bodyguards he picked and trained to stand watchdog over them.

And there were times when his concern for their well-being slid over into areas that had nothing to do with arms and assassinations.

This was looking—to his worried eyes, at least—like one of those times.

He was standing on the cold granite of the landing at the top of a set of spiraling tower stairs, outside a particular tower apartment in the Guildmembers Hall, the highest apartment in a tower reserved for the

Masterclass Mages. Sunlight poured through a sky-light above him, reflecting off the pale wooden paneling of the wall he faced. There was no door at the head of this helical staircase; there *had* been one, but the occupant of the apartment had spelled it away, presumably so that her privacy *could not* be violated. But although Trebenth could not enter, he *could* hear something of what was going on beyond that feature-less paneled wall.

Masterclass Sorceress Martis Orleva Kiriste of High Ridings, a chief instructress of the Academe, and a woman of an age *at least* equal to Trebenth's middle years was—giggling. Giggling like a giddy adolescent.

Mart hasn't been the same since she faced down Kelven, Ben gloomed, shifting his weight restlessly from his left foot to his right. *I thought at first it was just because she hadn't recovered yet from that stab-wound. Losing that much blood—gods, it would be enough to fuddle anyone's mind for a while. Then I thought it was emotional backlash from having been forced to kill somebody that was almost a substitute child for her. But then—she started acting odder instead of saner. First she requisitioned that outlander as her own, and then installed him in her quarters—and is making no secret that she's installed him in her bed as well. It's like she's lost whatever sense of proportion she had.*

Behind the honey-colored paneling Trebenth heard another muffled giggle, and his spirits slipped another notch. *I thought I'd finally found her the perfect bodyguard with that outlander Lyran; one that wouldn't get in her way. He was so quiet, so—so humble. Was it all a trick to worm his way into some woman's confidence? What the hell did I really bring in? What did I let latch onto her soul?*

He shifted his weight again, sweating with inde-cision. Finally he couldn't bear it any longer, and tapped with one knuckle, uncharacteristically hesitant, in the area where the door *had* been. "Go away," Martis called, the acid tone of her low voice clearly evident even through the muffling of the wood. "I am *not* on call. Go pester Uthedre."

"Mart?" Ben replied unhappily. "It's Ben. It isn't—" There was a shimmer of golden light, and the door popped into existence under his knuckles, in the fleeting instant between one tap and the next. Then it swung open so unexpectedly that he was left stupidly tapping empty air.

Beyond the door was Martis' sitting room; a tiny room, mostly taken up by a huge brown couch with overstuffed cushions. Two people were curled close together there, half-disappearing into the soft pillows. One was a middle-aged, square-faced woman, greying blond hair twined into long braids that kept coming undone. Beside her was a slender young man, his shoulder-length hair nearly the color of dark amber, his obliquely slanted eyes black and unfathomable. He looked—to Trebenth's mind—fully young enough to be Martis' son. In point of fact, he was her hireling bodyguard—and her lover.

"Ben, you old goat!" Martis exclaimed from her seat on the couch, "Why didn't you say it was you in the first place? I'd never lock you out, no matter what, but you *know* I'm no damn good at aura-reading."

To Trebenth's relief, Martis was fully and decently clothed, as was the young outland fighter Lyran seated beside her. She lowered the hand she'd used to gesture the door back into reality and turned the final flourish into a beckoning crook of her finger. With no little reluctance Trebenth sidled into the sun-flooded outermost room of her suite. She cocked her head to one side, her grey eyes looking suspiciously mischievous and bright, her generous mouth quirked in an expectant half-smile.

"Well?" she asked. "I'm waiting to hear what you came all the way up my tower to ask."

Trebenth flushed. "It's—about—"

"Oh my, you sound embarrassed. Bet I can guess. Myself and my far-too-young lover, hmm?"

"Mart!" Ben exclaimed, blushing even harder. "I—didn't—"

"Don't bother, Ben," she replied, lounging back against the cushions, as Lyran watched his superior with a disconcertingly serene and thoughtful expression on his lean face. "I figured it was all over High Ridings by now. Zaila's Toenails! Why is it that when some old goat of a *man* takes a young wench to his bed everyone chuckles and considers it a credit to his virility, but when an old *woman*—"

"You are *not* old," Lyran interrupted her softly, in an almost musical tenor.

"Flatterer," she said, shaking her head at him. "I know better. So, why is it when an *older* woman does the same, everyone figures her mind is going?"

Trebenth was rather at a loss to answer that far-too-direct question.

"Never mind, let it go. I suspect, though, that you're worried about what I've let leech onto me. Let me ask you a countering question. Is Lyran causing trouble? Acting up? Flaunting status—spending my gold like water? Boasting about his connections or—his 'conquest'?"

"Well," Ben admitted slowly, "No. He acts just like he did before; so quiet you hardly know he's there. Except—"

"Except what?"

"Some of the others have been goin' for *him*. At practice, mostly."

"And?" Beside her, Lyran shifted, and laid his right hand unobtrusively—but protectively—over the one of hers resting on the brown couch cushion between them.

"Everything stayed under control until this morning. Harverth turned the dirty side of his tongue on you 'stead of Lyran, seeing as he wasn't gettin' anywhere baiting the boy. Harverth was armed, Lyran wasn't."

Martis raised one eyebrow. "So? What happened?"

"I was gonna mix in, but they finished it before I could get involved. It didn't take long. Harverth's with the Healers. They tell me he *might* walk without limping in a year or so, but they won't promise. Hard to Heal shattered kneecaps."

Martis turned a reproachful gaze on the young, long-haired man beside her. Lyran flushed. "Pardon," he murmured. "This one was angered for your sake more than this one knew. This one lost both Balance and temper."

"You lost more'n that, boy," Ben growled, "You lost me a trained—"

"Blowhard," Martis interrupted him. "You forget that you assigned that dunderhead to me once—he's damned near useless, and he's a pain in the aura to a mage like me. You know damned well you've been on the verge of kicking that idiot out on his rear a half dozen times—you've told me so yourself! Well, now you've got an excuse to pension him off—it was *my* hireling and *my* so-called honor involved; deduct the bloodprice from my account and throw the bastard out of High Ridings. There, are you satisfied?"

Ben wasn't. "Mart," he said pleadingly, "It's not just that—"

"What is it? The puppies in your kennel still likely to go for Lyran?"

"No, not after this morning."

"What is it then? Afraid I'm going to become a laughingstock? Got news for you, Ben, I already *am*, and I don't give a damn. Or are you afraid *for* me, afraid that I'm making a fool of myself?"

Since that was exactly what Trebenth *had* been thinking, he flushed again, and averted *his* eyes from the pair on the sofa.

"Ben," Martis said softly, "when have you ever seen us acting as anything other than mage and hireling outside of my quarters? Haven't we at least kept the appearance of respectability?"

"I guess," he mumbled, hot with embarrassment.

"People would be talking even if there was *nothing* between us. They've talked about me ever since I got my Mastery. There were years at the beginning when everybody was *certain* I'd earned it in bed, not in the circles. And when you and I—they talked about that, too, didn't they? The only difference now is that I'm about half again older than Lyran. People just don't seem to like that, much. But my position is in no danger. When the push comes, it's my power the Guild cares about, not what damage I do to an already dubious reputation. And *I* don't care. I'm happy, maybe for the first time in years. Maybe in my life."

He looked up sharply. "Are you? Really? Are you sure?"

"I'm sure," she replied with absolute candor, as Lyran raised his chin slightly, and his eyes silently dared his superior to challenge the statement.

Trebenth sighed, and felt a tiny, irrational twinge of jealousy. After all, *he* had Margwynwy—but *he'd* never been able to bring that particular shine to Martis' eyes—not even at the height of their love affair. "All right, then," he said, resigned. "As long as you don't care about the gossip—"

"Not in the slightest."

"I guess I was out of line."

"No Ben," Martis replied fondly. "You're a friend. Friends worry about friends; I'm glad you care enough to worry. My wits haven't gone south, honestly."

"Then—I guess I'll go see about paying a certain slacker off and pitching him out."

✧   ✧   ✧

Martis gestured the door closed behind the towering Guard-serjant, then removed the door with another gesture, and turned back to her seatmate with frustration in her eyes. "Why didn't you tell me that you were being harassed?" Lyran shook his head; his light brown hair shimmered in the warm sun pouring through the skylight above his head.

"It didn't matter. Words are only as worthy as the speaker."

"It got beyond words."

"I am better than anyone except the Guild-serjant." It wasn't a boast, Martis knew, but a plain statement of fact. "What did I have to fear from harassment? It was only—" It was Lyran's turn to flush, although he continued to hold her gaze with his own eyes. "I could not bear to hear you insulted."

Something rather atavistic deep down inside glowed with pleasure at his words. "So you leapt to my defense, hmm?"

"How could I not? Martis—lady—love—" His eyes warmed to her unspoken approval.

She laughed, and leaned into the soft cushion behind her. "I suppose I'm expected to reward my defender now, hmm? Now that you've fought for my honor?"

He chuckled, and shook his head. "Silly and primitive of us, doubtless, but it does rouse up certain instinctive responses, no?"

She slid a little closer on the couch, and reached up to lace the fingers of both hands behind his neck, under his long hair. Not even the silk of his tunic was as soft as that wonderful hair. . . .

"You know good and well how I feel." The healing-magic of his people that he had used to save her life had bound their souls together; that was the reason why Lyran did *not* refer to himself in the third person when they were alone together. And it was why each tended to know now a little of what the other felt. It would have been rather futile to deny her feelings even if she'd wanted to . . . which she didn't.

"*Are* you happy, my Mage-lady?" She felt an unmistakable twinge of anxiety from him. "*Do* the words of fools hurt you? If they do—"

"They don't," she reassured him, coming nearer to him so that she could hold him closer and bury her face in that wonderful, magical hair. She wondered now how she could ever have thought it too long, and untidy, or why she had thought him effeminate. She breathed in the special scent of him; a hint of sunlight and spicy grasses. And she felt the tension of anxiety inside him turn to tension of another kind. His hands, strong, yet gentle, slid around her waist and drew her closer still.

But a few hours later there came a summons she could not ignore; a mage-message from the Council. And the moment the two of them passed her threshold it would have been impossible for anyone to have told that they were lovers from their demeanor. Martis was no mean actress—she was diplomat and teacher as well as sorceress, and both those professions often required the ability to play a part. And Lyran, with his incredible *mental* discipline, and a degree of training in control that matched and was in fact incorporated in his physical training, could have passed for an ice-sculpture. Only Martis could know for certain that his chill went no deeper than the surface.

He was her bodyguard; he was almost literally her possession until and unless he chose not to serve her. And as such he went with her everywhere—even into the hallows of the Council chamber. Just as the bodyguards of the five Councilors did.

The carved double doors of a wood so ancient as to have turned black swung open without a hand touching them, and she and Lyran entered the windowless Council Chamber. It was lit entirely by magelights as ancient as the doors, all still burning with bright yellow incandescence high up on the walls of white marble. The room was perfectly circular and rimmed with a circle of malachite; in the center was a second circle inlaid in porphyry in the white marble of the floor. Behind that circle was the half-circle of the Council table, of black-lacquered wood, and the five matching thronelike chairs behind it. All five of those chairs were occupied by mages in the purple robes of the Mage-Guild Council.

Only one of the Councilors, the cadaverous Masterclass Mage Ronethar Gethry, gave Lyran so much as a glance; and from the way Ronethar's eyes flickered from Lyran to Martis and back, the sorceress rather guessed that it was because of the gossip that he noticed her guard at all.

The rest ignored the swordsman, as they ignored their own hirelings, each standing impassively behind his master's chair, garbed from head to toe, as was Lyran, in Mage-Guild hireling red: red leathers, red linen—even one, like Lyran, in red silk.

The Councilors were worried; even Martis could read that much behind their impassive masks. They wasted no time on petty nonsense about her private life. What brought them all to the Council Chamber was serious business, not accusations about whom she was dallying with.

Not that they'd dare take *her* to task over it. She was the equal of any of the mages in those five seats; she could sit there behind the Council table any time she chose. She simply had never chosen to do so. They knew it, and she knew it, and they knew she knew. She was not accountable to them, or anything but her conscience, for her behavior. Only for her actions as the representative of the Guild.

The fact was that she didn't *want* a Council seat;

as a Masterclass mage she had little enough freedom as it was. Sitting on the Council would restrict it still further. The Masterclass mage served only the Guild, the powers of the Masterclass being deemed too dangerous to be put at hire.

"Martis." Rotund old Dabrel was serving as Chief this month; he was something less of an old stick than the others.

"Councilor," she responded. "How may I serve my Guild?"

"By solving a mystery," he replied. "The people of Lyosten have been acting in a most peculiar and disturbing fashion—"

"He means they've been finding excuses to put off a Guild inspection," sour-faced and acid-voiced Liavel interrupted. "First there was a fever—so they say—then a drought, then the road was blocked by a flood. It doesn't ring true; nobody else around Lyosten is having any similar troubles. We believe they're hiding something."

"Lyosten is a Free City, isn't it?" Martis asked. "Who's in charge?"

"The Citymaster—a man called Bolger Freedman."

"Not a Guildsman. A pity. That means we can't put pressure on him through his own Guild," Martis mused. "You're right, obviously; they must be covering up *something*, so what's the guess?"

"We think," Dabrel said, leaning over the table and steepling his fingertips together, "That their local mage has gone renegade in collusion with the townsfolk; that he's considering violating the Compacts against using magecraft in offensive manner against nonmages. They've been feuding off and on with Portravus for decades; we think they may be deciding to end the feud."

"And Portravus has no mage—" said mousy Herjes, looking as much frightened as worried. "Just a couple of hedge-wizards and some assorted Low Magick practitioners. And not a lot of money to spare to hire one."

Martis snorted. *"Just* what I wanted to hear. Why me?"

"You're known;" replied Dabrel. "They don't dare cause you any overt magical harm. You're one of the best at offensive and defensive magics. Furthermore, you can activate the Gates to get in fairly close to the town *before* they can think up another excuse. We'll inform them that you're coming about a day before you're due to arrive."

"And there's another factor," creaked ancient Cetallas. "Your hireling. The boy is good; damned good. Best I've seen in—can't remember when. No Free City scum is going to get past *him* to take you out. He's a healer of sorts, so Ben tells us. That's no bad thing to have about, a healer you can trust just in case some physical accident happens. And you must admit he's got a pretty powerful incentive to keep you alive." The old man wheezed a little, and quirked an amused eyebrow at the two of them. Martis couldn't help but notice the twinkle of laughter in his eyes. She bit her lip to keep from smiling. So the old bird still had some juice in him—and wasn't going to grudge her *her* own pleasures!

"You have a point," she admitted. "And yes, Lyran does have something more at stake with me than just his contract." She was rather surprised to see the rest of the Councilors nod soberly.

Well. Well, well! They may not like it—they may think I'm some kind of fool, or worse—but they've got to admit that what Lyran and I have can be pretty useful to the Guild. "How soon do you want us to leave?"

"Are you completely recovered from—"

"Dealing with Kelven? Physically, yes. Mentally, emotionally—to be honest, only time will tell. Betrayal; gods, that's not an easy thing to deal with."

"Admitted—and we're setting you up to deal with another traitor." Dabrel had the grace to look guilty.

"At least this one isn't one of my former favorite pupils," she replied, grimacing crookedly, "I don't even think I know him."

"You don't," Herjes said, "I trained him. He also is not anywhere near Kelven's potential, and he *isn't* dabbling in blood-magic. Speaking of which—have you recovered arcanely as well as physically?"

"I'm at full power. I can go any time."

"In the morning, then?"

"In the morning." She inclined her head slightly; felt the faintest whisper of magic brush her by.

Show-offs, she thought, as she heard the doors behind her open. *Two can play that game.*

"We will be on our way at dawn, Councilors," she said, carefully setting up the *rolibera* spell in her mind, and wrapping it carefully about both herself *and* Lyran. There weren't too many mages even at Masterclass level that could translate two people at once. She braced herself, formed the energy into a tightly coiled spring with her mind, then spoke one word as she inclined her head again— There was a flash of light behind her eyes, and a fluttery feeling in her stomach as if she had suddenly dropped the height of a man.

And she and Lyran stood side-by-side within the circle carved into the floor of her private workroom.

She turned to see the mask of indifference drop from him, and his thin, narrow face come alive with mingled humor and chiding.

"Must you always be challenging them, beloved?"

She set her mouth stubbornly. He shook his head. "Alas," he chuckled, "I fear if you stopped, I would no longer know you. Challenge and avoidance—" He held out his arms, and she flowed into them. "Truly, beloved," he murmured into her ear, as she pressed her cheek into the silk of his tunic shoulder, "we Balance each other."

✧ ✧ ✧

They would not be riding Jesalis and Tosspot, those beasts of foul temper and fiercely protective instincts. This was a mission which would depend as much on the impression they would give as their capabilities, and Tosspot and Jesalis would be unlikely to impress anyone. Instead, when they descended the tower stairs in the pale, pearly light of dawn, Martis found the grooms in the stone-paved courtyard holding the reins of two showy palfreys, a grey and a bay. Tethered behind the bay on a lead rope was a glossy mule loaded with packs. The harness of the grey was dyed a rich purple, and that of the bay was scarlet. Lyran approached the horses with care, for the eyes of the bay rolled with alarm at the sight of the stranger. He ran his hands over their legs once he could get near them, and walked slowly back to Martis' side with his arms folded, shaking his head a little.

"Hmm?" she asked.

"Worthless," he replied. "I hope we will not be needing to entrust our lives to them. No strength, no stamina—and worst of all, no sense."

"They're just for show," Martis frowned, feeling a little dubious herself. "We aren't supposed to have to do any hard riding, or long, except for the gallop to take us through the Gates. A day's ride to the first Gate, half a day to the second. In and out of both Gates, then a ride of less than half a day to the city."

"If all goes well. And what if all does not go well?"

"I—" Martis fell silent. "Well, that's why you're along."

Lyran looked back over his shoulder at the horses, and grimaced. "This one will do the best one can, Mage-lady," he said formally. "Will the Mage-lady mount?"

Martis had been doing more with Lyran's aid than her colleagues suspected. A few moons ago she would not have been able to mount unaided—now she

swung into her saddle with at least some of the grace
of her lover. The exercises he had been insisting she
practice had improved her strength, her wind, her
flexibility—she was nearly as physically fit as she'd
been twenty-odd years ago, when she'd first come to
the Academe.

Lyran mounted at nearly the same moment, and
his bay tried to shy sideways. It jerked the reins out
of the groom's hands, and danced backwards, then
reared. Lyran's mouth compressed, but that was the
only sign that he was disturbed that Martis could see.
The scarlet silk of his breeches rippled as he clamped
his legs around the bay gelding's barrel, and the reins
seemed to tighten of themselves as he forced the
gelding back down to the ground, and fought him to
a standstill. As the horse stood, sweating, sides heav-
ing, Lyran looked up at her.

"This one will do what this one can, Mage-lady,"
he repeated soberly.

The grey palfrey Martis rode was of a more placid
disposition, for which she was profoundly grateful. She
signed to the groom to release his hold and turned
its head to face the open wooden gate set into the
stone walls of the court. At Lyran's nod she nudged
it with her heels and sent it ambling out beneath the
portcullis.

They rode in single file through the city, Lyran
trailing the mule at a respectful distance from "his
employer." Four times the bay started and shied at
inconsequential commonplaces; each time Lyran had
to fight the beast back onto all four hooves and into
sweating good behavior. The last time seemed to
convince it that there was no unseating its rider, for
it did not make another attempt. Once outside the
city walls, they reversed their positions, with Lyran
and the mule going first. Ordinarily Martis would now
be spending her time in half-trance, gathering power
from the living things around her. But her mount was

not her faithful Tosspot, who could be relied upon to keep a falling-down drunk in the saddle—and Lyran's beast was all too likely to shy or dance again, and perhaps send her gelding off as well. So instead of gathering always-useful energy, she fumed and fretted, and was too annoyed even to watch the passing landscape.

They reached the Gate at sunset. The ring of standing stones in the center of the meadow stood out black against the flaming glow of the declining sun. The wide, weed-grown fields around them were otherwise empty; not even sheep cared to graze this near a Gate. The evening wind carried a foretaste of autumnal chill as it sighed through the grasses around them. Martis squinted against the bloody light and considered their options.

Lyran had finally decided to exhaust his misbehaving mount by trotting it in circles around her as they traveled down the road until it was too tired to fuss. Now it was docile, but plainly only because it was weary. It still rolled its eyes whenever a leaf stirred. The sorceress urged her gelding up beside his.

"Can you get one last run out of him?" Martis asked anxiously.

"Probably," Lyran replied. "Why?"

"I'd like to take this Gate now, if we can, while that misbegotten horse of yours is too tired to bolt."

He looked at her in that silent, blank-faced way he had when he was thinking. "What if he did bolt?"

"The gods only know where you'd end up," she told him frankly. "If he got out of my influence—I can't predict what point beyond the Gate you'd come out at, or even what direction it would be in."

"And if I can't get him to a gallop?"

"Almost the same—if you didn't keep within my aura you'd come out somewhere between here and where I'd land."

He reached out and touched her face with the tips of his fingers. "You seem tired, beloved."

"I *am* tired," she admitted, confessing to him what she would admit to no other living person. "But I'm not too tired to Gate-spell, and I think it's safer to do it now than it will be later."

"Then I will force this bundle of contrariness disguised as a horse into keeping up with you."

"Hold butter-brains here, would you?" she passed him the reins of her mount, not trusting it to stand firm on its own. She drew entirely into herself, centering all her concentration on the hoarded power within herself, drawing it gradually to the surface with unspoken words and careful mental probes. Her eyes were closed, but she could feel the energy stirring, flowing, coming up from—elsewhere—and beginning to trickle along the nerves of her spine. At first it was barely a tingle, but the power built up quickly until she was vibrating to its silent song.

At that point she opened the channels to her hands, raising her arms out in front of her and holding her hands out with the open palms facing the ring of standing stones.

The power surged along her arms and leapt for the ring of the Gate with an eagerness that was almost an emotion. She sang the words of the Gate-spell now, sang it in a barely audible whisper. Her eyes were half open, but she really wasn't paying a great deal of attention to anything but the flow of power from her to the Gate.

The ring of stones began to glow, glowing as if they were stealing the last of the sun's fire and allowing it to run upon their surfaces. The color of the fire began to lighten, turning from deep red to scarlet to a fiery orange. Then the auras surrounding each Gate-stone extended; reaching for, then touching, the auras beside it, until the circle became one pulsating ring of golden-orange light.

Martis felt the proper moment approaching, and signed to Lyran to hand her back her reins. She waited, weighing, judging—then suddenly spurred her mount into one of the gaps between the stones, with Lyran's gelding practically on top of her horse's tail.

They emerged into a forest clearing beneath a moon already high, exactly five leagues from the next Gate.

"Gods, I wish I had Tosspot under me," Martis muttered, facing the second Gate under a bright noontide sun. This one stood in the heart of the forest, and the stones were dwarfed by the stand of enormous pine trees that towered all about them. The sorceress was feeling depleted, and she had not been able to recuperate the energy she'd spent on the last spell.

"We could wait," Lyran suggested. "We could rest here, and continue on in the morning."

Martis shook her head with regret. "I only wish we could. But it isn't healthy to camp near a Gate—look at the way the magic's twisted those bushes over there, the ones growing up against the stones! And besides, we need to come as close to surprising our hosts as we can."

She coughed; there was a tickle in the back of her throat that threatened to turn into a cold. Lyran noted that cough, too, and tightened his mouth in unvoiced disapproval, but made no further objections. Martis handed him her reins, and began the second spell—But they emerged, not into a sunlit clearing as she'd expected, but into the teeth of the worst storm she'd ever seen.

Rain, cold as the rains of winter, lashed at them, soaking them to the skin in moments. It would have been too dark to see, except that lightning struck so often that the road was clearly lit most of the time. Lyran spurred his horse up beside the sorceress as she gasped for breath beneath the onslaught of the icy water. He'd pulled his cloak loose from the lashings that held it to his saddle and was throwing it over her shoulders before she even had recovered the wit to *think* about the fact that she needed it. The cloak was sodden in seconds, but it was wool—warm enough, even though wet. She stopped shivering a little, but the shock of chill coming on top of the strain of the spells had unbalanced her a little. She fumbled after her reins, but her mind wouldn't quite work; she couldn't seem to think where they should be going.

Lyran put his hand under her chin, and turned her face toward his. She blinked at him, at his searching expression as revealed by the flickers of lightning. Some rational little bit of her that hadn't been stunned hoped idly that he remembered what she'd told him once, about how mages sometimes went into spell-shock when they were low on energy and hit with unexpected physical conditions. This happened most frequently when they were ungrounded and uncentered—and the Gate-spell demanded that she be both when taking them in transit.

Evidently he did, for he took the reins out of her unresisting fingers and nudged his gelding into a nervy, shuddering walk, leaving her to cling to the saddle as best she could while he led her mount.

It was impossible to hear or be heard over the nearly continuous roar of the thunder, so she didn't even try to speak to him. She just closed her eyes and concentrated on getting herself centered and grounded again. So it was that she never noticed when the road approached the brink of a river—once peaceful, now swollen and angry with flood water. She knew that there *was* such a road, and such a river— she knew that they were to cross it before reaching Lyosten. She knew that there was a narrow, aged bridge that was still nonetheless sound, but she was too deeply sunk within herself to see it, as Lyran urged the horses onto its span.

But she *felt* the lightning-strike, so close it scorched the wood of the bridge not ten paces in front of them.

And as her eyes snapped open, she saw Lyran's horse rearing above her in complete panic—a darkly writhing shape that reared and thrashed—and toppled over onto *hers*. She had no time to react; she felt herself go numb and open-mouthed in fear, and then pain as all of them, horses, humans, and mule, crashed through the railing of the bridge to plunge into the churning water below. She flailed wildly with unfocused energy trying to form up something to catch them—and lost spell and all in the shock of hitting the raging water.

Martis pulled herself up onto the muddy bank, scraping herself across the rocks and tree-roots protruding from it, and dragging Lyran with her by the shoulder-fabric of his tunic. She collapsed, half-in, half-out of the water, too spent to go any farther. The swordsman pulled himself, coughing, up onto the bank beside her. A child of open plains, *he* couldn't swim.

Fortunately for both of them, Martis could. And equally fortunately, he'd had the wit to go limp when he felt her grabbing his tunic. The storm—now that the damage was done—was slackening.

"Are you all right?" she panted, turning her head and raising herself on her arms enough to be able to see him, while her teeth chattered like temple rattles.

Lyran had dragged himself up into a sitting position, and was clutching a sapling as if it were a lover. His eyes were bruised and swollen, one of them almost shut, and there was a nasty welt along the side of his face. He coughed, swallowed, nodded. "I think—yes."

"Good." She fell back onto the bank, cheek pressed into the mud, trying to keep from coughing herself. If she did—it felt as if she might well cough her aching lungs out. She fought the cough with closed eyes, the rain plastering hair and clothing flat to her skin.

This is witched weather; the power is everywhere, wild, undisciplined. How could that Lyosten mage have let himself get so out of control? But that was just a passing thought, unimportant. The important thing was the cold, the aching weariness. She was so cold now that she had gone beyond feeling it—

"Martis—"

She was drifting, drifting away, being carried off to somewhere where there was sun and warmth. In fact, she was actually beginning to feel warm, not cold. She felt Lyran shake her shoulder, and didn't care. All she wanted to do was sleep. She'd never realized how soft mud could be.

"Martis!" It was the sharp-edged fear in his voice as much as the stinging slap he gave her that woke her. She got her eyes open with difficulty.

"What?" she asked stupidly, unable to think.

"Beloved, *thena,* you are afire with fever," he said, pulling her into his arms and chafing her limbs to get the blood flowing. "I cannot heal disease, only wounds. Fight this—you must fight this, or you will surely die!"

"Ah—" she groaned, and tried to pummel the fog that clouded her mind away. But it was a battle doomed to be lost; she felt the fog take her, and drifted away again.

Lyran half-carried, half-dragged the mage up the last few feet of the road to the gates of Lyosten. The horses were gone, and the mule, and with them everything except what they had carried on their persons that had not been ripped away by the floodwaters. His two swords were gone; he had only his knife, his clothing, and the money belt beneath his tunic. Martis had only her robes; no implements of magic or healing, no cloak to keep her warm—

At least she had not succumbed to shock or the cold-death; she was intermittently conscious, if not coherent. But she was ill—very ill, and like to become worse.

The last few furlongs of road had been a waking nightmare; the rain stopped as if it had been shut off, but the breeze that had sprung up had chilled them even as it had dried their clothing. Once past the thin screen of trees lining the river, there had been nothing to buffer it. It hadn't helped that Lyran could see the bulk of Lyosten looming in the distance, dark grey against a lighter grey sky. He'd forced himself and Martis into motion, but more often than not he was supporting her; sheer exhaustion made them stagger along the muddy road like a pair of drunks, getting mired to the knees in the process. It was nearly sunset when they reached the gates of the city.

He left Martis leaning against the wood of the wall and went to pound on the closed gates themselves, while she slid slowly down to crouch in a miserable huddle, fruitlessly seeking shelter from the wind.

A man-sized door opened in the greater gate, and a surly, bearded fighter blocked it.

"What's the ruckus?" he growled.

Lyran drew himself up and tried not to shiver. "This one is guard to Martis, Master Sorceress and envoy of the Mages' Guild," he replied, his voice hoarse, his throat rasping. "There has been an accident—"

"Sure, tell me another one," the guard jeered, looking from Lyran, to the bedraggled huddle that was Martis, and back again. He started to close the portal. "You think I've never heard *that* one before? Go around to th' Beggar's Gate."

"Wait!" Lyran blocked the door with his foot, but before he could get another word out, the guard unexpectedly lashed out with the butt of his pike, catching him with a painful blow to the stomach. It knocked the wind out of him and caused him to land on his rump in the mud of the road. The door in the gate slammed shut.

Lyran lowered Martis down onto the pallet, and knelt beside her. He covered her with every scrap of ragged blanket or quilt that he could find. She was half out of her mind with fever now, and coughing almost constantly. The cheap lamp of rock-oil gave off almost as much smoke as light, which probably didn't help the coughing any.

"Martis?" he whispered, hoping against hope for a sane response.

This time he finally got one. Her eyes opened, and there was sense in them. "Lyr—" she went into a coughing fit. He helped her to sit up, and held a mug of water to her mouth. She drank, her hand pressed against his, and the hand was so hot it frightened him. *"Thena,"* he said urgently, "You are ill, very ill. I cannot heal sickness, only hurts. Tell me what I must do."

"Take me—to the Citymaster—" He shook his head. "I tried; they will not let me near. I cannot prove that I am what I say—"

"Gods. And I can't—magic to prove it."

"You haven't even been answering me." He put the cup on the floor and wedged himself in behind her, supporting her. She closed her eyes as if even the dim light of the lamp hurt them. Her skin was hot and dry, and tight-feeling, as he stroked her forehead. "The storm—witched."

"You said as much in raving, so I guessed it better to avoid looking for the city wizard. Tell me what I must do!"

"Is there—money—?"

"A little. A very little."

"Get—trevaine-root. Make tea."

He started. "And poison you? Gods and demons—!"

"Not poison." She coughed again."It'll put me—where I can trance. Heal myself. Only way."

"But—"

"Only way I know," she repeated, and closed her eyes. Within moments the slackness of her muscles told him she'd drifted off into delirium again.

He lowered her back down to the pallet, and levered himself to his feet. The bed and the lamp were all the furnishings this hole of a room had; Martis had bigger closets back at High Ridings. And he'd been lucky to find the room in the first place. The old woman who rented it to him had been the first person he'd accosted that had "felt" honest.

He blew out the lamp and made his way down to the street. Getting directions from his hostess, he headed for the marketplace. The ragged and threadbare folk who jostled him roused his anxiety to a fever-pitch. He sensed that many of them would willingly knife him from behind for little or no reason. He withdrew into himself, shivering mentally, and put on an icy shell of outward calm.

The streets were crowded; Lyran moved carefully within the flow of traffic, being cautious to draw no attention to himself. He was wearing a threadbare tunic and breeches nearly identical to a dozen others around him; his own mage-hireling silk was currently adorning Martis' limbs beneath her mage-robes. The silk was one more layer of covering against the chill—and he didn't like the notion of appearing in even stained mage-hireling red in public; not around here. He closed his mind to the babble and his nose to the stench of unwashed bodies, uncleaned privies, and garbage that thickened the air about him. But these people worried him; he had only his knife for

defense. What if some of this street-scum should learn
about Martis, and decide she was worth killing and
robbing? If he had his swords, or even just a single
sword of the right reach and weight, he could hold
off an army—but he didn't, nor could he afford one.
The only blades he'd seen yet within his scanty re-
sources were not much better than cheap metal clubs.

Finally he reached the marketplace. Trevaine-root
was easy enough to find, being a common rat-poison.
He chose a stall whose owner "felt" reasonably honest
and whose wares looked properly preserved, and
began haggling.

A few moments later he slid his hand inside his
tunic to extract the single coin he required from the
heart-breakingly light money-belt, separating it from
the others by feel. The herbalist handed over the
scrap of root bound up in a bit of old paper without a second glance; Lyran hadn't bought enough to
seem suspicious. But then, it didn't take much to
make a single cup of strong tea.

Lyran turned, and narrowly avoided colliding with
a scarred man, a man who walked with the air of a
tiger, and whose eyes were more than a little mad.
Lyran ducked his head, and willed himself invisible
with all his strength. If only he had a *sword*! The need
was beginning to be more than an itch—it was
becoming an ache.

Lyran was heading out of the market and back to
the boarding-house when he felt an unmistakable
mental "pull," not unlike the calling he had felt when
he first was moved to take up the Way of the sword,
the pull he had felt when he had chosen his Teacher.
It did not "feel" wrong, or unbalanced. Rather, it was
as if Something was sensing the need in him for a
means to protect Martis, and was answering that need.

Hardly thinking, he followed that pull, trusting to
it as he had trusted to the pull that led him to the
doorstep of the woman destined to be his Teacher,

and as he had followed the pull that had led him
ultimately to the Mage Guild at High Ridings and
to Martis. This time it led him down the twisting,
crooked path of a strangely silent street, a street
hemmed by tall buildings so that it scarcely saw the
sun; a narrow street that was wide enough only for
two people to pass abreast. And at the end of it—
for it proved to be a dead-end street, which accounted
in part for the silence—was an odd little junk shop.

There were the expected bins of rags, cracked
pottery pieces, the scavenged flotsam of a thousand
lives. Nothing ever went to waste in this quarter. Rags
could be patched together into clothing or quilts like
those now covering Martis; bits of crockery were
destined to be fitted and cemented into a crazy-paving
that would pass as a tiled floor. Old papers went to
wrap parcels, or to eke out a thinning shoe-sole. No,
nothing was ever thrown away here; but there was
more to this shop than junk, Lyran could sense it.
People could find what they *needed* here.

"You require something, lad," said a soft voice at
his elbow.

Lyran jumped—he hadn't sensed *any* presence at
his side—yet there was a strange little man, scarcely
half Lyran's height; a dwarf, with short legs, and blunt,
clever hands, and bright, birdlike eyes. And a kindness like that of the widow who had rented them her
extra room, then brought every bit of covering she
had to spare to keep Martis warm. "A sword," Lyran
said hesitantly. "This one needs a sword."

"I should think you do," replied the little man, after
a long moment of sizing Lyran up. "A swordsman generally does need a sword. And it can't be an ill-bal-
anced bludgeon, either—that would be worse than
nothing, eh, lad?"

Lyran nodded, slowly. "But this one—has but
little—" The man barked rather than laughed, but his
good humor sounded far more genuine than anything

coming from the main street and marketplace. "Lad, if you had money, you wouldn't be *here*, now, would you? Let me see what I can do for you."

He waddled into the shop door, past the bins of rags and whatnot; Lyran's eyes followed him into the darkness of the doorway, but couldn't penetrate the gloom. In a moment, the shopkeeper was back, a long, slim shape wrapped in oily rags in both his hands. He handed the burden to Lyran with a kind of courtly flourish.

"Here you be, lad," he said, "I think that may have been what was calling you."

The rags fell away, and the little man caught them before they hit the paving stones—

At first Lyran was conscious only of disappointment. The hilt of this weapon had once been ornamented, wrapped in gold wire, perhaps—but there were empty sockets where the gems had been, and all traces of gold had been stripped away.

"Left in pawn to me, but the owner never came back, poor man," the shopkeeper said, shaking his head. "A good man fallen on hard times—unsheath it, lad."

The blade was awkward in his hand for a moment, the hilt hard to hold with the rough metal bare in his palm—but as he pulled it from its sheath, it seemed to come almost alive; he suddenly found the balancing of it, and as the point cleared the sheath it had turned from a piece of dead metal to an extension of his arm.

He had feared that it was another of the useless dress-swords, the ones he had seen too many times, worthless mild steel done up in long-gone jewels and plating. This sword—this blade had belonged to a fighter, had been made for a swordsman. The balance, the temper were almost too good to be true. It more than equaled his lost twin blades, it surpassed them. With this one blade in hand he could easily have bested a twin-Lyran armed with his old sword-pair; that was the extent of the "edge" this blade could give him.

"How—how much?" he asked, mouth dry.

"First you must answer me true," the little man said softly. "You be the lad with the sick lady, no? The one that claimed the lady to be from the Mage Guild?"

Lyran whirled, stance proclaiming that he was on his guard. The dwarf simply held out empty hands. "No harm to you, lad. No harm meant. Tell me true, and the blade's yours for three copper bits. Tell me not, or tell me lie—I won't sell it. Flat."

"What if this one is not that person?" Lyran hedged.

"So long as the answer be true, the bargain be true."

Lyran swallowed hard, and followed the promptings of his inner guides. "This one—is," he admitted with reluctance. "This one and the lady are what this one claims—but none will heed."

The dwarf held out his hand, "Three copper bits," he said mildly. "And some advice for free."

Lyran fumbled out the coins, hardly able to believe his luck. The worst pieces of pot-metal pounded into the shape of a sword were selling for a silver— yet this strange little man had sold him a blade worth a hundred times that for the price of a round of cheese! "This one never rejects advice."

"But you may or may not heed it, eh?" The man smiled, showing a fine set of startlingly white teeth. "Right enough; you get your lady to tell you the story of the dragon's teeth. Then tell her that Bolger Freedman has sown them, but can't harvest them."

Lyran nodded, though without understanding. "There's some of us that never agreed with him. There's some of us would pay dearly to get shut of what we've managed to get into. Tell your lady that— and watch your backs. I'm not the only one who's guessed."

✧ ✧ ✧

Lyran learned the truth of the little man's words long before he reached the widow's boarding-house.

The gang of street-toughs lying in ambush for him were probably considered canny, crafty and subtle by the standards of the area. But Lyran knew that they were there as he entered the side-street; and he knew *where* they were moments before they attacked him.

The new sword was in his hands and moving as the first of them struck him from behind. It sliced across the thug's midsection as easily as if Lyran had been cutting bread, not flesh, and with just about as much resistance. While the bully was still falling, Lyran took out the one dropping on him from the wall beside him with a graceful continuation of that cut, and kicked a third rushing him from out of an alley, delivering a blow to his knee that shattered the kneecap, and then forced the knee to bend in the direction opposite to that which nature had intended for a human.

He couldn't get the blade around in time to deal with the fourth, so he ducked under the blow and brought the pommel up into the man's nose, shattering the bone and driving the splinters into the brain.

And while the fifth man stared in openmouthed stupefication, Lyran separated his body from his head.

Before anyone could poke a curious nose into the street to see what all the noise was about, Lyran vaulted to the top of the wall to his left, and from there to the roof of the building it surrounded. He scampered quickly over the roof and down again on the other side, taking the time to clean and sheath the sword and put it away before dropping down into the next street.

After all, he hadn't spent his childhood as a thief without learning something about finding unconventional escape routes.

About the time he had taken a half a dozen paces, alarm was raised in the next street. Rather than running away, Lyran joined the crowd that gathered about the five bodies, craning his neck like any of the people around him, wandering off when he "couldn't get a look."

A childhood of thieving had taught him the truth of what his people often said: "If you would be taken for a crow, join the flock and caw."

Lyran took the cracked mug of hot water from his hostess, then shooed her gently out. He didn't want her to see—and perhaps recognize—what he was going to drop into it. She probably wouldn't understand. For that matter, he didn't understand; he just trusted Martis.

His lover tossed her head on the bundle of rags that passed for a pillow and muttered, her face sweat-streaked, her hair lank and sodden. He soothed her as best he could, feeling oddly helpless.

When the water was lukewarm and nearly black, he went into a half trance and soul-called her until she woke. Again—to his relief—when he finally brought her to consciousness, there was foggy sense in her gray eyes.

"I have the tea, *thena*," he said, helping her into a sitting position. She nodded, stifling a coughing fit, and made a weak motion with her hand. Interpreting it correctly, he held the mug to her lips. She clutched at it with both hands, but her hands shook so that he did not release the mug, only let her guide it.

He lowered her again to the pallet when she had finished the foul stuff, sitting beside her and holding her hands in his afterwards.

"How long will this take?"

She shook her head. "A bit of time before the drug takes; after that, I don't know." She coughed, doubling over; he supported her.

"Have you ever known any story about 'dragon's teeth,' my lady?" he asked, reluctantly. "I—was advised to tell you that Bolger has sown the dragon's teeth, but cannot harvest them."

She shook her head slightly, a puzzled frown creasing her forehead—then her eyes widened. "Harvest! Gods! I—"

The drug chose that moment to take her; between one word and the next her eyes glazed, then closed. Lyran swore, in three languages, fluently and creatively. It was some time before he ran out of invective.

"*I* know 'bout dragon's teeth," said a high, young voice from the half-open door behind him. Lyran jumped in startlement for the second time that day. Truly, anxiety for Martis was dulling his edge!

He turned slowly, to see the widow's youngest son peeking around the doorframe.

"And would you tell this one of dragon's teeth?" he asked the dirty-faced urchin as politely as he could manage.

Encouraged, the youngster pushed the door open a little more. "You ain't never seen a dragon?" he asked.

Lyran shook his head, and crooked his finger. The boy sidled into the room, clasping his hands behind his back. To the widow's credit, only the child's face was dirty—the cut-down tunic he wore was threadbare, but reasonably clean. "There are no dragons in this one's homeland."

"Be there mages?" the boy asked, and at Lyran's negative headshake, the child nodded. "That be why. Dragons ain't natural beasts, they be mage-made. Don't breed, neither. You want 'nother dragon, you take tooth from a live dragon an' plant it. Only thing is, baby dragons come up hungry an' mean. Takes a tamed dragon to harvest 'em, else they go out killin' an feedin' an' get the taste fer fear. Then their brains go bad, an' they gotta be killed thesselves."

"This one thanks you," Lyran replied formally. The child grinned, and vanished.

Well, now he knew about dragon's teeth. The only problem was that the information made no sense—at least not to him! It had evidently meant something to Martis, though. She must have some bit of information that *he* didn't have.

He stroked the mage's damp forehead and sighed. At least the stuff hadn't killed her outright—he'd been half afraid that it would. And she *did* seem to be going into a proper trance; her breathing had become more regular, her pulse had slowed— Suddenly it was far too quiet in the street outside. Lyran was on his feet with his new sword in his hands at nearly the same moment that he noted the absence of sound. He slipped out the door, closing it carefully behind him once he knew that the musty hallway was "safe." The stairs that led downwards were at the end of that hall—but he had no intention of taking them.

Instead he glided soundlessly to the window at the other end of the hall; the one that overlooked the scrap of back yard. The shutters were open, and a careful glance around showed that the yard itself was empty. He sheathed the sword and adjusted the makeshift baldric so that it hung at his back, then climbed out onto the ledge, balancing there while he assessed his best path.

There was a cornice with a crossbeam just within reach; he got a good grip on it, and pulled himself up, chinning himself on the wood of the beam—his arms screamed at him, but he dared not make a sound. Bracing himself, he let go with his right hand and swung himself up until he caught the edge of the roof. Holding onto it with a death-grip he let go of the cornice entirely, got his other hand on the roof-edge, and half-pulled, half-scrambled up onto the roof itself. He lay there for one long moment, biting his lip to keep from moaning, and willing his arms back into their sockets.

When he thought he could move again, he slid over the roof across the splintery, sunwarmed shingles to the street-side, and peered over the edge.

Below him, as he had suspected, were a half-dozen armed men, all facing the door. Except for them, the street below was deserted.

There was one waiting at the blind side of the door. Lyran pulled his knife from the sheath in his boot and dropped on him.

The *crack* as the man's skull hit the pavement— he hadn't been wearing a helm—told Lyran that he wouldn't have to worry about slitting the fighter's throat.

Lyran tumbled and rolled as he landed, throwing the knife as he came up at the man he judged to be the leader. His aim was off—instead of hitting the throat it glanced off the fighter's chest-armor. But the move distracted all of them enough to give Lyran the chance to get his sword out and into his hands.

There was something wrong with these men; he knew that as soon as he faced them. They moved oddly; their eyes were not quite focused. And even in the heat of the day, when they must have been standing out in the sun for a good long time setting up their ambush, with one exception they weren't sweating.

Then Lyran noticed that, except for the man he'd thrown the dagger at—the man who *was* sweating—they weren't casting any shadows. Which meant that they were illusions. They could only harm him if he believed in them.

So he ignored them, and concentrated his attention on the leader. He went into a purely defensive stance and waited for the man to act.

The fighter, a rugged, stocky man with a wary look

to his eyes, sized him up carefully—and looked as if he wasn't happy with what he saw. Neither of them moved for a long, silent moment. Finally Lyran cleared his throat, and spoke.

"This one has no quarrel with any here, nor does this one's lady. You have done your best; this one has sprung the trap. There is no dishonor in retreat. Hireling to hireling, there is no contract violation."

The man straightened, looked relieved. "You—"

"No!"

The voice was high, cracking a little, and came from Lyran's left, a little distance up the street. It was a young voice; a breath later the owner emerged from the shadow of a doorway, and the speaker matched the voice. It was a white-blond boy, barely adolescent, dressed in gaudy silks; from behind him stepped two more children, then another pair. All of them were under the age of fifteen, all were dressed in rainbow hues—and all of them had wild, wide eyes that looked more than a little mad.

The man facing Lyran swallowed hard; *now* he was sweating even harder. Lyran looked at him curiously. It almost seemed as if he were *afraid* of these children! Lyran decided to act.

He stepped out into the street and placed himself between the man and the group of youngsters. "There has been no contract violation," he said levelly, meeting their crazed eyes, blue and green and brown, with his own. "The man has fulfilled what was asked." Behind him, he heard the fighter take to his heels once the attention of the children had switched from himself to Lyran. Lyran sighed with relief; that was one death, at least, that he would not have to Balance. "This one has no quarrel with you," he continued. "Why seek you this one?"

The children stared at him, a kind of insane affrontery in their faces, as if they could not believe that he would defy them. Lyran stood easily, blade held loosely in both hands, waiting for their response.

The blond, nearest and tallest, raised his hands; a dagger of light darted from his outstretched palms and headed straight for Lyran's throat—

But this was something a Mage Guild fighter was trained to defend against; fire daggers could not survive the touch of cold steel—

Lyran's blade licked out, and intercepted the dagger before it reached its target. It vanished when the steel touched it.

The child snarled, his mouth twisted into a grimace of rage ill-suited to the young face. Another dagger flew from his hands, and another; his companions sent darts of light of their own. Within moments Lyran was moving as he'd never moved in his life, dancing along the street, his swordblade blurring as he deflected dagger after dagger.

And still the fire-daggers kept coming, faster and faster—yet—

The air was growing chill, the sunlight thinning, and the faces of the children losing what little color they had possessed. Lyran realized then that they were draining themselves and everything about them for the energy to create the daggers. Even as the realization occurred to him, one of them made a choking sound and collapsed to the pavement, to lie there white and still.

If he could just hold out long enough, he *might* be able to outlast them! But the eldest of the group snarled when his confederate collapsed, and redoubled his efforts. Lyran found himself being pressed back, the light-daggers coming closer and closer before he was able to intercept them, his arms becoming leaden and weary—

He knew then that he would fail before they did.

And he saw, as he deflected a blade heading for

his heart, another heading for his throat—and he knew he would not be able to intercept this one.

He had an instant to wonder if it would hurt very much. Then there was a blinding flash of light.

He wasn't dead—only half-blind for a long and heart-stopping moment. And when his eyes cleared—

Martis stood in the doorway of the house that had sheltered them, bracing herself against the frame, her left palm facing him, her right, the children. Both he and the youngsters were surrounded by a haze of light; his was silver, theirs was golden.

Martis gestured, and the haze around him vanished. He dropped to the pavement, so weak with weariness that his legs could no longer hold him. She staggered over to his side, weaving a little.

"Are you going to be all right?" she asked. He nodded, panting. Her hair was out of its braids, and stringy with sweat, her robes limp with it. She knelt beside him for a moment; placed both her hands on his shoulders and looked long and deeply into his eyes. "Gods, love—that was close. Too close. Did they hurt you?"

He shook his head, and she stared at him as he'd sometimes seen her examine something for magic taint. Evidently satisfied by what she saw, she kissed him briefly and levered herself back up onto her feet.

His eyes blurred for a moment; when they refocused, he saw that the haze around the remaining four children had vanished, and that they had collapsed in a heap, crying, eyes no longer crazed. Martis stood, shoulders sagging just a little, a few paces away from them.

She cleared her throat. The eldest looked up, face full of fear—

But she held out her arms to them. "It wasn't your fault," she said, in a voice so soft only the children and Lyran could have heard the words, and so full of compassion Lyran scarcely recognized it. "I know it wasn't your fault—and I'll help you, if you let me."

The children froze—then stumbled to their feet and surrounded her, clinging to her sweat-sodden robes, and crying as if their hearts had been broken, then miraculously remended.

"—so Bolger decided that he had had enough of the Mage Guild dictating what mages could and could not do. He waited until the Lyosten wizard had tagged the year's crop of mage-Talented younglings, then had the old man poisoned."

The speaker was the dwarf—who Lyran now knew was one of the local earth-witches, a cheerful man called Kasten Ythres. They were enjoying the hospitality of his home while the Mage Guild dealt with the former Citymaster and the clutch of half-trained children he'd suborned.

Martis was lying back against Lyran's chest, wearily at ease within the protective circle of his arms. They were both sitting on the floor, in one corner by the fireplace in the earth-witch's common room; there were no furnishings here, just piles of flat pillows. Martis had found it odd, but it had reminded Lyran strongly of home.

It was an oddly charming house, like its owner: brown and warm and sunny; utterly unpretentious. Kasten had insisted that they relax and put off their mage-hireling act. "It's my damned house," he'd said, "And you're my guests. To the nether hells with so-called propriety!"

"How on earth did he think he was going to get them trained?" Martis asked.

Kasten snorted. "He thought he could do it out of books—and if that didn't work, he'd get one of us half-mages to do it for him. Fool."

"He sowed the dragon's teeth," Martis replied acidly, "he shouldn't have been surprised to get dragons."

"Lady—dragon's teeth?" Lyran said plaintively, still at a loss to understand.

Martis chuckled, and settled a little more comfortably against Lyran's shoulder. "I was puzzled for a moment, too, until I remembered that the storm that met us had been witched—and that the power that created it was out of control. Magic power has some odd effects on the mind, love—if you *aren't* being watched over and guided properly, it can possess you. That's why the tales about demonic possession; you get a Talented youngling or one who blooms late, who comes to power with no training—they go mad. Worst of all, they *know* they're going mad. It's bad—and you only hope you can save them before any real damage is done."

"Aye," Kasten agreed. "I suspect that's where the dragon's teeth tale comes from too—which is why I told your man there to remind you of it. The analogy being that the younglings are the teeth, the trained mage is the dragon. What I'd like to know is what's to do about this? You can't take the younglings to the Academe—and I surely couldn't handle them!"

"No, they're too powerful," Martis agreed. "They need someone around to train them *and* keep them drained, until they've gotten control over their powers instead of having the powers control them. We have a possible solution, though. The Guild has given me a proposition, but I haven't had a chance to discuss it with Lyran yet." She craned her head around to look at him. "How would you like to be a father for the next half-year or so?"

"Me?" he replied, too startled to refer to himself in third person.

She nodded. "The Council wants them to have training, but feels that they would be best handled in a stable, home-like setting. But their blood-parents are frightened witless of them. But you—you stood up to them, you aren't afraid of them—and you're kind, love. You have a wonderful warm heart. And you know how I feel about youngsters. The Council feels that we would be the best parental surrogates they're ever likely to find. If you're willing, that is."

Lyran could only nod speechlessly.

"And they said," Martis continued with great satisfaction in her voice, "that if you'd agree, they'd give you anything you wanted."

"Anything?"

"They didn't put any kind of limitation on it. They're worried; these are *very* Talented children. All five of the Councilors are convinced you and I are their only possible salvation."

Lyran tightened his arms around her. "Would they—would they give this one rank to equal a Masterclass mage?"

"Undoubtedly. You certainly qualify for Swordmaster—only Ben could better you, and he's a full Weaponsmaster. If you weren't an outlander, you'd *have* that rank already."

"Would they then allow this one to wed as he pleased?"

He felt Martis tense, and knew without asking why she had done so. She feared losing him so much—and feared that this was just exactly what was about to happen. But they were interrupted before he could say anything. "That and more!" said a voice from the door. It was the Chief Councilor, Dabrel, purple robes straining over his stomach. "Swordmaster Lyran, do you wish to be the young fool that I think you do?"

"If by that, the Mastermage asks if this one would wed the Master Sorceress Martis, then the Mastermage is undoubtedly correct," Lyran replied demurely, a smile straining at the corners of his mouth as he heard Martis gasp.

"Take her with our blessings, Swordmaster," the

portly mage chuckled. "Maybe you'll be able to mellow that tongue of hers with your sweet temper!"

"Don't I get any say in this?" Martis spluttered.

"Assuredly." Lyran let her go, and putting both hands on her shoulders, turned so that she could face him. "Martis, *thena,* lady of my heart and Balance of my soul, would you deign to share your life with me?"

She looked deeply and soberly into his eyes. "Do you mean that?" she whispered. "Do you really mean that?"

He nodded, slowly.

"Then—" she swallowed, and her eyes misted briefly. Then the sparkle of mischief that he loved came back to them, and she grinned. "Will you bloody well *stop* calling yourself 'this one' if I say yes?"

He sighed, and nodded again.

"Then that is an offer I will *definitely* not refuse!"

This story was written for the Grail anthology that was to be presented at the World Fantasy convention in Atlanta. Richard Gilliam, approached me and asked me if I would contribute. We discussed this idea, which I had almost immediately, and he loved it, so I wrote it. The book was later broken into two volumes and published as Grails of Light *and* Grails of Darkness.

The Cup and the Caldron

Rain leaked through the thatch of the hen-house; the same dank, cold rain that had been falling for weeks, ever since the snow melted. It dripped on the back of her neck and down her back under her smock. Though it was nearly dusk, Elfrida checked the nests one more time, hoping that one of the scrawny, ill-tempered hens might have been persuaded, by a miracle or sheer perversity, to drop an egg. But as she had expected, the nests were empty, and the hens resisted her attempts at investigation with nasty jabs of their beaks. They'd gotten quite adept at fighting, competing with and chasing away the crows who came to steal their scant feed over the winter. She came away from the hen-house with an empty apron and scratched and bleeding hands.

Nor was there remedy waiting for her in the cottage, even for that. The little salve they had must be hoarded against greater need than hers.

Old Mag, the village healer and Elfrida's teacher, looked up from the tiny fire burning in the pit in the center of the dirt-floored cottage's single room. At least the thatch here was sound, though rain dripped in through the smoke-hole, and the fire didn't seem to be warming the place any. Elfrida coughed on the smoke, which persisted in staying inside, rather than rising through the smoke-hole as it should.

Mag's eyes had gotten worse over the winter, and the cottage was very dark with the shutters closed. "No eggs?" she asked, peering across the room, as Elfrida let the cowhide down across the cottage door.

"None," Elfrida replied, sighing. "This spring—if it's this bad now, what will summer be like?"

She squatted down beside Mag, and took the share of barley-bread the old woman offered, with a crude wooden cup of bitter-tasting herb tea dipped out of the kettle beside the fire.

"I don't know," Mag replied, rubbing her eyes— Mag, who had been tall and straight with health last summer, who was now bent and aching, with swollen joints and rheumy eyes. Neither willow-bark nor eyebright helped her much. "Lady bless, darling, I don't know. First that killing frost, then nothing but rain—seems like what seedlings the frost didn't get, must've rotted in the fields by now. Hens aren't laying, lambs are born dead, pigs lay on their own young . . . what we're going to do for food come winter, I've no notion."

When Mag said "we," she meant the whole village. She was not only their healer, but their priestess of the Old Way. Garth might be hetman, but she was the village's heart and soul—as Elfrida expected to be one day. This was something she had chosen, knowing the work and self-sacrifice involved, knowing that the enmity of the priests of the White Christ might fall upon her. But not for a long time—Lady grant.

That was what she had always thought, but now

the heart and soul of the village was sickening, as the village around her sickened. But why?

"We made the proper sacrifices," Elfrida said, finally. "Didn't we? What've we done or not done that the land turns against us?"

Mag didn't answer, but there was a quality in her silence that made Elfrida think that the old woman knew something—something important. Something that she hadn't yet told her pupil.

Finally, as darkness fell, and the fire burned down to coals, Mag spoke.

"We made the sacrifices," she said. "But there was one—who didn't."

"Who?" Elfrida asked, surprised. The entire village followed the Old Way—never mind the High King and his religion of the White Christ. That was for knights and nobles and suchlike. Her people stuck by what they knew best, the turning of the seasons, the dance of the Maiden, Mother and Crone, the rule of the Horned Lord. And if anyone in the village had neglected their sacrifices, surely she or Mag would have known!

"It isn't just our village that's sickening," Mag said, her voice a hoarse, harsh whisper out of the dark. "Nor the county alone. I've talked to the other Wise Ones, to the peddlers—I talked to the crows and the owls and ravens. It's the whole land that's sickening, failing—and there's only one sacrifice can save the land."

Elfrida felt her mouth go dry, and took a sip of her cold, bitter tea to wet it. "The blood of the High King," she whispered.

"Which he will not shed, come as he is to the feet of the White Christ." Mag shook her head. "My dear, my darling girl, I'd hoped the Lady wouldn't lay this on us . . . I'd prayed she wouldn't punish us for his neglect. But 'tisn't punishment, not really, and I should've known better than to hope it wouldn't come.

Whether he believes it or not, the High King is tied to the land, and Arthur is old and failing. As he fails, the land fails—"

"But—surely there's something we can do?" Elfrida said timidly into the darkness.

Mag stirred. "If there is, I haven't been granted the answer," she said, after another long pause. "But perhaps—you've had Lady-dreams before, 'twas what led you to me. . . ."

"You want me to try for a vision?" Elfrida's mouth dried again, but this time no amount of tea would soothe it, for it was dry from fear. For all that she had true visions, when she sought them, the experience frightened her. And no amount of soothing on Mag's part, or encouragement that the—things—she saw in the dark waiting for her soul's protection to waver could not touch her, could ever ease that fear.

But weighed against her fear was the very real possibility that the village might not survive the next winter. If she was worthy to be Mag's successor, she must dare her fear, and dare the dreams, and see if the Lady had an answer for them since High King Arthur did not. The land and the people needed her and she must answer that need.

"I'll try," she whispered, and Mag touched her lightly on the arm.

"That's my good and brave girl," she said. "I knew you wouldn't fail us." Something on Mag's side of the fire rustled, and she handed Elfrida a folded leaf full of dried herbs.

They weren't what the ignorant thought, herbs to bring visions. The visions came when Elfrida asked for them—these were to strengthen and guard her while her spirit rode the night winds, in search of answers. Foxglove to strengthen her heart, moly to shield her soul, a dozen others, a scant pinch of each. Obediently, she placed them under her tongue, and while Mag chanted the names of the Goddess, Elfrida

closed her eyes, and released her all-too-fragile hold
on her body.

The convent garden was sodden, the ground turning to mush, and unless someone did something about
it, there would be nothing to eat this summer but
what the tithes brought and the King's Grace granted
them. Outside the convent walls, the fields were just
as sodden; so, as the Mother Superior said, "A tithe
of nothing is still nothing, and we must prepare to
feed ourselves." Leonie sighed, and leaned a little
harder on the spade, being careful where she put each
spadeful of earth. Behind the spade, the drainage
trench she was digging between each row of droop-
ing pea-seedlings filled with water. Hopefully, this
would be enough to keep them from rotting. Hopefully, there would be enough to share. Already the
eyes of the children stared at her from faces pinched
and hungry when they came to the convent for Mass,
and she hid the bread that was half her meal to give
to them.

Her gown was as sodden as the ground; cold and
heavy with water, and only the fact that it was made
of good wool kept it from chilling her. Her bare feet,
ankle-deep in mud, felt like blocks of stone, they were
so cold. She had kirtled her gown high to keep the
hem from getting muddied, but that only let the wind
get at her legs. Her hair was so soaked that she had
not even bothered with the linen veil of a novice; it
would only have flapped around without protecting
her head and neck any. Her hands hurt; she wasn't
used to this.

The other novices, gently born and not, were
desperately doing the same in other parts of the
garden. Those that could, rather; some of the gen-
tly-born were too ill to come out into the soaking,
cold rain. The sisters, as many as were able, were
outside the walls, helping a few of the local peasants

dig a larger ditch down to the swollen stream. The trenches in the convent garden would lead to it—and so would the trenches being dug in the peasants' gardens, on the other side of the high stone wall.

"We must work together," Mother Superior had said firmly, and so here they were, knight's daughter and villien's son, robes and tunics kirtled up above the knee, wielding shovels with a will. Leonie had never thought to see it.

But the threat of hunger made strange bedfellows. Already the convent had turned out to help the villagers trench their kitchen gardens. Leonie wondered what the village folk would do about the fields too large to trench, or fields of hay? It would be a cold summer, and a lean winter.

What had gone wrong with the land? It was said that the weather had been unseasonable—and miserable—all over the kingdom. Nor was the weather all that had gone wrong; it was said there was quarreling at High King Arthur's court; that the knights were moved to fighting for its own sake, and had brought their leman openly to many court gatherings, to the shame of the ladies. It was said that the Queen herself—

But Leonie did not want to hear such things, or even think of them. It was all of a piece, anyway; knights fighting among themselves, killing frosts and rain that wouldn't end, the threat of war at the borders, raiders and bandits within, and starvation and plague hovering over all.

Something was deeply, terribly wrong.

She considered that, as she dug her little trenches, as she returned to the convent to wash her dirty hands and feet and change into a drier gown, as she nibbled her meager supper, trying to make it last, and as she went in to Vespers with the rest.

Something was terribly, deeply wrong.

When Mother Superior approached her after

Vespers, she somehow knew that her feeling of *wrongness* and what the head of the convent was about to ask were linked.

"Leonie," Mother Superior said, once the other novices had filed away, back to their beds, "when your family sent you here, they told me it was because you had visions."

Leonie ducked her head and stared at her sandals. "Yes, Mother Magdalene."

"And I asked you not to talk about those visions in any way," the nun persisted. "Not to any of the other novices, not to any of the sister, not to Father Peregrine."

"Yes, Mother Magdalene—I mean, no Mother Magdalene—" Leonie looked up, flushing with anger. "I mean, I haven't—"

She knew why the nun had ordered her to keep silence on the subject; she'd heard the lecture to her parents through the door. The Mother Superior didn't believe in Leonie's visions—or rather, she was not convinced that they were really visions. "This could simply be a young woman's hysteria," she'd said sternly, "or an attempt to get attention. If the former, the peace of the convent and the meditation and prayer will cure her quickly enough—if the latter, well, she'll lose such notions of self-importance when she has no one to prate to."

"I know you haven't, child," Mother Magdalene said wearily, and Leonie saw how the nun's hands were blistered from the spade she herself had wielded today, how her knuckles were swollen, and her cheekbones cast into a prominence that had nothing to do with the dim lighting in the chapel. "I wanted to know if you still have them."

"Sometimes," Leonie said hesitantly. "That was how—I mean, that was why I woke last winter, when Sister Maria was elf-shot—"

"Sister Maria was not elf-shot," Mother Magdalene

said automatically. "Elves could do no harm to one who trusts in God. It was simply something that happens to the very old, now and again, it is a kind of sudden brain-fever. But that isn't the point. You're still having the visions—but can you still see things that you want to see?"

"Sometimes," Leonie said cautiously. "If God and the Blessed Virgin permit."

"Well, if God is ever going to permit it, I suspect He'd do so during Holy Week," Mother Magdalene sighed. "Leonie, I am going to ask you a favor. I'd like you to make a vigil tonight."

"And ask for a vision?" Leonie said, raising her head in sudden interest.

"Precisely." The nun shook her head, and picked up her beads, telling them through her fingers as she often did when nervous. "There is something wrong with us, with the land, with the kingdom—I want you to see if God will grant you a vision of *what*." As Leonie felt a sudden upsurge of pride, Mother Magdalene added hastily, "You aren't the only one being asked to do this—every order from one end of the kingdom to the other has been asked for visions from their members. I thought long and hard about asking this. But you are the only one in my convent who has ever—had a tendency to visions."

The Mother Superior had been about to say something else, Leonie was sure, for the practical and pragmatic Mother Magdalene had made her feelings on the subject of mysticism quite clear over the years. But that didn't matter—what did matter was that she was finally going to be able to release that pent-up power again, to soar on the angels' wings. Never mind that there were as many devils "out there" as angels; her angels would protect her, for they always had, and always would.

Without another word, she knelt on the cold stone before the altar, fixed her eyes on the bright little gilded cross above it, and released her soul's hold on her body.

"What did you see?" Mag asked, as Elfrida came back, shivering and spent, to consciousness. Her body was lying on the ground beside the fire, and it felt too tight, like a garment that didn't fit anymore—but she was glad enough to be in it again, for there had been *thousands* of those evil creatures waiting for her, trying to prevent her from reaching—

"The Cauldron," she murmured, sitting up slowly, one hand on her aching head. "There was a Cauldron "

"Of course!" Mag breathed. "The Cauldron of the Goddess! But—" It was too dark for Elfrida to see Mag, other than as a shadow in the darkness, but she somehow felt Mag's searching eyes. "What about the Cauldron? When is it coming back? Who's to have it? Not the High King, surely—"

"I'm—supposed to go look for it—" Elfrida said, vaguely. "That's what They said—I'm supposed to go look for it."

Mag's sharp intake of breath told her of Mag's shock. "But—no, I know you, when you come out of this," she muttered, almost as if to herself. "You can't lie. If you say They said for you to go, then go you must."

Elfrida wanted to say something else, to ask what it all meant, but she couldn't. The vision had taken too much out of her, and she was whirled away a second time, but this time it was not on the winds of vision, but into the arms of exhausted sleep.

"What did you see?" Mother Superior asked urgently. Leonie found herself lying on the cold stone before the altar, wrapped in someone's cloak, with something pillowed under her head. She felt very peaceful, as she always did when the visions released her, and very, very tired. There had been many demons out there, but as always, her angels had protected her. Still, she was glad to be back. There had never been quite so many of the evil things there before, and they had frightened her.

She had to blink a few times, as she gathered her memories and tried to make sense of them. "A cup," she said, hesitantly—then her eyes fell upon the Communion chalice on the altar, and they widened as she realized just what she truly *had* seen. "No—not a cup, *the* Cup! We're to seek the Grail! That's what They told me!"

"The Grail?" Mother Magdalene's eyes widened a little herself, and she crossed herself hastily. "Just before you—you dropped over, you reached out. I thought I saw—I thought I saw something faint, like a ghost of a glowing cup in your hands—"

Leonie nodded, her cheek against the rough homespun of the habit bundled under her head. "They said that to save the kingdom, we have to seek the Grail."

"We?" Mother Magdalene said, doubtfully. "Surely you don't mean—"

"The High King's knights and squires, some of the clergy—and—me—" Leonie's voice trailed off, as she realized what she was saying. "They said the knights will know already and that when you hear about it from Camelot, you'll know I was speaking the truth. But I don't *want* to go!" she wailed. "I don't! I—"

"I'm convinced of the truth now," the nun said. "Just by the fact that you don't want to go. If this had been a sham, to get attention, you'd have demanded special treatment, to be cosseted and made much of, not to be sent off on your own."

"But—" Leonie protested frantically, trying to hold off unconsciousness long enough to save herself from this exile.

"Never mind," the Mother Superior said firmly. "We'll wait for word from Camelot. When we hear it, then you'll go."

Leonie would have protested further, but Mother Magdalene laid a cool hand across her hot eyes, and sleep came up and took her.

Elfrida had never been this far from her home village before. The great forest through which she had been walking for most of the day did not look in the least familiar. In fact, it did not look like anything anyone from the village had ever described.

And why hadn't Mag brought her here to gather healing herbs and mushrooms?

The answer seemed clear enough; she was no longer in lands Mag or any of the villagers had ever seen.

She had not known which way to go, so she had followed the raven she saw flying away from the village. The raven had led her to the edge of the woods, which at the time had seemed quite ordinary. But the oaks and beeches had turned to a thick growth of fir; the deeper she went, the older the trees became, until at last she was walking on a tiny path between huge trunks that rose far over her head before properly branching out. Beneath those spreading branches, thin, twiggy growth reached out skeletal fingers like blackened bones, while the upper branches cut off most of the light, leaving the trail beneath shrouded in a twilight gloom, though it was midday.

Though she was on a quest of sorts, that did not mean she had left her good sense behind. While she was within the beech and oak forest, she had gleaned what she could on either side of the track. Her pack now held two double-handfuls each of acorns and beechnuts, still sound, and a few mushrooms. Two here, three or four there, they added up.

It was just as well, for the meager supply of journey-bread she had with her had been all given away by the end of the first day of her quest. A piece at

a time, to a child here, a nursing mother there . . .
but she had the freedom of the road and the forest;
the people she encountered were tied to their land
and could not leave it. Not while there was any
chance they might coax a crop from it.

They feared the forest, though they could not tell
Elfrida why. They would only enter the fringes of it,
to feed their pigs on acorns, to pick up deadfall.
Further than that, they would not go.

Elfrida had known for a long time that she was
not as magical as Mag. She had her visions, but that
was all; she could not see the power rising in the
circles, although she knew it was there, and could
sometimes feel it. She could not see the halos of light
around people that told Mag if they were sick or well.
She had no knowledge of the future outside of her
visions, and could not talk to the birds and animals
as Mag could.

So she was not in the least surprised to find that
she could sense nothing about the forest that indi-
cated either good or ill. If there was something here,
she could not sense it. Of course, the gloom of the
fir-forest was more than enough to frighten anyone
with any imagination. And while nobles often claimed
that peasants had no more imagination than a block
of wood—well, Elfrida often thought that nobles had
no more sense than one of their high-bred, high-
strung horses, that would break legs, shying at
shadows. Witless, useless—and irresponsible. How
many of them were on their lands, helping their
liegemen and peasants to save their crops? Few
enough; most were idling their time away at the High
King's Court, gambling, drinking, wenching, playing
at tourneys and other useless pastimes. And she would
wager that the High King's table was not empty; that
the nobles' children were not going pinch-faced and
hungry to bed. The religion of the White Christ had
divorced master from man, noble from villager,

making the former into a master in truth, and the latter into an income-producing slave. The villager was told by his priest to trust in God and receive his reward in heaven. The lord need feel no responsibility for any evils he did or caused, for once they had been confessed and paid for—usually by a generous gift to the priest—his God counted them as erased. The balance of duty and responsibility between the vassal and his lord was gone.

She shook off her bitter thoughts as nightfall approached. Without Mag's extra abilities Elfrida knew she would have to be twice as careful about spending the night in this place. If there were supernatural terrors about, she would never know until they were on her. So when she made her little camp, she cast circles around her with salt and iron, betony and rue, writing the runes as clear as she could, before she lit her fire to roast her nuts.

But in the end, when terror came upon her, it was of a perfectly natural sort.

Leonie cowered, and tried to hide in the folds of her robe. Her bruised face ached, and her bound wrists were cut and swollen around the thin twine the man who had caught her had used to bind her.

She had not gotten more than two days away from the convent—distributing most of her food to children and the sick as she walked—when she had reached the edge of the forest, and her vague visions had directed her to follow the path through it. She had seen no signs of people, nor had she sensed anything about the place that would have caused folk to avoid it. That had puzzled her, so she had dropped into a walking trance to try and sort out what kind of a place the forest was.

That was when someone had come up behind her and hit her on the head.

Now she knew why ordinary folk avoided the forest; it was the home of bandits. And she knew what her fate was going to be. Only the strength of the hold the chieftain had over his men had kept her from that fate until now. He had decreed that they would wait until all the men were back from their errands—and then they would draw lots for their turns at her. . . .

Leonie was so terrified that she was beyond thought; she huddled like a witless rabbit inside her robe and prayed for death.

"What's *this?*" the bandit chief said, loudly, startling her so that she raised her head out of the folds of her sleeves. She saw nothing at first; only the dark bulking shapes of men against the fire in their midst. He laughed, long and hard, as another of his men entered their little clearing, shoving someone in front of him. "By Satan's arse! The woods are sprouting wenches!"

Elfrida caught her breath at the curse; so, these men were not "just" bandits—they were the worst kind of bandit, nobles gone beyond the law. Only one who was once a follower of the White Christ would have used his adversary's name as an exclamation. No follower of the Old Way, either Moon or Blood-path would have done so.

The brigand who had captured her shoved her over to land beside another girl—and once again she caught her breath, as her talisman-bag swung loose on its cord, and the other girl shrunk away, revealing the wooden beads and cross at the rope that served her as a belt. Worse and worse—the girl wore the robes of one who had vowed herself to the White Christ! There would be no help there . . . if she were not witless before she had been caught, she was probably frightened witless now. Even if she would accept help from the hands of a "pagan."

✧ ✧ ✧

Leonie tried not to show her hope. Another girl!
Perhaps between the two of them, they could manage to win free!

But as the girl was shoved forward, to drop to the
needles beside Leonie, something swung free of her
robe to dangle over her chest. It was a little bag, on
a rawhide thong.

And the bandit chief roared again, this time with
disapproval, seizing the bag and breaking the thong
with a single, cruelly hard tug of his hand. He tossed
it out into the darkness and backhanded the outlaw
who had brought the girl in.

"You witless bastard!" he roared. "You brought in
a witch!" A *witch?*

Leonie shrunk away from her fellow captive. A
witch? Blessed Jesu—this young woman would be just
as pleased to see Leonie raped to death! She would
probably call up one of her demons to help!

As the brigand who had been struck shouted and
went for his chief's throat, and the others gathered
around, yelling encouragement and placing bets, she
closed her eyes, bowed her head, and prayed. *Blessed
Mother of God! hear me. Angels of grace, defend us.
Make them forget us for just a moment. . . .*

As the brainless child started in fear, then pulled
away, bowed her head, and began praying, Elfrida
kept a heavy hand on her temper. Bad enough that
she was going to die—and in a particularly horrible
way—but to have to do it in such company!

But—suddenly the outlaws were fighting. One of
them appeared to be the chief; the other the one who
had caught her. And they were ignoring the two girls
as if they had somehow forgotten their existence. . . .

Blessed Mother, hear me. Make it so.

The man had only tied her with a bit of leather,
no stronger than the thong that had held her herb-bag.

If she wriggled just right, bracing her tied hands against her feet, she could probably snap it.

She prayed, and pulled. And was rewarded with the welcome release of pressure as the thong snapped.

She brought her hands in front of her, hiding them in her tunic, and looked up quickly; the fight had involved a couple more of the bandits. She and the other girl were in the shadows now, for the fire had been obscured by the men standing or scuffling around it. If she crept away quickly and quietly—

No sooner thought than done. She started to crawl away, got as far as the edge of the firelight, then looked back.

The other girl was still huddled where she had been left, eyes closed. Too stupid or too frightened to take advantage of the opportunity to escape.

If Elfrida left her there, they probably wouldn't try to recapture her. They'd have one girl still, and wouldn't go hunting in the dark for the one that had gotten away. . . .

Elfrida muttered an oath, and crawled back.

Leonie huddled with the witch-girl under the shelter of a fallen tree, and they listened for the sounds of pursuit. She had been praying as hard as she could, eyes closed, when a painful tug on the twine binding her wrists had made her open her eyes.

"Well, come *on!*" the girl had said, tugging again. Leonie had not bothered to think about what the girl might be pulling her into, she had simply followed, crawling as best she could with her hands tied, then getting up and running when the girl did.

They had splashed through a stream, running along a moonlit path, until Leonie's sides ached. Finally the girl had pulled her off the path and shoved her under the bulk of a fallen tree, into a little dug-out den she would never have guessed was there. From the musky smell, it had probably been made by a fox or badger.

Leonie huddled in the dark, trying not to sob, concentrating on the pain in her side and not on the various fates the witch-girl could have planned for her.

Before too long, they heard shouts in the distance, but they never came very close. Leonie strained her ears, holding her breath, to try and judge how close their pursuers were, and jumped when the witch-girl put a hand on her.

"Don't," the girl whispered sharply. "You won't be going far with your hands tied like that. Hold still! I'm not going to hurt you."

Leonie stuttered something about demons, without thinking. The girl laughed.

"If I had a demon to come when I called, do you think I would have let a bastard like that lay hands on me?" Since there was no logical answer to that question, Leonie wisely kept quiet. The girl touched her hands, and then seized them; Leonie kept herself from pulling away, and a moment later, felt the girl sawing at her bonds with a bit of sharp rock. Every so often the rock cut into Leonie instead of the twine, but she bit her lip and kept quiet, gratitude increasing as each strand parted. "What were you doing out here, anyway?" the girl asked. "I thought they kept your kind mewed up like prize lambs."

"I had a vision—" Leonie began, wondering if by her words and the retelling of her holy revelation, the witch-girl might actually be converted to Christianity. It happened that way all the time in the tales of the saints, after all. . . .

So while the girl sawed patiently at the bonds with the sharp end of the rock, Leonie told her everything, from the time she realized that something was wrong, to the moment the bandit took her captive. The girl stayed silent through all of it, and Leonie began to hope that she *might* bring the witch-girl to the Light and Life of Christ.

The girl waited until she had obviously come to

the end, then laughed, unpleasantly. "Suppose, just suppose," she said, "I were to tell you that the *exact same* vision was given to me? Only it isn't some mystical cup that this land needs, it's the Cauldron of Cerridwen, the ever-renewing, for the High King refuses to sacrifice himself to save his kingdom as the Holy Bargain demands and only the Cauldron can give the land the blessing of the Goddess."

The last of the twine snapped as she finished, and Leonie pulled her hands away. "Then I would say that your vision is wrong, evil," she retorted. "There is no goddess, only the Blessed Virgin—"

"Who is one face of the Goddess, who is Maiden, Mother and Wise One," the girl interrupted, her words dripping acid. "Only a fool would fail to see that. And your White Christ is no more than the Sacrificed One in one of *His* many guises—it is the Cauldron the land needs, not your apocryphal Cup—"

"Your cauldron is some demon-thing," Leonie replied, angrily. "Only the Grail—"

Whatever else she was going to say was lost, as the tree-trunk above them was riven into splinters by a bolt of lightning that blinded and deafened them both for a moment.

When they looked up, tears streaming from their eyes, it was to see something they both recognized as The Enemy.

Standing over them was a shape, outlined in a glow of its own. It was three times the height of a man, black and hairy like a bear, with the tips of its outstretched claws etched in fire. But it was not a bear, for it wore a leather corselet, and its head had the horns of a bull, the snout and tusks of a boar, dripping foam and saliva, and its eyes, glowing an evil red, were slitted like a goat's.

Leonie screamed and froze. The witch-girl seized her bloody wrist, hauled her to her feet, and ran with her stumbling along behind.

The beast roared and followed after. They had not gotten more than forty paces down the road, when the witch-girl fell to the ground with a cry of pain, her hand slipping from Leonie's wrist.

Her ankle— Leonie thought, but no more, for the beast was shambling towards them. She grabbed the girl's arm and hauled her to her feet; draped her arm over her own shoulders, and dragged her erect. Up ahead there was moonlight shining down on something—perhaps a clearing, and perhaps the beast might fear the light—

She half-dragged, half-guided the witch-girl towards that promise of light, with the beast bellowing behind them. The thought crossed her mind that if she dropped the girl and left her, the beast would probably be content with the witch and would not chase after Leonie. . . .

No, she told herself, and stumbled onward.

They broke into the light, and Leonie looked up— And sank to her knees in wonder.

Elfrida fell beside the other girl, half blinded by tears of pain, and tried to get to her feet. The beast— she had to help Leonie up, they had to run—

Then she looked up.

And fell again to her knees, this time stricken not with pain, but with awe. And though she had never felt *power* before, she felt it now; humming through her, blood and bone, saw it in the vibration of the air, in the purity of the light streaming from the Cup—

The Cup held in the hand of a man, whose gentle, sad eyes told of the pain, not only of His own, but of the world's, that for the sake of the world, He carried on His own shoulders.

Leonie wept, tears of mingled joy and fear—joy to be in the Presence of One who was all of Light

and Love, and fear, that this One was She and not
He—and the thing that she held, spilling over the
Light of Love and Healing was Cauldron and not
Cup.

I was wrong— she thought, helplessly.

Wrong? said a loving, laughing Voice. *Or simply—
limited in vision?*

And in that moment, the Cauldron became a Cup,
and the Lady became the Lord, Jesu—then changed
again, to a man of strange, draped robes and slanted
eyes, who held neither Cup nor Cauldron, but a cup-
shaped Flower with a jeweled heart—a hawk-headed
creature with a glowing stone in His hand—a black-
skinned Woman with a bright Bird—

And then to another shape, and another, until her
eyes were dazzled and her spirit dizzied, and she
looked away, into the eyes of Elfrida. *The witch-girl—
Wise Girl* whispered the Voice in her mind, *and
Quest-Companion*—looked similarly dazzled, but the
joy in her face must surely mirror Leonie's. The girl
offered her hand, and Leonie took it, and they turned
again to face—

A Being of light, neither male nor female, and a
dazzling Cup as large as a Cauldron, the veil covering it barely dimming its brilliance.

Come, the Being said, *you have proved yourselves
worthy.*

Hand in hand, the two newest Grail Maidens rose,
and followed the shining beacon into the Light.

It was inevitable that the Holy Grail anthology would spawn an Excalibur anthology. I kept promising to write the story and things got in the way . . . like other deadlines! But bless their hearts, they held a place for me, and here is the story itself. It's not at all like the Grail story; in fact, it's not a very heroic story, which may surprise some people.

Once and Future

Michael O'Murphy woke with the mother of all hangovers splitting his head in half, churning up his stomach like a winter storm off the Orkneys, and a companion in his bed.

What in Jaysus did I do last night?

The pain in his head began just above his eyes, wrapped around the sides, and met in the back. His stomach did not bear thinking about. His companion was long, cold, and unmoving, but very heavy.

I took a board to bed? Was I that hard up for a sheila? Michael, you're slipping!

He was lying on his side, as always. The unknown object was at his back. At the moment it was no more identifiable than a hard presence along his spine, uncomfortable and unyielding. He wasn't entirely certain he wanted to find out exactly what it was until he mentally retraced his steps of the previous evening. Granted, this was irrational, but

178

a man with the mother of all hangovers is not a
rational being.

The reason for his monumental drunk was clear
enough in his mind; the pink slip from his job at the
docks, presented to him by the foreman at the end
of the day. *That would be yesterday, Friday, if I
haven't slept the weekend through.*

He wasn't the only bloke cashiered yesterday;
they'd laid off half the men at the shipyard. *So it's
back on the dole, and thank God Almighty I didn't
get serious with that little bird I met on holiday. Last
thing I need is a woman nagging at me for losing me
job and it wasn't even me own fault.* Depression piled
atop the splitting head and the foul stomach. Michael
O'Murphy was not the sort of man who accepted the
dole with any kind of grace other than ill.

He cracked his right eye open, winced at the stab
of light that penetrated into his cranium, and squinted
at the floor beside his bed.

Yes, there was the pink slip, crumpled into a wad,
beside his boots—and two bottles of Jameson's, one
empty, the other half full and frugally corked.

*Holy Mary Mother of God. I don't remember shar-
ing out that often, so I must've drunk most of it myself. No wonder I feel like a walk through Purgatory.*

He closed his eye again, and allowed the whiskey
bottle to jog a few more memories loose. So, he'd
been sacked, and half the boys with him. And they'd
all decided to drown their sorrows together.

*But not at a pub, and not at pub prices. You can't
get royally, roaring drunk at a pub unless you've got
a royal allowance to match. So we all bought our
bottles and met at Tommy's place.*

There'd been a half-formed notion to get shel-
lacked there, but Tommy had a car, and Tommy
had an idea. He'd seen some nonsense on the telly
about "Iron Johns" or some such idiocy, over in
America—

*Said we was all downtrodden and "needed to get
in touch with our inner selves"; swore that we had
to get "empowered" to get back on our feet, and
wanted to head out into the country—* There'd been
some talk about "male bonding" ceremonies, pounding
drums, carrying on like a lot of Red Indians—and
drinking of course. Tommy went on like it was some
kind of communion; the rest of them had already
started on their bottles before they got to Tommy's,
and at that point, a lot of pounding and dancing half-
naked and drinking sounded like a fine idea. So off
they went, crammed into Tommy's aging Morris Minor
with just enough room to get their bottles to their
lips.

At some point they stopped and all piled out;
Michael vaguely recalled a forest, which might well
have been National Trust lands and it was a mercy
they hadn't been caught and hauled off to gaol.
Tommy had gotten hold of a drum somewhere; it
was in the boot with the rest of the booze. They
all grabbed bottles and Tommy got the drum, and
off they went into the trees like a daft May Day
parade, howling and carrying on like bleeding loon-
ies.

How Tommy made the fire—and why it hadn't been
seen, more to the point!—Michael had not a clue. He
remembered a great deal of pounding on the drum,
more howling, shouting and swearing at the bosses of
the world, a lot of drinking, and some of the lads strip-
ping off their shirts and capering about like so many
monkeys. *About then was when I got an itch for some
quiet.* He and his bottles had stumbled off into the
trees, following an elusive moonbeam, or so he thought
he remembered. The singing and pounding had faded
behind him, and in his memory the trees loomed the
way they had when he was a nipper and everything
seemed huge. *They were like trees out of the old tales,
as big as the one they call Robin Hood's Oak in*

Sherwood. There was only one way to go since he didn't even consider turning back, and that was to follow the path between them, and the fey bit of moonlight that lured him on.

Was there a mist? I think there was. Wait! That was when the real path appeared. There had been mist, a curious, blue mist. It had muffled everything, from the sounds of his own footsteps to the sounds of his mates back by the fire. Before too very long, he might have been the only human being alive in a forest as old as time and full of portentous silence.

He remembered that the trees thinned out at just about the point where he was going to give up his ramble and turn back. He had found himself on the shores of a lake. It was probably an ordinary enough pond by daylight, but last night, with the mist drifting over it and obscuring the farther shore, the utter and complete silence of the place, and the moonlight pouring down over everything and touching everything with silver, it had seemed . . . uncanny, a bit frightening, and not entirely in the real world at all.

He had stood there with a bottle in each hand, a monument to inebriation, held there more by inertia than anything else, he suspected. He could still see the place as he squeezed his eyes shut, as vividly as if he stood there at that moment. The water was like a sheet of plate glass over a dark and unimaginable void; the full moon hung just above the dark mass of the trees behind him, a great round Chinese lantern of a moon, and blue-white mist floated everywhere in wisps and thin scarves and great opaque billows. A curious boat rested by the bank not a meter from him, a rough-hewn thing apparently made from a whole tree-trunk and shaped with an axe. Not even the reeds around the boat at his feet moved in the breathless quiet.

Then, breaking the quiet, a sound; a single splash in the middle of the lake. Startled, he had seen an arm rise up out of the water, beckoning.

He thought, of course, that someone had fallen in, or been swimming and took a cramp. One of his mates, even, who'd come round to the other side and taken a fancy for a dip. It never occurred to him to go back to the others for help, just as it never occurred to him not to rush out there to save whoever it was.

He dropped his bottles into the boat at his feet, and followed them in. He looked about for the tether to cast off, but there wasn't one—looked for the oars to row out to the swimmer, but there weren't any of those, either. Nevertheless, the boat was moving, and heading straight for that beckoning arm as if he was willing it there. And it didn't seem at all strange to him that it was doing so, at least, not at the time.

He remembered that he'd been thinking that whoever this was, she'd fallen in fully clothed, for the arm had a long sleeve of some heavy white stuff. And it had to be a she—the arm was too white and soft to be a man's. It wasn't until he got up close, though, that he realized there was nothing showing *but* the arm, that the woman had been under an awfully long time—and that the arm sticking up out of the water was holding something.

Still, daft as it was, it wasn't important— He'd ignored everything but the arm, ignored things that didn't make any sense. As the boat got within range of the woman, he'd leaned over the bow so far that *he* almost fell in, and made a grab for that upraised arm.

But the hand and wrist slid through his grasp somehow, although he was *sure* he'd taken a good, firm hold on them, and he fell back into the boat, knocking himself silly against the hard wooden bottom, his hands clasped tight around whatever it was she'd been holding. He saw stars, and more than stars, and when he came to again, the boat was back against the bank, and there was no sign of the woman.

But he had her sword.

Her sword? I had her sword?

Now he reached behind him to feel the long, hard length of it at his back.

By God—it is a sword!

He had no real recollection of what happened after that; he must have gotten back to the lads, and they all must have gotten back to town in Tommy's car, because here he was.

In bed with a sword.

I've heard of being in bed with a battle-axe, but never a sword.

Slowly, carefully, he sat up. Slowly, carefully, he reached into the tumble of blankets and extracted the drowning woman's sword.

It was real, it looked old, and it was damned heavy. He hefted it in both hands, and grunted with surprise. If this was the kind of weapon those old bastards used to hack at one another with in the long-ago days that they made films of, there must have been as much harm done by breaking bones as by whacking bits off.

It wasn't anything fancy, though, not like you saw in the flicks or the comics; a plain, black, leather-wrapped hilt, with what looked like brass bits as the cross-piece and a plain, black leather-bound sheath. Probably weighed about as much as four pry-bars of the same length put together.

He put his hand to the hilt experimentally, and pulled a little, taking it out of the sheath with the vague notion of having a look at the blade itself.

PENDRAGON!

The voice shouted in his head, an orchestra of nothing but trumpets, and all of them played at top volume.

He dropped the sword, which landed on his toes. He shouted with pain, and jerked his feet up reflexively, and the sword dropped to the floor, half out of its sheath. "What the *hell* was that?" he howled, grabbing his abused toes in both hands, and rocking back and forth a little. He was hardly expecting an answer, but he got one anyway.

It was I, Pendragon.

He felt his eyes bugging out, and he cast his gaze frantically around the room, looking for the joker who'd snuck inside while he was sleeping. But there wasn't anyone, and there was nowhere to hide. The rented room contained four pieces of furniture—his iron-framed bed, a cheap deal bureau and nightstand, and a chair. He bent over and took a peek under the bed, feeling like a frightened old aunty, but there was nothing there, either.

You're looking in the wrong place.

"I left the radio on," he muttered, "that's it. It's some daft drama. Gawd, I hate those BBC buggers!" He reached over to the radio on the nightstand and felt for the knob. But the radio was already off, and cold, which meant it hadn't *been* on with the knob broken.

Pendragon, I am on the floor, where you dropped me.

He looked down at the floor. The only things besides his boots were the whiskey bottles and the sword.

"I never heard of no Jameson bottles talking in a bloke's head before," he muttered to himself, as he massaged his toes, "and me boots never struck up no conversations before."

Don't be absurd, said the voice, tartly. *You know what I am, as you know what you are.*

The sword. It had to be the sword. "And just what am I, then?" he asked it, wondering when the boys from the Home were going to come romping through the door to take him off for a spot of rest. *This is daft. I must have gone loopy. I'm talking to a piece of metal, and it's talking back to me.*

You are the Pendragon, the sword said patiently, and waited. When he failed to respond except with an uncomprehending shrug, it went on—but with far less patience. *You are the Once and Future King. The Warrior Against the Darkness.* It waited, and he still had no notion what it was talking about.

You are ARTHUR, it shouted, making him wince. *You are King Arthur, Warleader and Hero!*

"Now it's *you* that's loopy," he told it sternly. "I don't bloody well think! King Arthur indeed!"

The only recollection of King Arthur he had were things out of his childhood—stories in the schoolbooks, a Disney flick, Christmas pantomimes. Vague images of crowns and red-felt robes, of tin swords and papier-mache armor flitted through his mind— and talking owls and daft magicians. "King Arthur! Not likely!"

You are! the sword said, sounding desperate now. *You are the Pendragon! You have been reborn into this world to be its Hero! Don't you remember?*

He only snorted. "I'm Michael O'Murphy, I work at the docks, I'll be on the dole on Monday, and I don't bloody think anybody needs any bloody more Kings these days! They've got enough troubles with the ones they've—*Gawd!*"

He fell back into the bed as the sword bombarded his mind with a barrage of images, more vivid than the flicks, for he was *in* them. Battles and feasts, triumph and tragedy, success and failure—a grim stand against the powers of darkness that held for the short space of one man's lifetime.

It all poured into his brain in the time it took for him to breathe twice. And when he sat up again, he remembered.

All of it.

He blinked, and rubbed his mistreated head. "Gawd!" he complained. "You might warn a lad first!"

Now do you believe? The sword sounded smug.

Just like the nuns at his school, when they'd gotten done whapping him "for his own good."

"I believe you're damn good at shoving a lot of rubbish into a man's head and making him think it's his," he said stubbornly, staring down at the shining expanse of blade, about ten centimeter's worth, that protruded out of the sheath. "I still don't see where all this makes any difference, even if I *do* believe it."

If the sword could have spluttered, it probably would have. *You don't—you're Arthur! I'm Excalibur! You're supposed to take me up and use me!*

"For what?" he asked, snickering at the mental image of prying open tins of beans with the thing. "You don't make a good pry-bar, I can't cut wood with you even if I had a wood stove, which I don't, nobody's going to believe you're a fancy saw-blade, and there's laws about walking around with something like you strapped to me hip. What do I do, fasten a sign to you, and go on a protest march?"

You—you— Bereft of words, the sword resorted to another flood of images. Forewarned by the last one, Michael stood his ground.

But this time the images were harder to ignore.

He saw himself taking the sword and gathering his fighters to his side—all of his friends from the docks, the ones who'd bitched along with him about what a mess the world was in. He watched himself making an army out of them, and sending them out into the streets to clean up the filth there. He saw himself as the leader of a new corps of vigilantes who tracked down the pushers, the perverts, the thugs and the punks and gave them all a taste of what they had coming to them.

He saw his army making the city safe for people

to live in, saw them taking back the night from the Powers of Evil.

He saw more people flocking to his banner and his cause, saw him carrying his crusade from city to city, until a joyous public threw the House of Hanover out of Buckingham Palace and installed him on the throne, and a ten-year-old child could carry a gold bar across the length of the island and never fear a robber or a molester.

Or try this one, if that doesn't suit you!

This time he saw himself crossing to Ireland, confronting the leadership of every feuding party there, and defeating them, one by one, in challenge-combat. He saw himself bringing peace to a land that had been torn by strife for so long that there wasn't an Irish child alive that didn't know what a knee-capper was. He saw the last British Tommy leaving the island with a smile on his face and a shamrock in his lapel, withdrawing in good order since order itself had been restored. He saw plenty coming back to the land, prosperity, saw Ireland taking a major role in the nations of the world, and "Irish honor" becoming a byword for "trust." Oh, this was cruel, throwing a vision like that in his face! He wasn't for British Rule, but the IRA was as bad as the PLO by his lights—and there wasn't anything he could do about either.

Until now.

Or here—widen your horizons, lift your eyes beyond your own sordid universe!

This time he started as before, carried the sword to Ireland and restored peace there, and went on—on to the Continent, to Eastern Europe, taking command of the UN forces there and forcing a real and lasting peace by the strength of his arm. Oh, there was slaughter, but it wasn't a slaughter of the innocents but of the bastards that drove the fights, and in the end that same ten-year-old child could start in Galway and end in

Sarejevo, and no one would so much as dirty the lace on her collar or offer her an unkind word.

The sword released him, then, and he sat blinking on his shabby second-hand bed, in his dingy rented room, still holding his aching toes in both hands. It all seemed so tawdry, this little world of his, and all he had to do to earn a greater and brighter one was to reach out his hand.

He looked down at the sword at the side of his bed, and the metal winked smugly up at him. "You really think you have me now, don't you," he said bitterly to it.

It said nothing. It didn't have to answer.

But he had answers enough for all the temptations in his own mind. Because now he *remembered* Arthur— and Guinevere, and Lancelot and Agravaine and Morgaine.

And Mordred.

Oh yes. He had no doubt that there would be a Mordred out there, somewhere, waiting for him the moment he took up the sword. He hadn't been any too careful, AIDS notwithstanding, and there could be any number of bastards scattered from his seed. Hell, there would be a Mordred even if it *wasn't* his son. For every Warrior of the Light there was a Warrior of the Dark; he'd seen that quite, quite clearly. For every Great Friend there was always the Great Betrayer—hadn't Peter betrayed Christ by denying him? For every Great Love there was the Great Loss.

It would *not* be the easy parade of victories the sword showed him; he was older and far, far wiser than the boy-Arthur who'd taken Excalibur the last time. He was not to be dazzled by dreams. The *most* likely of the scenarios to succeed was the first—some bloke in New York had done something like that, called his lads the "Guardian Angels"—and even *he* hadn't succeeded in cleaning up more than a drop or two of the filth in one city, let alone hundreds.

That scenario would only last as long as it took some punk's parents to sue him. What good would a sword be in court, eh? What would he do, slice the judge's head off?

And this was the age of the tabloids, of smut-papers. They'd love him for a while, then they'd decide to bring him down. If they'd had a time with Charles and Di, what would they do with him—and Guinevere, and Lancelot—and Mordred?

For Mordred and Morgaine were surely here, and they might even have got a head start on him. They could be waiting for him to appear, waiting with hired thugs to take him out.

For that matter, Mordred might be a lawyer, ready for him at this very moment with briefs and brief-case, and he'd wind up committed to the loony asylum before he got two steps! Or he might be a smut reporter, good at digging up dirt. His own, real past wouldn't make a pretty sight on paper.

Oh no. Oh, no.

"I don't think so, my lad," he said, and before the sword could pull any clever tricks, he reached down, and slammed it home in the sheath.

Three hours and six aspirins later, he walked into the nearest pawn shop with a long bundle wrapped in old newspapers under his arm. He handed it across the counter to the wizened old East Indian who kept the place.

The old boy unwrapped the papers, and peered at the sword without a hint of surprise. God alone knew he'd probably seen stranger things pass across his counter. He slid it out of its sheath and examined the steel before slamming it back home. Only then did he squint through the grill at Michael.

"It's mild steel. Maybe antique, maybe not, no way of telling. Five quid," he said. "Take it or leave it."

"I'll take it," said the Pendragon.

This is one of those fun ones. I submitted this to Andre Norton for her Magic in Ithkar *braided anthology for Another Company; this was during that time when braided anthologies (otherwise known as "shared worlds") were Hot Stuff. I didn't know if I had a hope of getting in, but I tried—and she accepted it! Later, since* Magic in Ithkar *only made it to volume two, and I really liked the concept of the Free Bards, this became the basis for the "Bardic Voices" series I do for Baen. This is a case where I was able to "file the serial numbers off" and do a rewrite to fit the story into an entirely original world; you can't always do that, but sometimes it works.*

Fiddler Fair

All the world comes to Ithkar Fair.

That's what they said, anyway—and it certainly seemed that way to Rune, as she traveled the Trade Road down from her home near the Galzar Pass. She wasn't walking on the dusty, hard-packed road itself; she'd likely have been trampled by the press of beasts, then run over by the carts into the bargain. Instead, she walked with the rest of the foot-travelers on the road's verge. It was no less dusty, what grass there had been had long since been trampled into powder by all the feet of the pilgrims and fairgoers, but at least a traveler was able to move along without risk of acquiring hoofprints on his anatomy.

Rune was close enough now to see the gates of the Fair itself, and the Fair-ward beside them. This seemed like a good moment to separate herself from the rest of the throng, rest her tired feet, and plan her next moves before entering the grounds of the Fair.

She elbowed her way out of the line of people, some of whom complained and elbowed back, and moved away from the road to a place where she had a good view of the Fair and a rock to sit on. The sun beat down with enough heat to be felt through her soft leather hat as she plopped herself down on the rock and began massaging her tired feet while she looked the Fair over.

It was a bit overwhelming. Certainly it was much bigger than she'd imagined it would be. It was equally certain that there would be nothing dispensed for free behind those log palings, and the few coppers Rune had left would have to serve to feed her through the three days of trials for admission to the Bardic Guild. After that—

Well, after that, she should be an apprentice, and food and shelter would be for her master to worry about. If not—

She refused to admit the possibility of failing the trials. She couldn't—the Three surely *wouldn't* let her fail. Not after getting this far.

But for now, she needed somewhere to get herself cleaned of the road-dust, and a place to sleep, both with no price tags attached. Right now, she was the same gray-brown from head to toe, the darker brown of her hair completely camouflaged by the dust, or at least it felt that way. Even her eyes felt dusty.

She strolled down to the river, her lute thumping her shoulder softly on one side, her pack doing the same on the other. Close to the docks the water was muddy and roiled; there was too much traffic on the river to make an undisturbed bath a viable possibility, and too many wharf-rats about to make leaving one's belongings a wise move. She backtracked upstream a bit, while the noise of the Fair faded behind her, crossed over the canal and went hunting the rapids that the canal bypassed. The bank of the river was wilder here, and overgrown, not like the carefully tended area of the canalside. Finally she found a place where the river had cut a tiny cove into the bank. It was secluded; trees overhung the water, their branches making a good thick screen that touched the water, the ground beneath them bare of growth, and hollows between some of the roots just big enough to cradle her sleeping roll. Camp, bath, and water, all together, and within climbing distance on one of the trees was a hollow big enough to hide her bed-roll and those belongings she didn't want to carry into the Fair.

She waited until dusk fell before venturing into the river and kept her eyes and ears open while she scrubbed herself down. Once clean, she debated whether or not to change into the special clothing she'd brought tonight; it might be better to save it— then the thought of donning the sweat-soaked, dusty traveling gear became too distasteful, and she rejected it out of hand.

She felt strange and altogether different once she'd put the new costume on. Part of that was due to the materials—except for when she'd tried the clothing on for fit, this was the first time she'd ever worn silk and velvet. Granted, the materials were all old; bought from a second-hand vendor and cut down from much larger garments. The velvet of the breeches wasn't *too* rubbed; the ribbons on the sleeves of the shirt and the embroidery should cover the faded places, and the vest should cover the stain on the back panel completely. Her hat, once the dust was beaten out of it and the plumes she'd snatched from the tails

of several disgruntled roosters were tucked into the
band, looked brave enough. Her boots, at least, were
new, and when the dust was brushed from them,
looked quite well. She tucked her remaining changes
of clothing and her bedroll into her pack, hid the lot
in the tree-hollow, and felt ready to face the Fair.

The Fair-ward at the gate eyed her carefully.
"Minstrel?" he asked suspiciously, looking at the lute
and fiddle she carried in their cases, slung from her
shoulders.

She shook her head. "Here for the trials, m'lord."

"Ah," he appeared satisfied. "You come in good
time, boy. The trials begin tomorrow. The Guild has
its tent pitched hard by the main gate of the Temple;
you should have no trouble finding it."

The wizard of the gate looked bored, ignoring her.
Rune did not correct the Fair-ward's assumption that
she was a boy; it was her intent to pass as male until
she'd safely passed the trials. She'd never heard of
the Bardic Guild admitting a girl, but so far as she'd
been able to determine, there was nothing in the rules
and Charter of the Guild preventing it. So once she'd
been accepted, once the trials were safely passed,
she'd reveal her sex, but until then, she'd play the
safe course.

She thanked him, but he had already turned his
attention to the next in line. She passed inside the
log walls and entered the Fair itself.

The first impressions she had were of noise and
light; torches burned all along the aisle she traversed;
the booths to either side were lit by lanterns, candles,
or other, more arcane methods. The crowd was noisy;
so were the merchants. Even by torchlight it was plain
that these were the booths featuring shoddier goods;
secondhand finery, brass jewelry, flash and tinsel. The
entertainers here were—surprising. She averted her
eyes from a set of dancers. It wasn't so much that
they wore little but imagination, but the *way* they

were dancing embarrassed even her; and a tavern-bred child has seen a great deal in its life.

She kept a tight grip on her pouch and instruments, tried to ignore the crush, and let the flow of fairgoers carry her along.

Eventually the crowd thinned out a bit (though not before she'd felt a ghostly hand or two try for her pouch and give it up as a bad cause). She followed her nose then, looking for the row that held the cookshop tents and the ale-sellers. She hadn't eaten since this morning, and her stomach was lying in uncomfortably close proximity to her spine.

She learned that the merchants of tavern-row were shrewd judges of clothing; hers wasn't fine enough to be offered a free taste, but wasn't poor enough to be shooed away. Sternly admonishing her stomach to be less impatient, she strolled the length of the row twice, carefully comparing prices and quantities, before settling on a humble tent that offered meat pasties (best not ask what beast the meat came from, not at these prices) and fruit juice or milk as well as ale and wine. Best of all, it offered seating at rough trestle-tables as well. Rune took her flaky pastry and her mug of juice (no wine or ale for her; not even had she the coppers to spare for it. She dared not be the least muddle-headed, not with a secret to keep and a competition on the morn), and found herself a spot at an empty table where she could eat and watch the crowd passing by. The pie was more crust than meat, but it was filling and well-made and fresh; that counted for a great deal. She noted with amusement that there were two sorts of the clumsy, crude clay mugs. One sort, the kind they served the milk and juice in, was ugly and shapeless (too ugly to be worth stealing) but was just as capacious as the exterior promised. The other, for wine and ale, was just the same ugly shape and size on the *outside* (though a different shade of toad-back green), but had a far thicker bottom, effectively reducing the interior capacity by at least a third.

"Come for the trials, lad?" asked a quiet voice in her ear. Rune jumped, nearly knocking her mug over, and snatching at it just in time to save the contents from drenching her shopworn finery (and however would she have gotten it clean again in time for the morrow's competition?). There hadn't been a sound or a hint of movement or even the shifting of the bench to warn her, but now there was a man sitting beside her.

He was of middle years, red hair going to gray, smile-wrinkles around his mouth and grey-green eyes, with a candid, triangular face. Well, that said nothing; Rune had known highwaymen with equally friendly and open faces. His dress was similar to her own; leather breeches instead of velvet, good linen instead of worn silk, a vest and a leather hat that could have been twin to hers, knots of ribbon on the sleeves of his shirt—and the neck of a lute peeking over his shoulder. A Minstrel!

Of the Guild? Rune rechecked the ribbons on his sleeves, and was disappointed. Blue and scarlet and green, not the purple and silver of a Guild Minstrel, nor the purple and gold of a Guild Bard. This was only a common songster, a mere street-player. Still, he'd bespoken her kindly enough, and the Three knew not everyone with the music-passion had the skill or the talent to pass the trials—

"Aye, sir," she replied politely. "I've hopes to pass; I think I've the talent, and others have said as much."

His eyes measured her keenly, and she had the disquieting feeling that her boy-ruse was fooling *him* not at all. "Ah well," he replied, "There's a-many before you have thought the same, and failed."

"That may be—" she answered the challenge in his eyes, "but I'd bet fair coin that none of *them* fiddled for a murdering ghost, and not only came out by the grace of their skill but were rewarded by that same spirit for amusing him!"

"Oh, so?" a lifted eyebrow was all the indication he gave of being impressed, but somehow that lifted brow conveyed volumes. "You've made a song of it, surely?"

"Have I not! It's to be my entry for the third day of testing."

"Well then—" He said no more than that, but his wordless attitude of waiting compelled Rune to unsling her fiddlecase, extract her instrument, and tune it without further prompting.

"It's the fiddle that's my first instrument," she said apologetically, "And since 'twas the fiddle that made the tale—"

"Never apologize for a song, child," he admonished, interrupting her. "Let it speak out for itself. Now let's hear this ghost-tale."

It wasn't easy to sing while fiddling, but Rune had managed the trick of it some time ago. She closed her eyes a half-moment, fixing in her mind the necessary changes she'd made to the lyrics—for unchanged, the song would have given her sex away—and began.

"I sit here on a rock, and curse
my stupid, bragging tongue,
And curse the pride that would not let
me back down from a boast
And wonder where my wits went,
when I took that challenge up
And swore that I would go
and fiddle for the Skull Hill Ghost!"

Oh, aye, that had been a damn fool move—to let those idiots who patronized the tavern where her mother worked goad her into boasting that there wasn't anyone, living or dead, that she couldn't cozen with her fiddling. Too much ale, Rune, and too little sense. And

too tender a pride, as well, to let them rub salt in the
wound of being the tavern wench's bastard.

> "It's midnight, and there's not a sound
>   up here upon Skull Hill
> Then comes a wind that chills my blood
>   and makes the leaves blow wild"

Not a good word choice, but a change that had
to be made—that was one of the giveaway verses.

> "And rising up in front of me,
>   a thing like shrouded Death.
> A voice says, 'Give me reason why
>   I shouldn't kill you, child.'"

Holy Three, that thing had been ghastly; cold and
old and totally heartless; it had smelled of Death and
the grave, and had shaken her right down to her
toenails. She made the fiddle sing about what words
alone could never convey, and saw her audience of
one actually shiver.

The next verse described Rune's answer to the
spirit, and the fiddle wailed of fear and determina-
tion and things that didn't rightly belong on earth.
Then came the description of that night-long, lightless
ordeal she'd passed through, and the fiddle shook with
the weariness she'd felt, playing the whole night long,
and the tune rose with dawning triumph when the
thing not only didn't kill her outright, but began to
warm to the music she'd made. Now she had an
audience of more than one, though she was only half
aware of the fact.

> "At last the dawnlight strikes my eyes;
>   I stop, and see the sun.
> The light begins to chase away
>   the dark and midnight cold—

And then the light strikes something more—
  I stare in dumb surprise—
For where the ghost had stood
   there is a heap of shining gold!"

The fiddle laughed at Death cheated, thumbed its nose at spirits, and chortled over the revelation that even the dead could be impressed and forced to reward courage and talent.

Rune stopped, and shook back brown locks dark with sweat, and looked about her in astonishment at the applauding patrons of the cooktent. She was even more astonished when they began to toss coppers in her open fiddlecase, and the cooktent's owner brought her over a full pitcher of juice and a second pie.

"I'd a brought ye wine, laddie, but Master Talaysen there says ye go to trials and mustna be a-muddled," she whispered as she hurried back to her counter.

"I hadn't meant—"

"Surely this isn't the first time you've played for your supper, child?" the minstrel's eyes were full of amused irony.

"Well, no, but—"

"So take your well-earned reward and don't go arguing with folk who have a bit of copper to fling at you, and who recognize the Gift when they hear it. No mistake, youngling, you *have* the Gift. And sit and eat; you've more bones than flesh. A good tale, that."

"Well," Rune blushed, "I did exaggerate a bit at the end. 'Twasn't gold, it was silver. But silver won't rhyme. And it was that silver that got me here— bought me my second instrument, paid for lessoning, kept me fed while I was learning. I'd be just another tavern-musician, otherwise—"

"Like me, you are too polite to say?" the minstrel smiled, then the smile faded. "There are worse things, child, than to be a free musician. I don't think there's

much doubt your Gift will get you past the trials—
but you might not find the Guild to be all you think
it to be."

Rune shook her head stubbornly, wondering
briefly why she'd told this stranger so much, and
why she so badly wanted his good opinion. "Only
a Guild Minstrel would be able to earn a place in
a noble's train. Only a Guild Bard would have the
chance to sing for royalty. I'm sorry to contradict
you, sir, but I've had my taste of wandering, singing my songs out only to know they'll be forgotten
in the next drink, wondering where my next meal
is coming from. I'll never get a secure life except
through the Guild, and I'll never see my songs live
beyond me without their patronage."

He sighed. "I hope you never regret your decision,
child. But if you should—or if you need help, ever—
well, just ask for Talaysen. I'll stand your friend."

With those surprising words, he rose soundlessly,
as gracefully as a bird in flight, and slipped out of
the tent. Just before he passed out of sight among
the press of people, Rune saw him pull his lute
around and begin to strum it. She managed to hear
the first few notes of a love-song, the words rising
golden and glorious from his throat, before the crowd
hid him from view and the babble of voices obscured
the music.

Rune was waiting impatiently outside the Guild
tent the next morning, long before there was anyone
there to take her name for the trials. It was, as the
Fair-ward had said, hard to miss; purple in the main,
with pennons and edgings of silver and gilt. Almost—
too much; almost gaudy. She was joined shortly by
three more striplings, one well-dressed and confident,
two sweating and nervous. More trickled in as the
sun rose higher, until there was a line of twenty or
thirty waiting when the Guild Registrar, an old and

sour-looking scribe, raised the tent-flap to let them file inside. He wasn't wearing Guild colors, but rather a robe of dusty brown velvet; a hireling therefore.

He took his time, sharpening his quill until Rune was ready to scream with impatience, before looking her up and down and asking her name.

"Rune, child of Lista Jesaril, tavernkeeper." That sounded a trifle better than her mother's *real* position, serving wench.

"From whence?"

"Karthar, East and North—below Galzar Pass."

"Primary instrument?"

"Fiddle."

"Secondary?"

"Lute."

He raised an eyebrow; the usual order was lute, primary; fiddle, secondary. For that matter, fiddle wasn't all that common even as a secondary instrument.

"And you will perform—?"

"First day, primary, 'Lament Of The Maiden Esme.' Second day, secondary, 'The Unkind Lover.' Third day, original, 'The Skull Hill Ghost.'" An awful title, but she could hardly use the *real* name of "Fiddler Girl." "Accompanied on primary, fiddle."

"Take your place."

She sat on the backless wooden bench trying to keep herself calm. Before her was the raised wooden platform on which they would all perform; to either side of it were the backless benches like the one she warmed, for the aspirants to the Guild. The back of the tent made the third side, and the fourth faced the row of well-padded chairs for the Guild judges. Although she was first here, it was inevitable that they would let others have the preferred first few slots; there would be those with fathers already in the Guild, or those who had coins for bribes. Still, she shouldn't have to wait too long—rising with the dawn would give her that much of an edge, at least.

She got to play by midmorning. The "Lament" was perfect for fiddle, the words were simple and few, and the wailing melody gave her lots of scope for improvisation. The row of Guild judges, solemn in their tunics or robes of purple, white silk shirts trimmed with gold or silver ribbon depending on whether they were Minstrels or Bards, were a formidable audience. Their faces were much alike: well-fed and very conscious of their own importance; you could see it in their eyes. As they sat below the platform and took unobtrusive notes, they seemed at least mildly impressed. Even more heartening, several of the boys yet to perform looked satisfyingly worried when she'd finished.

She packed up her fiddle and betook herself briskly out—to find herself a corner of Temple Wall to lean against as her knees sagged when the excitement that had sustained her wore off. It was several long moments before she could get her legs to bear her weight and her hands to stop shaking. It was then that she realized that she hadn't eaten since the night before—and that she was suddenly ravenous. Before she'd played, the very thought of food had been revolting.

The same cookshop tent as before seemed like a reasonable proposition. She paid for her breakfast with some of the windfall-coppers of the night before; this morning the tent was crowded and she was lucky to get a scant corner of a bench to herself. She ate hurriedly and joined the strollers through the Fair.

Once or twice she thought she glimpsed the red hair of Talaysen, but if it was he, he was gone by the time she reached the spot where she had thought he'd been. There were plenty of other street-singers, though. She thought wistfully of the harvest of coin she'd garnered the night before as she noted that

none of them seemed to be lacking for patronage.
But now that she was a duly registered entrant in the
trials, it would be going against custom, if not the
rules, to set herself up among them.

So instead she strolled, and listened, and made
mental notes for further songs. There was many a tale
she overheard that would have worked well in song-
form; many a glimpse of silk-bedecked lady, strangely
sad or hectically gay, or velvet-clad lord, sly and
foxlike or bold and pompous, that brought snatches
of rhyme to mind. By early evening her head was
crammed full—and it was time to see how the Guild
had ranked the aspirants of the morning.

The list was posted outside the closed tent-flaps,
and Rune wasn't the only one interested in the outcome of the first day's trials. It took a bit of time to
work her way in to look, but when she did—

By the Three! There she was, "Rune of Karthar"—
listed *third*.

She all but floated back to her river-side tree-roost.

The second day of the trials was worse than the first;
the aspirants performed in order, lowest ranking to
highest. That meant that Rune had to spend most of
the day sitting on the hard wooden bench, clutching
the neck of her lute in nervous fingers, listening to
contestant after contestant and sure that each one was
much better on his secondary instrument than she was.
She'd only had a year of training on it, after all. Still,
the song she'd chosen was picked deliberately to play
up her voice and de-emphasize her lute-strumming.
It was going to be pretty difficult for any of these
others to match her high contralto, (a truly cunning
imitation of a boy's soprano) since most of them had
passed puberty.

At long last her turn came. She swallowed her
nervousness as best she could, took the platform, and
began.

Privately she thought it was a pretty silly song. Why on earth any man would put up with the things that lady did to him, and all for the sake of a "kiss on her cold, quiet hand" was beyond her. Still, she put all the acting ability she had into it, and was rewarded by a murmur of approval when she'd finished.

"That voice—I've seldom heard one so pure at that late an age!" she overheard as she packed up her instrument. "If he passes the third day—you don't suppose he'd agree to become castrati, do you? I can think of half a dozen courts that would pay red gold to have him."

She smothered a smile—imagine their surprise to discover that it would *not* be necessary to eunuch her to preserve her voice!

She lingered to listen to the last of the entrants, then waited outside for the posting of the results.

She nearly fainted to discover that she'd moved up to second place.

"I told you," said a quiet voice in her ear. "But are you still sure you want to go through with this?"

She whirled, to find the minstrel Talaysen standing behind her, the sunset brightening his hair and the soft shadows on his face making him appear scarcely older than she.

"I'm sure," she replied firmly. "One of the judges said today that he could think of half a dozen courts that would pay red gold to have my voice."

"Bought and sold like so much mutton? Where's the living in that? Caged behind high stone walls and never let out of the sight of m'lord's guards, lest you take a notion to sell your services elsewhere? Is *that* the life you want to lead?"

"Trudging down roads in the pouring cold rain, frightened half to death that you'll take sickness and ruin your voice—maybe for good? Singing with your stomach growling so loud it drowns out the song?

Watching some idiot with half your talent being clad
in silk and velvet and eating at the high table, while
you try and please some brutes of guardsmen in the
kitchen in hopes of a few scraps and a corner by the
fire?" she countered. "No thank you. I'll take my
chances with the Guild. Besides, where else would
I be able to *learn?* I've got no more silver to spend
on instruments or teaching."

"There are those who would teach you for the love
of it—welladay, you've made up your mind. As you
will, child," he replied, but his eyes were sad as he
turned away and vanished into the crowd again.

Once again she sat the hard bench for most of the
day, while those of lesser ranking performed. This
time it was a little easier to bear; it was obvious from
a great many of these performances that few, if any,
of the boys had the Gift to create. By the time it was
Rune's turn to perform, she judged that, counting
herself and the first-place holder, there could only
be five real contestants for the three open Bardic
apprentice slots. The rest would be suitable only as
Minstrels; singing someone else's songs, unable to
compose their own.

She took her place before the critical eyes of the
judges, and began.

She realized with a surge of panic as she finished
the first verse that they did *not* approve. While she
improvised, she mentally reviewed the verse, trying
to determine what it was that had set those slight
frowns on the Judicial faces.

Then she realized; *boasting.* Guild Bards simply did
not admit to being boastful. Nor did they demean
themselves by reacting to the taunts of lesser beings.
Oh, Holy Three—

Quickly she improvised a verse on the folly of
youth; of how, had she been older and wiser, she'd
never have gotten herself into such a predicament.

She heaved an invisible sigh of relief as the frowns disappeared.

By the last chorus, they were actually nodding and smiling, and one of them was tapping a finger in time to the tune. She finished with a flourish worthy of a Master, and waited, breathlessly. And they *applauded*. Dropped their dignity and *applauded*.

The performance of the final contestant was an anticlimax.

None of them had left the tent since this last trial began. Instead of a list, the final results would be announced, and they waited in breathless anticipation to hear what they would be. Several of the boys had already approached Rune, offering smiling congratulations on her presumed first-place slot. A hush fell over them all as the chief of the judges took the platform, a list in his hand.

"First place, and first apprenticeship as Bard—Rune, son of Lista Jesaril of Karthar—"

"Pardon, my lord—" Rune called out clearly, bubbling over with happiness and unable to hold back the secret any longer. "—but it's not son—it's *daughter*."

She had only a split second to take in the rage on their faces before the first staff descended on her head.

They flung her into the dust outside the tent, half-senseless, and her smashed instruments beside her. The passersby avoided even looking at her as she tried to get to her feet, and fell three times. Her right arm dangled uselessly; it hurt so badly that she was certain that it must be broken, but it hadn't hurt half as badly when they'd cracked it as it had when they'd smashed her fiddle; that had broken her heart. All she wanted to do now was to get to the river and throw herself in. With any luck at all, she'd drown.

But she couldn't even manage to stand.

"Gently, lass," firm hands took her and supported

her on both sides, "Lady be my witness, if ever I thought they'd have gone this far, I'd never have let you go through with this farce."

She turned her head, trying to see through tears of pain, both of heart and body, with eyes that had sparks dancing before them. The man supporting her on her left she didn't recognize, but the one on the right—

"T-Talaysen?" she faltered.

"I told you I'd help if you needed it, did I not? I think you have more than a little need at the moment—"

"Th-they broke my fiddle, Talaysen. And my lute. They broke them, and they broke my arm."

"Oh, Rune, lass—" There were tears in *his* eyes, and yet he almost seemed to be laughing as well. "If *ever* I doubted you'd the makings of a Bard, you just dispelled those doubts. *First* the fiddle, *then* the lute—and only *then* do you think of your own hurts. Ah, come away lass, come where people can care for such a treasure as you—"

Stumbling through darkness, wrenched with pain, carefully supported and guided on either side, Rune was in no position to judge where or how far they went. After some unknown interval however, she found herself in a many-colored tent, lit with dozens of lanterns, partitioned off with curtains hung on wires that criss-crossed the entire dwelling. Just now most of these were pushed back, and a mixed crowd of men and women greeted their entrance with cries of welcome that turned to dismay at the sight of her condition.

She was pushed down into an improvised bed of soft wool blankets and huge, fat pillows, while a thin, dark girl dressed like a gypsy bathed her cuts and bruises with something that stung, then numbed them, and a gray-bearded man tsk'd over her arm, prodded it once or twice, then, without warning, pulled it into alignment. When he did that, the pain was so incredible that Rune nearly fainted.

By the time the multi-colored fire-flashing cleared from her eyes, he was binding her arm up tightly with thin strips of wood, while the girl was urging her to drink something that smelled of herbs and wine.

Before she had a chance to panic, Talaysen reappeared as if conjured at her side.

"Where—"

"You're with the Free Bards—the *real* Bards, not those pompous pufftoads with the Guild," he said. "Dear child, I thought that all that would happen to you was that those inflated bladders of self-importance would give you a tongue-lashing and throw you out on your backside. If I'd had the slightest notion that they'd do *this* to you, I'd have kidnapped you away and had you drunk insensible till the trials were over. I may never forgive myself. Now, drink your medicine."

"But how—why—who *are* you?" Rune managed between gulps.

"'What are you?' I think might be the better place to start. Tell her, will you, Erdric?"

"We're the Free Bards," said the gray-bearded man, "As Master Talaysen told you—he's the one who banded us together, when he found that there were those who, like himself, had the Gift and the Talent but were disinclined to put up with the self-aggrandizement and politics and foolish slavishness to form of Guild nonsense. We go where we wish and serve— or not serve—who we will, and sing as we damn well please and no foolishness about who'll be offended. We also keep a sharp eye out for youngsters like you, with the Gift, and with the spirit to fight the Guild. We've had our eye on you these three years now."

"You—but how?"

"Myself, for one," said a new voice, and a bony fellow with hair that kept falling into his eyes joined the group around her. "You likely don't remember me, but I remember you—I heard you fiddle in your tavern when I was passing through Karthar, and I passed the word."

"And I'm another." This one, Rune recognized; he was the man that sold her her lute, who had seemed to have been a gypsy peddler selling new and used instruments. He had also unaccountably stayed long enough to teach her the rudiments of playing it.

"You see, we keep an eye out for all the likely lads and lasses we've marked, knowing that soon or late, they'd come to the trials. Usually, though, they're not so stubborn as you." Talaysen smiled.

"I should hope to live!" the lanky fellow agreed. "They made the same remark my first day about wanting to have me stay a liltin' soprano the rest of me days. That was enough for me!"

"And they wouldn't even give *me* the same notice they'd have given a flea," the dark girl laughed. "Though I hadn't the wit to think of passing myself off as a boy for the trials."

"But—why are you—together?" Rune asked, bewildered.

"We band together to give each other help; a spot of silver to tide you over an empty month, a place to go when you're hurt or ill, someone to care for you when you're not as young as you used to be," the gray-haired Erdric said. "And to teach, and to learn. And we have more and better patronage than you, or even the Guild suspect; not everyone finds the precious style of the Guild songsters to their taste, especially the farther you get from the large cities. Out in the countryside, away from the decadence of courts, they like their songs, like their food, substantial and heartening."

"But why does the Guild let you get away with this, if you're taking patronage from them?" Rune's apprehension, given her recent treatment, was real and understandable.

"Bless you, child, they couldn't do without us!" Talaysen laughed. "No matter what you think, there isn't an original, creative Master among 'em! Gwena, my heart, sing her 'The Unkind Lover'—your version, I mean, the real and original."

Gwena, the dark girl, flashed dazzling white teeth in a vulpine grin, plucked a gittern from somewhere behind her, and began.

Well, it was the same melody that Rune had sung, and some of the words—the best phrases—were the same as well. But this was no ice-cold princess taunting her poor knightly admirer with what he'd never touch; no, this was a teasing shepherdess seeing how far she could harass her cowherd lover, and the teasing was kindly meant. And what the cowherd claimed at the end was a good deal more than a "kiss on her cold, quiet hand." In fact, you might say with justice that the proceedings got downright heated!

"That 'Lament' you did the first day's another song they've twisted and tormented; most of the popular ballads the Guild touts as their own are ours," Talaysen told her with a grin.

"As you should know, seeing as you've written at least half of them!" Gwena snorted.

"But what would you have done if they had accepted me anyway?" Rune wanted to know.

"Oh, you wouldn't have lasted long; can a caged thrush sing? Soon or late, you'd have done what I did—escaped your gilded cage, and we'd have been waiting."

"Then, *you* were a Guild Bard?" Somehow she felt she'd known that all along. "But I never hear of one called Talaysen, and if the 'Lament' is yours—"

"Well, I changed my name when I took my freedom. Likely though, you wouldn't recognize it—"

"Oh she wouldn't, you think? Or are you playing mock-modest with us again?" Gwena shook back her abundant black hair. "I'll make it known to you that you're having your bruises tended by Master Bard Merridon, himself."

"Merridon?" Rune's eyes went wide as she stared at the man, who coughed, deprecatingly. "But—but— I thought Master Merridon was supposed to have gone into seclusion—"

"The Guild would hardly want it known that their pride had rejected 'em for a pack of gypsy jonglers, now would they?" the lanky fellow pointed out.

"So, can I tempt you to join with us, Rune, lass?" the man she'd known as Talaysen asked gently.

"I'd like—but I can't," she replied despairingly. "How could I keep myself? It'll take months for my arm to heal. And—my instruments are splinters, anyway." She shook her head, tears in her eyes. "They weren't much, but they were all I had. I'll have to go home; they'll take me in the tavern. I can still turn a spit and fill a glass one-handed."

"Ah lass, didn't you hear Erdric? We take care of each other—we'll care for you till you're whole again—" The old man patted her shoulder, then hastily found her a rag when scanning their faces brought her belief—and tears.

"As for the instruments—" Talaysen vanished and returned again as her sobs quieted. "—I'll admit to relief at your words. I was half-afraid you'd a real attachment to your poor, departed friends. 'They're splinters, and I loved them' can't be mended, but 'They're splinters and they were all I had' is a different tune altogether. What think you of these twain?"

The fiddle and lute he laid in her lap weren't new, nor were they the kind of gilded, carved and ornamented dainties Guild musicians boasted, but they held their own kind of quiet beauty, a beauty of mellow wood and clean lines. Rune plucked a string on each, experimentally, and burst into tears again. The tone was lovely, smooth and golden, and these were the kind of instruments she'd never dreamed of touching, much less owning.

When the tears had been soothed away, the various medicines been applied both internally and externally, and introductions made all around, Rune found herself once again alone with Talaysen—or Merridon, though on reflection, she liked the name she'd first known him by better. The rest had drawn curtains on their wires close in about her little corner, making an alcove of privacy. "If you'll let me join you—" she said, shyly.

"Let!" he laughed. "Haven't we made it plain enough we've been trying to lure you like coney-catchers? Oh, you're one of us, Rune, lass. You'll not escape us now!"

"Then—what am I supposed to do?"

"You heal, that's the first thing. The second, well, we don't have formal apprenticeships amongst us. By the Three, there's no few things you could serve as Master in, and no question about it! You could teach most of us a bit about fiddling, for one—"

"But—" she looked and felt dismayed, "—one of the reasons I wanted to join the Guild was to *learn!* I can't read nor write music; there's so many instruments I can't play—" her voice rose to a soft wail "—how am I going to learn if a Master won't take me as an apprentice?"

"Enough! Enough! No more weeping and wailing, my heart's over-soft as it is!" he said hastily. "If you're going to insist on being an apprentice, I suppose there's nothing for it. Will I do as a Master to you?"

Rune was driven to speechlessness, and could only nod.

"Holy Three, lass, you make a liar out of me, who swore never to take an apprentice! Wait a moment." He vanished around the curtain for a moment, then returned. "Here—" He set down a tiny harp. "This can be played one-handed, and learning the ways of her will keep you too busy to bedew me with any more tears while your arm mends. Treat her gently— she's my own very first instrument, and she deserves respect."

Rune cradled the harp in her good arm, too awe-stricken to reply.

"We'll send someone in the morning for your things, wherever it is you've cached 'em. Lean back there—oh, it's a proper nursemaid I am—" He made her comfortable on her pillows, covering her with blankets and moving her two—no, three—new instruments to a place of safety, but still within sight. He seemed to understand how seeing them made her feel. "We'll find you clothing and the like as well. That sleepy-juice they gave you should have you nodding shortly. Just remember one thing before you doze off. I'm not going to be an easy Master to serve; you won't be spending your days lazing about, you know! Come morning, I'll set you your very first task. You'll teach *me*—" his eyes lighted with unfeigned eagerness "—that ghost-song!"

Not long after I was accepted into the Magic in Ithkar *anthology, the late Robert Adams who was the co-editor asked me to participate in his* Friends of the Horseclans *anthologies as well. I was happy to, since I liked Robert a great deal, and this was the result, which appeared in Volume Two.*

Robert was an odd duck; you either liked him and chuckled over his eccentricities, or you passionately hated him. His most popular books, the "Horseclans" series, have not weathered the change in political climate well. For some background, they are set in a distant future following a nuclear war in which (apparently) the U.S. and the Soviet Union both bombed each other back to the Stone Age. The hero of the earliest books is immortal and telepathic, having evidently stood in the right place at the wrong time as one of the nukes hit. He decides to single-handedly bring civilization in the U.S. back up to par, mostly by uniting the remains of the population with the Native Americans who, being on remote reservations, survived intact. The villains of the books are the Greeks, who sustained very little damage, since it seems that none of the greater powers thought they were worth bombing back to the Stone Age. They proceed to flourish and conquer in the tradition of Alexander, eventually moving on to the North American continent. However, thanks to better living through radiation, there are telepathic horses and mutated, large cats in North America, both of which have teamed up with the Horseclans-folk.

In those more innocent times, no one raised the objection that all that long-term radiation would probably render the population sterile rather than producing beneficial mutations; the concept of Nuclear Winter hadn't even occurred to anyone. But the possibility of a Third World/First Nuclear War was very real.

One of the obsessions of the more devoted of Horseclans fans was to try and figure out just what the real place-names and proper names were of the locations and characters; Robert had some formula by which he took English names and places, distorted and then phonetically re-spelled them. Some of them I never could figure out.

At any rate, it occurred to me that there was another, highly mobile ethnic group that could have survived Robert's WWIII by being outside the cities; the gypsies, who would have strenuously resisted being absorbed into the Horseclans as they have strenuously resisted being absorbed into every other culture they have come into contact with.

The Enemy of My Enemy

The fierce heat radiating from the forge was enough to deaden the senses all by itself, never mind the creaking and moaning of the bellows and the steady tap-tapping of Kevin's youngest apprentice out in the yard working at his assigned horseshoe. The stoutly-built stone shell was pure hell to work in from May to October; you could open windows and doors to the fullest, but heat soon built up to the point where thought ceased, the mind went numb, and the world narrowed to the task at hand.

But Kevin Floyd was used to it, and he was alive enough to what was going on about him that he sensed that someone had entered his smithy, although he dared not interrupt his work to see who it was. This was a commissioned piece—and one that could cost him dearly if he did a less-than-perfect job of completing it. Even under the best of circumstances the tempering of a swordblade was always a touchy bit of business. The threat of his overlord's wrath—and the implied loss of his shop—did not make it less so.

So he dismissed the feeling of eyes on the back of his neck, and went on with the work stolidly. For the moment he would ignore the visitor as he ignored the heat, the noise, and the stink of scorched leather and many long summers' worth of sweat—horse-sweat and man-sweat—that permeated the forge. Only when the blade was safely quenched and lying on the anvil for the next step did he turn to see who his visitor was.

He almost overlooked her entirely, she was so small, and was tucked up so invisibly in the shadowy corner where he kept oddments of harness and a pile of leather scraps. Dark, nearly black eyes peered up shyly at him from under a tangled mop of curling black hair as she perched atop his heap of leather bits, hugging her thin knees to her chest. Kevin didn't recognize her.

That, since he knew every man, woman and child in Northfork by name, was cause for a certain alarm.

He made one step toward her. She shrank back into the darkness of the corner, eyes going wide with fright. He sighed. "Kid, I ain't gonna hurt you—"

She looked terrified. Unfortunately, Kevin frequently had that effect on children, much as he liked them. He looked like a red-faced, hairy ogre, and his voice, rough and harsh from years of smoke and shouting over the forge-noise, didn't improve the impression he made. He tried again.

"Where you from, huh? Who's your kin?"

She stared at him, mouth set. He couldn't tell if it was from fear or stubbornness, but was beginning to suspect the latter. So he persisted, and when she made an abortive attempt to flee, shot out an arm to bar her way. He continued to question her, more harshly now, but she just shook her head at him, frantically, and plastered herself against the wall. She was either too scared now to answer, or wouldn't talk out of pure cussedness.

"Jack," he finally shouted in exasperation, calling

for his helper, who was around the corner outside the forge, manning the bellows. "Leave it for a minute and c'mere."

A brawny adolescent sauntered in the door from the back, scratching at his mouse-colored hair. "What—" he began.

"Where's this come from?" Kevin demanded. "She ain't one of ours, an' I misdoubt she came with the King."

Jack snorted derision. "King, my left—"

Kevin shared his derision, but cautioned—"When he's here, you call him what he wants. No matter he's King of only about as far as he can see, he's paid for mercs enough to pound you inta the ground like a tent-peg if you make him mad. Or there's worse he could do. What the hell good is my journeyman gonna be with only one hand?"

Jack twisted his face in a grimace of distaste. He looked about as intelligent as a brick wall, but his sleepy blue eyes hid the fact that he missed very little. HRH King Robert the Third of Trihtown had *not* impressed him. "Shit. Ah hell; King, then. Naw, she ain't with his bunch. I reckon that youngun came with them trader jippos this mornin'. She's got that look."

"What jippos?" Kevin demanded. "Nobody told me about no jippos—"

"Thass cause you was in here, poundin' away at His Highass's sword when they rode in. It's them same bunch as was in Five Point last month. Ain't no wants posted on 'em, so I figgered they was safe to let be for a bit."

"Aw hell—" Kevin glanced at the waiting blade, then at the door, torn by duty and duty. There hadn't been any news about traders from Five Points, and bad news *usually* traveled faster than good—but— dammit, he had responsibility. As the duly appointed Mayor, it was his job to cast his eye over any strangers to Northfork, apprise them of the town laws, see that they knew troublemakers got short shrift. And he knew damn well what Willum Innkeeper would have to say about his dealing with them so tardily as it was—pissant fool kept toadying up to King Robert, trying to get himself appointed Mayor.

Dammit, he thought furiously. *I didn't want the damn job, but I'll be sheep-dipped if I'll let that suckass take it away from me with his rumor-mongering and back-stabbing. Hell, I have to go deal with these jippos, and quick, or he'll be on my case again—*

On the other hand, to leave King Robert's sword three-quarters finished—

Fortunately, before he could make up his mind, his dilemma was solved for him.

A thin, wiry man, as dark as the child, appeared almost magically, hardly more than a shadow in the doorway; a man so lean he barely blocked the strong sunlight. He could have been handsome but for the black eyepatch and the ugly keloid scar that marred the right half of his face. For the rest, he was obviously no native of any town in King Robert's territory; he wore soft riding boots, baggy pants of a wild scarlet, embroidered shirt and vest of blue and black, and a scarlet scarf around his neck that matched the pants. Kevin was surprised he hadn't scared every horse in town with an outfit like that.

"Your pardon—" the man said, with so thick an accent that Kevin could hardly understand him "—but I believe something of ours has strayed here, and was too frightened to leave."

Before Kevin could reply, he had turned with the swift suddenness of a lizard and held out his hand to the girl, beckoning her to his side. She flitted to him with the same lithe grace he had displayed, and half hid behind him. Kevin saw now that she wasn't as young as he'd thought; in late adolescence—it was her slight build and lack of height that had given him the impression that she was a child.

"I sent Chali aseeing where there be the smithy," the man continued, keeping his one eye on Kevin and his arm about the girl's shoulders. "For we were atold to seek the Townman there. And dear she loves the forge-work, so she stayed to be awatching. She meant no harm, God's truth."

"Well neither did I," Kevin protested, "I was just trying to ask her some questions, an' she wouldn't answer me. I'm the Mayor here, I gotta know about strangers—"

"Again, your pardon," the man interrupted, "But she *could not* give answers. Chali has been mute for long since—show, mouse—"

At the man's urging the girl lifted the curls away from her left temple to show the unmistakable scar of a hoofmark.

Aw, hellfire. Big man, Kevin, bullying a *little cripple.* Kevin felt about as high as a horseshoe nail. "Shit," he said awkwardly. "Look, I'm sorry—hell, how was *I* to know?"

Now the man smiled, a wide flash of pearly white teeth in his dark face. "You could not. Petro, I am. I lead the Rom."

"Kevin Floyd; I'm Mayor here."

The men shook hands; Kevin noticed that this Petro's grip was as firm as his own. The girl had relaxed noticeably since her clansman's arrival, and now smiled brightly at Kevin, another flash of white against dusky skin. She was dressed much the same as her leader, but in colors far more muted; Kevin was grateful, as he wasn't sure how much more of that screaming scarlet his eyes could take.

He gave the man a quick run-down of the rules; Petro nodded acceptance. "What of your faiths?" he asked, when Kevin had finished. "Are there things we must or must not be adoing? Is there Church about?"

Kevin caught the flash of a gold cross at the man's throat. Well, hey—no wonder he said "Church" like it was poison. A fellow Christer—not like those damn Ehleen priests. This was a simple one-barred cross, not the Ehleen two-barred. "Live and let be" was a Christer's motto "a godly man converts by example, not words nor force"—which might well be why there were so few of them. Kevin and his family were one of only three Christer families in town, and Christer traders weren't that common, either. "Nothing much," he replied. "King Robert, he didn't go in for religion last I heard. So, what's your business here?"

"We live, what else?" Petro answered matter-of-factly. "We have livestock for trading. Horses, mules, donkeys—also metal-work."

"Don't know as I care for that last," Kevin said dubiously, scratching his sweaty beard.

"Na, na, not iron-work," the trader protested. "Light metals. Copper, brass—ornament, mostly. A few kettles, pans."

"Now *that* sounds a bit more like! Tell you—you got conshos, harness-studs, that kinda thing? You willin' to work a swap for shoein'?"

"The shoes, not the shoeing. Our beasts prefer the hands they know."

"Done." Kevin grinned. He was good enough at tools or weaponwork, but had no talent at ornament, and knew it. He could make good use of a stock of pretty bits for harnesses and the like. Only one frippery could he make, and that was more by accident than anything else. And since these people were fellow Christers and he was short a peace-offering— He usually had one in his apron pocket; he felt around among the horseshoe nails until his hand encountered a shape that wasn't a nail, and pulled it out.

"Here, missy—" he said apologetically. "Little somethin' fer scarin' you."

The girl took the cross made of flawed horseshoe

nails into strong, supple fingers, with a flash of delight in her expressive eyes.

"Hah! A generous apology!" Petro grinned. "And you cannot know how well comes the fit."

"How so?"

"It is said of my people, when the Christ was to be killed, His enemies meant to silence Him lest He rouse His followers against them. The evil ones made four nails—the fourth for His heart. But one of the Rom was there, and stole the fourth nail. So God blessed us in gratitude to awander wherever we would."

"Well, hey." Kevin returned the grin, and a thought occurred to him. Ehrik was getting about the right size to learn riding. "Say, you got any ponies, maybe a liddle horse gettin' on an' gentle? I'm lookin' for somethin' like that for m'boy."

The jippo regarded him thoughtfully. "I think, perhaps yes."

"Then you just may see me later on when I finish this."

Chali skipped to keep up with the wiry man as they headed down the dusty street toward the *tsera* of their *kumpania*. The town, of gray wood-and-stone buildings enclosed inside its shaggy log palisade depressed her and made her feel trapped—she was glad to be heading out to where the *kumpania* had made their camp. Her eyes were flashing at Petro with the only laughter she could show. *You did not tell him the rest of the tale, Elder Brother,* she mindspoke. *The part that tells how the good God then granted us the right to steal whatever we needed to live.*

"There is such a thing as telling more truth than a man wishes to hear," Petro replied. "Especially to *Gaje.*"

Huh. But not all Gaje. *I have heard a different tale from you every time we come to a new holding. You*

*tell us to always tell the whole of the truth to the
Horseclans folk, no matter how bitter.*

"They are not *Gaje.* They are not *o phral,* either,
but they are not *Gaje.* I do not know what they are,
but one does not lie to them."

*But why the rule? We have not seen Horseclans
since before I can remember,* she objected.

"They are like the Wind they call upon—they go
where they will. But they have the *dook.* So it is wise
to be prepared for meeting them at all times."

I would like to see them, one day.

He regarded her out of the corner of his eye. "If
I am still *rom baro,* you will be hidden if we meet
them. If I am not, I hope you will be wise and hide
yourself. They have *dook,* I tell you—and I am not
certain that I wish them to know that we also have
it."

She nodded, thoughtfully. The Rom had not survived this long by giving away secrets. *Do you think
my dook is greater than theirs? Or that they would
seek me out if they knew of it?*

"It could be. I know they value such gifts greatly.
I am not minded to have you stolen from us for the
sake of the children you could bear to one of them."

She clasped her hands behind her, eyes looking
downward at the dusty, trampled grass as they passed
through the open town gate. This was the first time
Petro had ever said anything indicating that he
thought her a woman and not a child. Most of the
kumpania, including Petro's wife Sara and their boy
Tibo, treated her as an odd mixture of child and *phuri
dai.* Granted, she *was* tiny; perhaps the same injury
that had taken her voice had kept her small. But she
was nearly sixteen winters—and still they reacted to
her body as to that of a child's, and to her mind as
to that of a *drabarni* of sixty. As she frowned a little,
she pondered Petro's words, and concluded they were
wise. Very wise. That the Rom possessed *draban* was

not a thing to be bandied about. That her own *dook* was as strong as it was should rightly be kept secret as well.

Yes, rom baro, I *will do* as *you advise,* she replied.

Although he did not mindspeak her in return, she knew he had heard everything she had told him perfectly well. She had so much *draban* that any human and most beasts could hear her when she chose. Petro could hear and understand her perfectly, for though his mindspeech was not as strong as hers, he would have heard her even had he been mind-deaf.

That he had no strong *dook* was not unusual; among the Rom, since the Evil Days, it was the women that tended to have more *draban* than the men. That was one reason why females had come to enjoy all the freedoms of a man since that time— when his wife could make a man feel every blow, he tended to be less inclined to beat her . . . when his own eyes burned with every tear his daughter shed, he was less inclined to sell her into a marriage with someone she feared or hated.

And when she could blast you with her own pain, she tended to be safe from rape.

As she skipped along beside Petro on the worn ruts that led out of the palisade gate and away from town, she was vaguely aware of every mind about her. She and everyone else in the *kumpania* had known for a very long time that her *dook* was growing stronger every year, perhaps to compensate for her muteness. Even the herd-guard horses, those wise old mares, had been impressed, and it took a great deal to impress *them!*

Petro sighed, rubbing the back of his neck absently, and she could read his surface thoughts easily. *That was an evil day, when ill-luck led us to the settlement of the Chosen. A day that ended with poor Chali sense-less—her brother dead, and Chali's parents captured*

*and burned as witches. And every other able-bodied,
weapons-handy member of the* kumpania *either
wounded or too busy making sure the rest got away
alive to avenge the fallen.* She winced as guilt flooded
him as always.

*You gave your eye to save me, Elder Brother. That
was more than enough.*

"I could have done more. I could have sent others
with your mama and papa. I could have taken
everyone away from that sty of pigs, that nest of—
I will *not* call them Chosen of God. Chosen of o *Beng*
perhaps—"

And o Beng *claims his own, Elder Brother. Are we
not* o phral? *We have more patience than all the* Gaje
in the world. We will see the day when o Beng *takes
them.* Chali was as certain of that as she was of the
sun overhead and the grass beside the track.

Petro's only reply was another sigh. He had less
faith than she. He changed the subject that was
making him increasingly uncomfortable. "So, when
you stopped being a frighted *tawnie juva*, did you
touch the *qajo*, the Townsman's heart? Should we sell
him old Pika for his little son?"

I think yes. He is a good one, for Gaje. *Pika will
like him; also, it is nearly fall, and another winter
wandering would be hard on his bones.*

They had made their camp up against a stand of
tangled woodland, and a good long way off from the
palisaded town. The camp itself could only be seen
from the top of the walls, not from the ground. That
was the way the Rom liked things—they preferred
to be apart from the *Gaje.*

The *tsera* was within shouting distance by now, and
Petro sent her off with a pat to her backside. The
vurdon, those neatly built wooden wagons, were
arranged in a precise circle under the wilderness of
trees at the edge of the grasslands, with the common
fire neatly laid in a pit in the center. Seven wagons,

seven families—Chali shared Petro's. Some thirty seven
Rom in all—and for all they knew, the last Rom in the
world, the only Rom to have survived the Evil Days.

But then, not a great deal had survived the Evil
Days. Those trees, for instance, showed signs of
having once been a purposeful planting, but so many
generations had passed since the Evil Days they were
now as wild as any forest.

Chali headed, not for the camp, but for the unpick-
eted string of horses grazing beyond. She wanted to
sound out Pika. If he was willing to stay here, this
Mayor Kevin would have his gentle old pony for his
son, and cheap at the price. Chali knew Pika would
guard any child in his charge with all the care he would
give one of his own foals. Pika was a stallion, but Chali
would have trusted a tiny baby to his care.

Petro trusted her judgment in matters of finding
their horses homes; a few months ago she had allowed
him to sell one of their saddlebred stallions and a
clutch of mares to mutual satisfaction on the part of
horses, Rom, and buyers. Then it had been a series
of sales of mules and donkeys to folk who wound up
treating them with good sense and more consideration
than they gave to their own well-being. And in Five
Points she had similarly placed an aging mare Petro
had raised from a filly, and when Chali had helped
the *rom baro* strain his meager *dook* to bid her fare-
well, Lisa had been nearly incoherent with gratitude
for the fine stable, the good feeding, the easy work.

Horses were bred into Chali's blood, for like the
rest of this *kumpania*, she was of the Lowara
natsiyi—and the Lowara were the Horsedealers.
Mostly, anyway, though there had been some Kalderash,
or Coppersmiths, among them in the first years. By
now the Kalderash blood was spread thinly through
the whole *kumpania*. Once or twice in each
generation there were artificers, but most of *rom
baro* Petro's people danced to Lowara music.

She called to Pika without even thinking his name, and the middle-aged pony separated himself from a knot of his friends and ambled to her side. He rubbed his chestnut nose against her vest and tickled her cheek with his whiskers. His thoughts were full of the hope of apples.

No apples, greedy pig! Do you like this place? Would you want to stay?

He stopped teasing her and stood considering, breeze blowing wisps of mane and forelock into his eyes and sunlight picking out the white hairs on his nose. She scratched behind his ears, letting him take his own time about it.

The grass is good, he said, finally. *The Gaje horses are not ill-treated. And my bones ache on cold winter mornings, lately. A warm stable would be pleasant.*

The blacksmith has a small son—she let him see the picture she had stolen from the *qajo's* mind, of a blond-haired, sturdily built bundle of energy. *The* gajo *seems kind.*

The horses here like him, came the surprising answer. *He fits the shoe to the hoof, not the hoof to the shoe. I think I will stay. Do not sell me cheaply.*

If Chali could have laughed aloud, she would have. Pika had been Romano's in the rearing—and he shared more than a little with that canny trader. *I will tell Romano—not that I need to. And don't forget, prala, if you are unhappy*—

Ha! the pony snorted with contempt. *If I am unhappy, I shall not leave so much as a hair behind me!*

Chali fished a breadcrust out of her pocket and gave it to him, then strolled in the direction of Romano's *vurdon*. When this *kumpania* had found itself gifted with *dook*, with more *draban* than they ever dreamed existed, it had not surprised them that they could speak with their horses; Lowara Rom had practically been able to do that before. But *draban* had granted them advantages they had never *dared* hope for—

Lowara had been good at horsestealing; now only the Horseclans could better them at it. All they needed to do was to sell one of their four-legged brothers into the hands of the one they wished to . . . relieve of the burdens of wealth. All the Lowara horses knew how to lift latches, unbar gates, or find the weak spot in any fence. And Lowara horses were as glib at persuasion as any of their two-legged friends. Ninety-nine times out of a hundred, the Lowara would return to the *kumpania* trailing a string of converts.

And if the *kumpania* came across horses that *were* being mistreated . . .

Chali's jaw tightened. That was what had set the Chosen at their throats.

She remembered that day and night, remembered it far too well. Remembered the pain of the galled beasts that had nearly driven her insane; remembered how she and Toby had gone to act as decoys while her mother and father freed the animals from their stifling barn.

Remembered the anger and fear, the terror in the night, and the madness of the poor horse that had been literally goaded into running her and Toby down.

It was just as well that she had been comatose when the "Chosen of God" had burned her parents at the *stake—that* might well have driven her completely mad.

That anger made her sight mist with red, and she fought it down, lest she broadcast it to the herd. When she had it under control again, she scuffed her way slowly through the dusty, flattened grass, willing it out of her and into the ground. She was so intent on controlling herself that it was not until she had come within touching distance of Romano's brightly-painted *vurdon* that she dared to look up from the earth.

Romano had an audience of children, all gathered about him where he sat on the tail of his wooden wagon. She tucked up against the worn side of it, and waited in the shade without drawing attention to herself, for he was telling them the story of the Evil Days.

"So old Simza, the *drabarni,* she spoke to the *rom baro* of her fear, and a little of what she had seen. Giorgi was her son, and he had *dook* enough that he believed her."

"Why shouldn't he have believed her?" tiny Ami wanted to know.

"Because in those days *draban* was weak, and even the *o phral* did not always believe in it. We were different, even among Rom. We were one of the smallest and least of *kumpania* then; one of the last to leave the old ways—perhaps that is why Simza saw what she saw. Perhaps the steel carriages the Rom had taken to, and the stone buildings they lived in, would not let *draban* through."

"Steel carriages? *Rom chal,* how would such a thing move? What horse could pull it?" That was Tomy, skeptical as always.

"I do not know—I only know that the memories were passed from Simza to Yanni, to Tibo, to Melalo, and so on down to me. If you would see, look."

As he had to Chali when she was small, as he did to every child, Romano the Storyteller opened his mind to the children, and they saw, with their *dook,* the dim visions of what had been. And wondered.

"Well, though there were those who laughed at him, and others of his own *kumpania* that left to join those who would keep to the cities of the *Gaje,* there were enough of them convinced to hold to the *kumpania.* They gave over their *Gaje* ways and returned to the old wooden *vurdon,* pulled by horses, practicing their old trades of horsebreeding and metal work, staying strictly away from the cities. And the irony is that it was the *Gaje* who made this possible, for they had become mad with fascination for the ancient days and had begun creating festivals than the Yanfi *kumpania* followed about."

Again came the dim sights—half-remembered music, laughter, people in wilder garments than ever the Rom sported.

"Like now?" asked one of the girls. "Like markets and trade-days?"

"No, not like now; these were special things, just for amusement, not really for trade. I am not certain I understand it; they were all a little mad in those times. Well, then the Evil Days came . . ."

Fire, and red death; thunder and fear—more people than Chali had ever seen alive, fleeing mindlessly the wreckage of their cities and their lives.

"But the *kumpania* was safely traveling out in the countryside, with nothing needed that they could not make themselves. Some others of the Rom remembered us and lived to reach us; Kalderash, mostly."

"And we were safe from *Gaje* and their mad ways?"

"When have the Rom ever been safe?" he scoffed. "No, if anything, we were in more danger yet. The *Gaje* wanted our horses, our *vurdon*, and *Gaje* law was not there to protect us. And there was disease, terrible disease that killed more folk than the Night of Fire had. One sickly *gajo* could have killed us all. No, we hid at first, traveling only by night and keeping off the roads, living where man had fled or died out."

These memories were clearer, perhaps because they were so much closer to the way the *kumpania* lived now. Hard years, though, and fear-filled—until the Rom learned again the weapons they had forgotten. The bow. The knife. And learned to use weapons they had never known like the sharp hooves of their four-legged brothers.

"We lived that way until the old weapons were all exhausted. Then it was safe to travel openly, and to trade; we began traveling as we do now—and now life is easier. For true God made the *Gaje* to live so that we might borrow from them what we need. And that is the tale."

Chali watched with her *dook* as Romano reached out with his mind to all the children seated about him; and found what he had been looking for. Chali felt his exultation; of all the children to whom Romano had given his memories and his stories, there was one in whose mind the memories were still as clear as they were when they had come from Romano's. Tomy had the *draban* of the Storyteller; Romano had found his successor.

Chali decided that it was wiser not to disturb them for now, and slipped away so quietly that they never knew she had been there.

The scout for Clan Skaht slipped into the encampment with the evening breeze and went straight to the gathering about Chief's fire. His prairiecat had long since reported their impending arrival, so the raidleaders had had ample time to gather to hear him.

"Well, I have good news and bad news," Daiv Mahrtun of Skaht announced, sinking wearily to the bare earth across the fire from his Chief. "The good news is that these Dirtmen look lazy and ripe for the picking—the bad news is that they've got traders with 'em, so the peace-banners are up. And I mean to tell you, they're the weirdest damn traders I ever saw. Darker than any Ehleenee—dress like no clan I know—and—" He stopped, not certain of how much more he wanted to say—and if he'd be believed.

Tohnee Skaht snorted in disgust, and spat into the fire. "Dammit anyway—if we break trade-peace—"

"Word spreads fast," agreed his cousin Jahn. "We may have trouble getting other traders to deal with us if we mount a raid while this lot's got the peace-banners up."

There were nearly a dozen clustered about the firepit; men and a pair of women, old and young—but all of them were seasoned raiders, regardless of age. And all of them were profoundly disappointed by the results of Daiv's scouting foray.

"Which traders?" Tohnee asked after a long moment of thought. "Anybody mention a name or a clan you recognized?"

Daiv shook his head emphatically. "I tell you, they're not like any lot I've ever seen *or* heard tell of. They got painted wagons, and they ain't the big tradewagons; more, they got whole families, not just the menfolk—and they're horsetraders."

Tohnee's head snapped up. "Horse—"

"Before you ask, I mindspoke their horses." This was a perfect opening for the most disturbing of Daiv's discoveries. "*This* oughta curl your hair. *The horses wouldn't talk to me.* It wasn't 'cause they couldn't, and it wasn't 'cause they was afraid to. It was like I was maybe an enemy—was surely an outsider, and maybe not to be trusted. Whoever, whatever these folks are, they got the same kind of alliance with their horses as we have with ours. And *that's* plainly strange."

"Wind and Sun—dammit Daiv, if I didn't know you, I'd be tempted to call you a liar!" That was Dik Krooguh, whose jaw was hanging loose with total astonishment.

"Do the traders mindspeak?" Tohnee asked at nearly the same instant.

"I dunno," Daiv replied, shaking his head, "I didn't catch any of 'em at it, but that don't mean much. My guess would be they do, but I can't swear to it."

"I think maybe we need more facts—" interrupted Alis Skaht. "If they've got horse-brothers, I'd be inclined to say they're not likely to be a danger to us—but we can't count on that. Tohnee?"

"Mm," he nodded. "Question is, how?"

"I took some thought to that," Daiv replied. "How about just mosey in open-like? Dahnah and I could come in like you'd sent us to trade with 'em." Dahnah was Daiv's twin sister; an archer with no peer in the clan, and a strong mindspeaker. "We could hang around for a couple of days without making 'em too suspicious. And a pair of Horseclan kids doin' a little dickerin ain't gonna make the Dirtmen *too* nervous. Not while the peace-banners are up."

Tohnee thought that over a while, as the fire cast weird shadows on his stony face. "You've got the sense to call for help if you end up needing it—and you've got Brighttooth and Stubtail backing you."

The two young prairiecats lounging at Daiv's side purred agreement.

"All right—it sounds a good enough plan to me," Tohnee concluded, while the rest of the sobered clansfolk nodded, slowly. "You two go in at first morning light and see what you can find. And I know I don't need to tell you to be careful, but I'm telling you anyway.

Howard Thomson, son of "King" Robert Thomson, was distinctly angered. His narrow face was flushed, always a bad sign, and he'd been drinking, which was worse. When Howard drank, he thought he owned the world. Trouble was, he was almost right, at least in this little corner of it. His two swarthy merc-bodyguards were between Kevin and the doors.

Just what I didn't need, Kevin thought bleakly, taking care that nothing but respect showed on his face, *a damn-fool touchy idiot with a brat's disposition tryin' to put me between a rock and a hard place.*

"I tell you, my father sent me expressly to fetch him that blade, *boy.*" Howard's face was getting redder by the minute, matching his long, fiery hair.

"You'd better hand it over *now*, before you find yourself lacking a hand."

I'll just bet he sent you, Kevin growled to himself, *Sure he did. You just decided to help yourself, more like—and leave me to explain to your father where his piece went, while you deny you ever saw me before.*

But his outwardly cool expression didn't change as he replied, stolidly, "Your pardon, but His Highness gave *me* orders that I was to put it into no one's hands but his. And he hasn't sent me written word telling me any different."

Howard's face enpurpled as Kevin obliquely reminded him that the Heir *couldn't* read or write. Kevin waited for the inevitable lightning to fall. Better he should get beaten to a pulp than that King Robert's wrath fall on Ehrik and Keegan, which it would if he gave in to Howard. What with Keegan being pregnant—better a beating. He tensed himself and waited for the order.

Except that, just at the moment when Howard was actually beginning to splutter orders to his two merc-bodyguards to take the blacksmith apart, salvation, in the form of Petro and a half-dozen strapping jippos came strolling through the door to the smithy. They were technically unarmed, but the long knives at their waists were a reminder that this was only a technicality.

"*Sarishan, gajo,*" he said cheerfully. "We have brought you your pony—"

Only then did he seem to notice the Heir and his two bodyguards.

"Why, what is this?" he asked with obviously feigned surprise. "Do we interrupt some business?"

Howard growled something obscene—if he started something *now* he would be breaking trade-peace, and no trader would deal with him *or* his family again without an extortionate bond being posted. For one moment Kevin feared that his temper might get the better of him anyway, but then the young man pushed past the jippos at the door and stalked into the street, leaving his bodyguards to follow as they would.

Kevin sagged against his cold forge, only now breaking into a sweat. "By all that's holy, man," he told Petro earnestly, "your timing couldn't have been better! You saved me from a beatin', and that's for damn sure!"

"Something more than a beating," the jippo replied, slowly, "—or I misread that one. I do not think we will sell any of our beasts *there*, no. But—" he grinned suddenly "—we lied, I fear. We did not bring the pony—we brought our other wares."

"You needed six men to carry a bit of copperwork?" Kevin asked incredulously, firmly telling himself that he would *not* begin laughing hysterically out of relief.

"Oh no—but I was *not* of a mind to carry back horseshoes for every beast in our herd by myself! I am *rom baro*, not a packmule!"

Kevin began laughing after all, laughing until his sides hurt.

Out of gratitude for their timely appearance, he let them drive a harder bargain with him than he normally would have allowed, trading shoes and nails for their whole equippage for about three pounds of brass and copper trinkets and a set of copper pots he knew Keegan would lust after the moment she saw them. And a very pretty little set of copper jewelry to brighten her spirit; she was beginning to show, and subject to bouts of depression in which she was certain her pregnancy made her ugly in his eyes. This bit of frippery might help remind her that she was anything but. He agreed to come by and look at the pony as soon as he finished a delivery of his own. He was going to take no chances on Howard's return; he was going to deliver that sword himself, now, and straight into Robert's palsied hands!

✧   ✧   ✧

"So if that one comes, see that he gets no beast nor thing of ours," Petro concluded. "Chali, you speak to the horses. Most like, he will want the king stallion, if any."

Chali nodded. *We could say Bakro is none of ours—that he's a wild one that follows our mares.*

Petro grinned approval. "Ha, a good idea! That way nothing of blame comes on us. For the rest—we wish to leave only Pika, is that not so?" The others gathered about him in the shade of his *vurdon* murmured agreement. They had done well enough with their copper and brass jewelry, ornaments and pots and with the odd hen or vegetable or sack of grain that had found a mysterious way into a Rom kettle or a *vurdon*.

"Well then, let us see what we can do to make them unattractive."

Within the half hour the Rom horses, mules and donkeys little resembled the sleek beasts that had come to the call of their two-legged allies. Coats were dirty, with patches that looked suspiciously like mange; hocks were poulticed, and looked swollen; several of the wise old mares were ostentatiously practicing their limps, and there wasn't a hide of an attractive color among them.

And anyone touching them would be kicked at, or *nearly* bitten—the horses were not minded to have their two-legged brothers punished for *their* actions. Narrowed eyes and laid-back ears gave the lie to the hilarity within. No one really knowledgeable about horses would want to come near this lot.

And just in time, for Howard Thomson rode into the camp on an oversized, dun-colored dullard of a gelding only a few moments after the tools of their deceptions had been cleaned up and put away. Chali briefly touched the beast's mind to see if it was being mistreated, only to find it nearly as stupid as one of the mongrels that infested the village.

He surveyed the copper trinkets with scorn, and the sorry herd of horses with disdain. Then his eye lit upon the king stallion.

"You there—trader—" he waved his hand at the proud bay stallion, who looked back at this arrogant two-legs with the same disdain. "How much for that beast there?"

"The noble prince must forgive us," Petro fawned, while Chali was glad, for once, of her muteness; she did not have to choke on her giggles as some of the others were doing. "But that one is none of ours. He is a wild one; he follows our mares, which we permit in hopes of foals like him."

"Out of nags like *those?* You hope for a miracle, man!" Howard laughed, as close to being in good humor as Petro had yet seen him. "Well, since he's none of yours, you won't mind if my men take him—"

Hours later, their beasts were ready to founder, the king stallion was still frisking like a colt, and none of them had come any closer to roping him than they had been when they started. The Rom were nearly bursting, trying to contain their laughter, and Howard was purple again.

Finally he called off the futile hunt, wrenched at the head of his foolish gelding, and spurred it back down the road to town . . .

And the suppressed laughter died, as little Ami's youngest brother toddled into the path of the lumbering monster—and Howard grinned and spurred the gelding at him—hard.

Kevin was nearly to the trader's camp when he saw the baby wander into the path of Howard's horse—and his heart nearly stopped when he saw the look on the Heir's face as he dug his spurs savagely into his gelding's flanks.

The smith didn't even think—he just *moved.* He frequently fooled folk into thinking he was slow and clumsy because of his size; now he threw himself at the child with every bit of speed and agility he possessed.

He snatched the toddler, curled protectively around it, and turned his dive into a frantic roll. As if everything had been slowed by a magic spell, he saw the horse charging at him and every move horse and rider made. Howard sawed savagely at the gelding's mouth, trying to keep it on the path. But the gelding shied despite the bite of the bit; foam-flecks showered from its lips, and the foam was spotted with blood at the corners of its mouth. It half-reared, and managed to avoid the smith and his precious burden by a hair—one hoof barely scraped Kevin's leg—then the beast was past, thundering wildly toward town.

Kevin didn't get back home until after dark—and he was not entirely steady on his feet. The stuff the Rom drank was a bit more potent than the beer and wine from the tavern, or even his own home-brew. Pacing along beside him, lending a supporting shoulder and triumphantly groomed to within an inch of his life and adorned with red ribbons, was the pony, Pika.

Pika was a gift—Romano wouldn't accept a single clipped coin for him. Kevin was on a first-name basis with all of the Rom now, even had a mastered a bit of their tongue. Not surprising, that—seeing as they'd sworn brotherhood with him.

He'd eaten and drunk with them, heard their tales, listened to their wild, blood-stirring music—felt as if he'd come home for the first time. Rom, that was what they called themselves, not "jippos,"—and "o phral," which meant "the people," sort of. They danced for him—and he didn't wonder that they wouldn't sing or dance before outsiders. It would be far too easy for dullard *gajo* to get the wrong idea from some of those dances—the women and girls danced with the freedom of the wind and the wildness of the storm—and to too many men, "wild" and "free" meant "loose." Kevin had just been entranced by a way of life he'd never dreamed existed.

Pika rolled a not-unsympathetic eye at him as he stumbled, and leaned in a little closer to him. Funny about the Rom and their horses—you'd swear they could read each other's minds. They had an affinity that was bordering on witchcraft—

Like that poor little mute child, Chali. Kevin had seen with his own eyes how wild the maverick stallion had been—at least when Howard and his men had been chasing it. But he'd also seen Chali walk up to him, pull his forelock, and hop aboard his bare back as if he were no more than a gentle, middle-aged pony like Pika. And then watched the two of them pull some trick riding stunts that damn near pulled the eyes out of his sockets. It was riding he'd remember for a long time, and he was right glad he'd seen it. But he devoutly hoped Howard hadn't. Howard hadn't but one of his men had.

Daiv and Dahnah rode up to the trader's camp in the early morning, leaving Brighttooth and Stubtail behind them as eyes to the rear. The camp appeared little different from any other they'd seen—at first glance. Then you noticed that the wagons were small, shaped almost like little houses on wheels, and painted like rainbows. They were almost distracting enough to keep you from noticing that there wasn't a beast around the encampment, not donkey nor horse, that was hobbled or picketed.

I almost didn't believe you, Daivie, his sister said into his mind, wonderingly.

His mare snorted; so did he. *Huh. Thanks a lot, sis. You catch any broad-beaming?*

She shook her head, almost imperceptibly, as her mount shifted a little. *Not so much as a stray thought—*

her own thought faded for a moment, and she bit her lip. *Now that I think of it, that's damned odd. These people are buttoned up as tight as a yurt in a windstorm.*

Which means what? He signaled Windstorm to move up beside Snowdancer.

Either they're naturally shielded as well as the best mindspeaker I ever met, yet they do have the gift. And the first is about as likely as Brighttooth sitting down to dinner with an Ehleenee priest.

Only if the priest was my dinner, sister, came the mischievous reply from the grassland behind them. With the reply came the mock disgust and nausea from Stubtail that his littermate would even *contemplate* such a notion as eating vile-tasting Ehleenee flesh.

So where does that leave us? Daiv asked.

We go in, do a little dickering, and see if we can eavesdrop. And I'll see if I can get any more out of the horses that you did.

Fat chance! he replied scornfully, but followed in the wake of her mare as she urged her into the camp itself.

The fire on the hearth that was the only source of light in Howard's room crackled. Howard lounged in his throne-like chair in the room's center. His back was to the fire, which made him little more than a dark blot to a petitioner, and cast all the available light on a petitioner's face.

Howard eyed the lanky tavern-keeper who was now kneeling before him with intense speculation. "You say the smith's been consorting with the heathen traders?"

"More than traders, m'lord," Willum replied humbly. "For the past two days there's been a brace of horse barbarians with the traders as well. I fear this means no good for the town."

"I knew about the barbarians," Howard replied, leaning back in his padded chair and staring at the flickering shadows on the wall behind Willum thoughtfully. Indeed he did know about the barbarians—twins they were, with hair like a summer sun; he'd spotted the girl riding her beast with careless grace, and his loins had ached ever since.

"I fear he grows far too friendly with them, m'lord. His wife and child spend much of the day at the trader's camp. I think that, unlike those of us who are loyal, he has forgotten where his duties lie."

"And you haven't, I take it?" Howard almost smiled.

"M'lord knows I am but an honest tavernkeeper—"

"And has the honest tavernkeeper informed my father of this possibly treacherous behavior?"

"I tried," Willum replied, his eyes not quite concealing his bitterness. "I have *been* trying for some time now. King Robert will not hear a word against the man."

"King Robert is a senile old fool!" Howard snapped viciously, jerking upright where he sat so that the chair rocked and Willum sat back on his heels in startlement. "King Robert is far too readily distracted by pretty toys and pliant wenches." His own mouth turned down with a bitterness to equal Willum's— for the talented flame-haired local lovely that had been gracing *his* bed had deserted it last night for his father's. Willum's eyes narrowed, and he crept forward on his knees until he almost touched Howard's leg. "Perhaps," he whispered, so softly that Howard could barely hear him, "it is time for a change of rulers—"

Chali had been banished to the forest as soon as the bright golden heads of the Horseclan twins had been spotted in the grasslands beyond the camp. She was not altogether unhappy with her banishment— she had caught an unwary thought from one of them,

and had shivered at the strength of it. Now she did
not doubt the *rom baro's* wisdom in hiding her. *Dook*
that strong would surely ferret out her own, and had
rather not betray the secret gifts of her people until
they knew more about the intent of these two. So
into the forest she had gone, with cloak and firestarter
and sack of food and necessaries.

Nor was she alone in her exile; Petro had deemed
it wiser not to leave temptation within Howard's reach,
and sent Bakro, the king stallion, with her. They had
decided to explore the woods—and had wandered far
from the encampment. To their delight and surprise,
they had discovered the remains of an apple orchard
deep in the heart of the forest—the place had gone
wild and reseeded itself several times over, and the
apples themselves were far smaller than those from
a cultivated orchard, hardly larger than crabapples.
But they were still sweet—and most of them were
ripe. They both gorged themselves as much as they
dared on the crisp, succulent fruits, until night had
fallen. Now both were drowsing beneath a tree in
Chali's camp, sharing the warmth of her fire, and
thinking of nothing in particular—

—when the attack on the Rom *tsera* came.

Chali was awake on the instant, her head ringing
with the mental anguish of the injured—and God, oh
God, the dying! Bakro wasn't much behind her in
picking up the waves of torment. He screamed, a
trumpeting of defiance and rage. She grabbed a
handful of mane and pulled herself up onto his back
without being consciously aware she had done so, and
they crashed off into the darkness to the source of
that agony.

But the underbrush they had threaded by day was
a series of maddening tangles by night; Bakro's headlong dash ended ignominiously in a tangle of vine,
and when they extricated themselves from the clawing
branches, they found their pace slowed to a fumbling

crawl. The slower they went, the more frantic they felt, for it was obvious from what they were being bombarded with that the Rom were fighting a losing battle. And one by one the voices in their heads lost strength. Then faded.

Until finally there was nothing.

They stopped fighting their way through the brush, then, and stood, lost in shock, in the blackness of the midnight forest—utterly, completely alone.

Dawn found Chali on her knees, exhausted, face tear-streaked, hands bruised from where she'd been pounding them on the ground, over and over. Bakro stood over her, trembling; trembling not from fear or sorrow, but from raw, red hatred. *His* herd had survived, though most had been captured by the enemy two-legs. But his two-leg herd—Chali was all he had left.

He wanted *vengeance*—and he wanted it now.

Slowly the hot rage of the stallion penetrated Chali's grief.

I hear you, pralà, *I do hear you*, she sent slowly, fumbling her way out of the haze of loss that had fogged her mind. *Kill!* the stallion trumpeted with mind and voice. *Kill them all!*

She clutched her hands at her throat, and encountered the thong that held the little iron cross. She pulled it over her head, and stared at it, dully. What good was a God of forgiveness in the light of this slaughter? She cast the cross—and all it implied—from her, violently.

She rose slowly to her feet, and put a restraining hand on the stallion's neck. He ceased his fidgeting and stood absolutely still, a great bay statue.

We will have revenge, pralà, *I swear it*, she told him, her own hatred burning as high as his, *but we shall have it wisely*.

Kevin was shoved and kicked down the darkened corridor of the King's manorhouse with brutal indifference, smashing up against the hard stone of the walls only to be shoved onward again. His head was near to splitting, and he'd had at least one tooth knocked out, the flat, sweet taste of blood in his mouth seemed somehow unreal.

He was angry, frightened—and bewildered. He'd awakened to distant shouts and screams, run outside to see a red glow in the direction of the Rom camp—then he'd been set upon from behind. Whoever it was that had attacked him clubbed him into apparent submission. Then he had his hands bound behind him—and his control broke; he began fighting again, and was dragged, kicking and struggling, up to the manorhouse. He'd seen, when his vision had cleared, that his attackers were some of King Robert's own mercs. He'd stumbled and nearly fallen on his face from the shock—he'd figured that the town had been taken by Ehleenee or some marauding band—

The door to King Robert's quarters opened and Kevin was shoved through it, skidding on the flagstone floor to land sprawling on his face at someone's feet.

"And here is the last of the suspects, my lord," he heard Willum say unctuously. He wrenched himself up onto his knees by brute force. Lounging at his ease in King Robert's favorite chair was Howard, sumptuously clad and playing with his father's new sword. Beside, him, in the blue and red of Howard's livery, was Willum.

"What the hell is that shit supposed to mean, asshole?" Kevin was too angry to mind his tongue, and a blow from one of the mercs behind him threw him onto his face again, made his brains rattle in his head and jarred his teeth to their sockets. His vision swam and he saw double for a long moment.

He pulled himself back into a semi-kneeling posture with aching difficulty.

"Keep a civil tongue in your head in the presence of your King, boy," Willum told him, with a faint smile. "You're suspected of conspiring with those false traders—"

"To what? Invade the town? Don't make me laugh!" Kevin snorted. "Take over with a handful of men when—what the hell do you mean, *King?*"

"My father has met with an accident," Howard purred, polishing the blade of the sword he held with a soft cloth. The steel glinted redly in the firelight. "He went mad, it seems. I was forced to defend myself. I have witnesses—"

Willum nodded, and it seemed to Kevin that there was a glint of balefire in the back of the man's eyes.

"So *I* am King now—by right of arms. I have declared that those so-called traders were no such thing at all—and I have eliminated their threat."

Slowly Kevin began to understand what it was he was saying. "You—good God—that camp was mostly women, children—"

"The spawn of vipers will grow to be vipers."

"You broke trade-peace! You *murdered* innocent people, babies in their beds!"

"That hardly sounds like the words of a loyal subject—"

"Loyal my ass! *They* deserved my loyalty—all *you* should get is the contempt of every honest man in this town! We're the ones who're gonna suffer because of what you just did! *You broke your sworn word, you bastard!*" Bound hands or not, Kevin lunged for the two of them—

His arms were caught and blows rained down on his head and shoulders. Still he fought, screaming obscenities, and only being clubbed half-unconscious kept him from getting to the oathbreakers and tearing their throats out with his teeth.

When he stopped fighting, he was thrown back at Howard's feet. He lay only half-conscious on the cold stone floor, and through a mist of dancing sparks could see that Howard was purple again.

"Take him out and make an example of him," the patricide howled. "Burn him—hang him—tear his guts out!"

"No—" Willum laid a restraining hand on his ruler's arm. "Not a good idea—you *might* make him a martyr for those who would doubt you. No, I have a better idea. Did we get the horse barbarians as well? I seem to remember that you ordered them to be taken."

The new King regained his normal coloring. "Only the boy," Howard pouted, calming. "The girl managed to get herself killed. Damn! I *wanted* that little bitch! I thought about having the boy gelded and sold—"

"Good, do that. We'll put it out that it was the horse barbarians that killed the traders—and that the smith conspired with them to raid both the traders and the town. We'll have it that the boy confessed. I'll have my men start passing the word. Then, by afternoon when the story is spreading, we'll put this fool and his family out of the gates—banish them. The barbarians aren't likely to let him live long, and they certainly aren't likely to give an ear to any tales he might tell."

Howard nodded, slowly. "Yes—yes, indeed! Willum, you are going to go far in my service."

Willum smiled, his eyes cast humbly down. From his vantage point on the floor, Kevin saw the balefire he thought he'd glimpsed leap into a blaze before being quenched. "I always intended to, my lord."

Chali crept in to the remains of the camp in the gray light before dawn and collected what she could. The wagons were charred ruins; there were no bodies. She supposed, with a dull ache in her soul, that the murderers had dragged the bodies off to be looted and burned. She hoped that the *mule* would haunt their killers to the end of their days—

There wasn't much left, a few bits of foodstuff, of clothing, other oddments—certainly not enough to keep her through the winter—but then, she would let the winter take care of itself. She had something more to concern her.

Scrabbling through the burned wood into the secret compartments built into the floor of every *vurdon*, she came up with less of use than she had hoped. She had prayed for weapons. What she mostly found was coin; useless to her.

After searching until the top of the sun was a finger's length above the horizon and dangerously near to betraying her, she gave up the search. She *did* manage to collect a bow and several quivers' worth of arrows—which was what she wanted most. Chali had been one of the best shots in the *kumpania.* Now the *Gaje* would learn to dread her skill.

She began her one-person reign of terror when the gates opened in late morning.

She stood hidden in the trees, obscured by the foliage, but well within bowshot of the gates, an arrow nocked, a second loose in her fingers, and two more in her teeth. The stallion stood motionless at her side. She had managed to convince the creatures of the woods about her that she was nothing to fear—so a blackbird sang within an arm's length of her head, and rabbits and squirrels hopped about in the grass at the verge of the forest, unafraid. Everything looked perfectly normal. The two men opening the gates died with shafts in their throats before anyone realized that there was something distinctly out of the ordinary this morning.

When they *did* realize that there was something wrong, the stupid *Gaje* did exactly the wrong thing; instead of ducking into cover, they ran to the bodies. Chali dropped two more who trotted out to look.

Then they realized that they were in danger, and scrambled to close the gates again. She managed to get a fifth before the gates closed fully and the bar on the opposite side dropped with a *thud* that rang across the plain, as they sealed themselves inside.

Now she mounted on Bakro, and arrowed out of cover. Someone on the walls shouted, but she was out of range before they even had time to realize that she was the source of the attack. She clung to Bakro's back with knees clenched tightly around his barrel, pulling two more arrows from the quiver slung at her belt. He ran like the wind itself, past the walls and around to the back postern-gate before anyone could warn the sleepy townsman guarding it that something was amiss.

She got him, too, before someone slammed the postern shut, and picked off three more injudicious enough to poke their heads over the walls.

Now they were sending arrows of their own after her, but they were poor marksmen, and their shafts fell short. She decided that they were bad enough shots that she dared risk retrieving *their* arrows to augment her own before sending Bakro back under the cover of the forest. She snatched at least a dozen sticking up out of the grass where they'd landed, leaning down as Bakro ran, and shook them defiantly at her enemies on the walls as they vanished into the underbrush.

Chali's vengeance had begun.

Kevin was barely conscious; only the support of Pika on one side and Keegan on the other kept him upright. Ehrik was uncharacteristically silent, terribly frightened at the sight of his big, strong father reduced to such a state.

King Howard and his minions had been "generous;" piling as much of the family's goods on the pony's back as he could stand before sending the little group out the gates. In cold fact that had been Willum's work, and it hadn't been done out of kindness; it had been done to make them a more tempting target for the horse barbarians or whatever strange menace it was that now had them hiding behind their stout wooden walls. That much Kevin could remember; and he waited in dull agony for arrows to come at them from out of the forest.

But no arrows came; and the pathetic little group, led by a little boy who was doing his best to be brave, slowly made their way up the road and into the grasslands.

Chali mindspoke Pika and ascertained that the smith had had nothing to do with last night's slaughter—that in fact, he was being cast out for objecting to it. So she let him be—besides, she had other notions in mind.

She couldn't keep them besieged forever—but she could make their lives pure hell with a little work.

She found hornets' nests in the orchard; she smoked the insects into slumberous stupefication, then took the nests down, carefully. With the help of a scrap of netting and two springy young saplings, she soon had an improvised catapult. It wasn't very accurate, but it didn't have to be. All it had to do was get those nests over the palisade.

Which it did.

The howls from within the walls made her smile for the first time that day.

Next she stampeded the village cattle by beaming pure fear into their minds, sending them pounding against the fence of their corral until they broke it down, then continuing to build their fear until they ran headlong into the grasslands. They might come back; they might not. The villagers would have to send men out to get them.

They did—and she killed one and wounded five more before their fire drove her back deeper into the forest.

They brought the cattle inside with them—barely half of the herd she had sent thundering away. That made Chali smile again. With the cattle would come vermin, noise, muck—and perhaps disease.

And she might be able to add madness to that—

Bakro? she broadbeamed, unafraid now of being overheard. *Have you found the mind-sick weed yet?*

But to her shock, it was not Bakro who answered her.

Daiv struggled up out of a darkness shot across with lances of red agony. It hurt even to think—and it felt as if every bone in his body had been cracked in at least three places. For a very long time he lay without even attempting to move, trying to assess his real condition and whereabouts through a haze of pain. Opening his eyes did not lessen the darkness, but an exploratory hand to his face told him that although the flesh was puffed and tender, his eyes were probably not damaged. And his nose told him of damp earth. So he was probably being held in a pit of some kind, one with a cover that let in no light. Either that, or it was still dark—

Faint clanks as he moved and his exploring fingers told him that chains encircled his wrists and ankles. He tried to lever himself up into a sitting position, and quickly gave up the idea; his head nearly split in two when he moved it, and the bones of his right arm grated a little.

He started then to mindcall to Dahnah—then he remembered.

Hot, helpless tears burned his eyes; scalded along the raw skin of his face. He didn't care. *Wind—oh Wind.*

For he remembered that Dahnah was dead, killed

defending two of the trader's tiny children. And uselessly, for the children had been spitted seconds after she had gone down. She'd taken one of the bastards with her though—and Stubtail had accounted for another before they'd gotten him as well.

But Daiv couldn't remember seeing Brighttooth's body—perhaps the other cat had gotten away!

He husbanded his strength for a wide-beam call, opened his mind—

And heard the stranger.

Bakro? came the voice within his mind, strong and clear as any of his kin could send. *Have you found the mind-sick weed yet?*

He was so startled that he didn't think—he just answered. *Who are you?* he beamed. *Please—who are you?*

Chali stood, frozen, when the stranger's mind touched her own—then shut down the channel between them with a ruthless, and somewhat frightened haste. She kept herself shut down, and worked her way deeper into the concealment of the forest, worming her way into thickets so thick that a rabbit might have had difficulty in getting through. There she sat, curled up in a ball, shivering with reaction.

Until Bakro roused her from her stupor with his own insistent thought.

I *have found the mind-sick weed,* drabarni, *and something else as well.* She still felt dazed and confused. *What* she replied, raising her head from her knees. And found herself looking into a pair of large, golden eyes.

Kevin had expected that the Horseclan folk would find them, eventually. What he had not expected was that they would be kind to him and his family.

He had a moment of dazed recognition of what and who it was that was approaching them across the waving grass. He pushed himself away from the pony, prepared to die defending his loved ones—

And fell over on his face in a dead faint.

When he woke again he was lying on something soft, staring up at blue sky, and there were two attentive striplings carefully binding up his head. When they saw he was awake, one of them frowned in concentration, and a Horseclan warrior strolled up in the next moment.

"You're damn lucky we found you," he said, speaking slowly so that Kevin could understand him. He spoke Merikan, but with an odd accent, the words slurring and blurring together. "Your mate was about t' fall on her nose, and your little one had heat-sick. Not to mention the shape *you* were in."

Kevin started to open his mouth, but the man shook his head. "Don't bother; what the pony didn't tell us, your mate did." His face darkened with anger. "I knew Dirtmen were rotten—but this! Only one thing she didn't know—there were two of ours with the traders—"

The nightmare confrontation with Howard popped into Kevin's mind, and he felt himself blanch, fearing that this friendly barbarian would slit his throat the moment he knew the truth.

But the moment the memory surfaced, the man went absolutely rigid; then leapt to his feet, shouting. The camp boiled up like a nest of angry wasps— Kevin tried to rise as his two attendants sprang to *their* feet.

Only to pass into oblivion again.

Chali stared into the eyes of the great cat, mesmerized.

My brother is within those walls, the cat said to her, *And I am hurt. You must help us.* True, the cat was hurt; a long cut along one shoulder, more on her flanks.

Chali felt anger stirring within her at the cat's imperious tone. *Why should I help you?* she replied. *Your quarrel is nothing to me!*

The cat licked her injured shoulder a moment, then caught her gaze again. *We have the same enemy,* she said shortly.

Chali pondered that for a moment. *And the enemy of my enemy—is my friend?*

The cat looked at her with approval. *That,* she said, purring despite the pain of her wounds, *is wisdom.*

Daiv had just about decided that the mind-call he'd caught had been a hallucination born of pain, when the stranger touched him again.

He snatched at the tentatively proffered thought-thread with near-desperation. *Who are you?* he gasped. *Please—*

Gently, brother— came a weaker mind-voice, joining the first. And that was one he knew!

Brighttooth!

The same. Her voice strengthened now, and carried an odd other-flavor with it, as if the first was somehow supporting her. *How is it with you?*

He steadied himself, willing his heart to stop pounding. *Not good. They've put chains on my arms and legs; my right arm's broken, I think—where are you? Who's with you?*

A friend. Two friends. We are going to try and free you. No-Voice says that she is picking up the thoughts of those Dirteaters regarding you, and they are not pleasant.

He shuddered. He'd had a taste of those thoughts himself, and he rather thought he'd prefer being sent to the Wind.

We are going to free you, my brother, Brighttooth

continued. *I cannot tell you how, for certain—but it will be soon; probably tonight. Be ready.*

It was well past dark. Chali, aided by Bakro, reached for the mind of Yula, the cleverest mare of the Rom herd. Within a few moments she had a good idea of the general lay of things inside the stockaded village, at least within the mare's line-of-sight—and she knew *exactly* where the Horseclans boy was being kept. They'd put him in an unused grain pit a few feet from the corral where the horses had been put. Yula told Chali that they had all been staying very docile, hoping to put their captors off their guard. *Well done!* Chali applauded. *Now, are you ready for freedom? More than ready,* came the reply. *Do we free the boy as well?* There was a definite overtone to the mare's mind-voice that hinted at rebellion if Chali answered in the negative.

Soft heart for hurt colts, hmm, elder sister? Na, we free him. How is your gate fastened? Contempt was plain. *One single loop of rawhide! Fools! It is not even a challenge!*

Then here is the plan. . . .

About an hour after full dark, when the nervous guards had begun settling down, the mare ambled up to the villager who'd been set to guard the grain pit.

"Hey old girl," he said, surprised at the pale shape looming up out of the darkness, like a ghost in the moonlight. "How in hell did *you* get. . . . "

He did not see the other, darker shape coming in behind him. The hooves of a second mare lashing into the back of his head ended his sentence and his life.

At nearly the same moment, Brighttooth was going over the back wall of the stockade. She made a run at the stallion standing rock-steady beneath the wall, boosting herself off the scavenged saddle Bakro wore. There was a brief sound of a scuffle; then the cat's thoughts touched Chali's.

The guard is dead. He tasted awful.

Chali used Bakro's back as the cat had, and clawed her own way over the palisade. She let herself drop into the dust of the other side, landing as quietly as she could, and searched the immediate area with mind touch.

Nothing and no-one.

She slid the bar of the gate back, and let Bakro in, and the two of them headed for the stockade and the grain-pits. The cat was already there.

If it had not been for the cat's superior night-sight, Chali would not have been able to find the latch holding it. The wooden cover of the pit was heavy; Chali barely managed to get it raised. Below her she could see the boy's white face peering up at her, just touched by the moonlight.

Can you climb? she asked.

Hell, no, he answered ruefully.

Then I must come down to you.

She had come prepared for this; there was a coil of scavenged rope on Bakro's saddle. She tied one end of it to the pommel and dropped the other down into the pit, sliding down to land beside the boy.

Once beside him, she made an abrupt reassessment. *Not* a boy. A young man; one who might be rather handsome under the dirt and dried blood and bruises. She tied the rope around his waist as he tried, awkwardly, to help.

From above came an urgent mind-call. *Hurry,* Brighttooth fidgeted. *The guards are due to report and have not. They sense something amiss.*

We're ready, she answered shortly. Bakro began backing, slowly. She had her left arm around the young man's waist, holding him steady and guiding him, and held to the rope with the other, while they "walked" up the side of the pit. It was hardly graceful—and Chali was grateful that the pit was not too deep—but at length they reached the top. Her shoulders were screaming in agony, but she let go of

him and caught the edge with that hand, then let go
of the rope and hung for a perilous moment on the
verge before hauling herself up. She wanted to lie
there and recover, but there was no time—

*They have found the dead one! Texal o rako lengo
gortiano!* she spat. The young man was trying to get
himself onto the rim; she grabbed his shoulders while
he hissed softly in pain and pulled him up beside her.
What? he asked, having sensed something.

No time! she replied, grabbing his shoulder and
shoving him at Bakro. She threw herself into the
saddle, and wasted another precious moment while
Bakro knelt and she pulled at the young man again,
catching him off-balance and forcing him to fall face-
down across her saddle-bow like a sack of grain.
NOW, my wise ones! NOW!

The last was broad-beamed to all the herd—and
even as the perimeter guards began shouting their
discovery, and torches began flaring all over the
town, the Rom horses began their stampede to
freedom.

The cat was already ahead of them, clearing the way
with teeth and flashing claws; her task was to hold the
gate against someone trying to close it. Chali clung to
Bakro's back with aching legs—she was having her
hands full trying to keep the young man from falling
off. He was in mortal agony, every step the stallion took
jarring his hurts without mercy, but he was fastened
to her leg and stirrup-iron like a leech.

The herd was in full gallop now—sweeping everything and everyone aside. There was only one thing
to stop them.

The narrowness of the postern gate—only three
horses could squeeze through at any one time. If
there was anyone with a bow and good sense, he
would have stationed himself there.

Chali heard the first arrow. She felt the second hit
her arm. She shuddered with pain, ducked, and

spread herself over the body in front of her, trying to protect her passenger from further shots.

Bakro hesitated for a moment, then shouldered aside two mules and a donkey to bully his own way through the gate.

But not before Chali had taken a second wound, and a third, and a fourth.

"I'll say this much for you, Dirtman, you're stubborn." The Horseclan warrior's voice held grudging admiration as it filtered out of the darkness beside Kevin. He had been detailed to ride at the smith's left hand and keep him from falling out of his saddle. He had obviously considered this duty something of an embarrassing ordeal. Evidently he didn't think it was anymore.

Kevin's face was white with pain, and he was nearly blind to everything around him, but he kept his seat. "Don't call me that. I told you—after what they did to my blood-brothers, *I'm not one of them.* I'm with you—all the way. If that means fighting, I'll fight. Those oathbreaking, child-murdering bastards don't deserve anything but a grave. They ain't even human anymore, not by my way of thinking."

That was a long speech for him, made longer still by the fact that he had to gasp bits of it out between flashes of pain. But he meant it, every word—and the Horseclansman took it at face value, simply nodding, slowly.

"I just—" A shout from the forward scout stopped them all dead in their tracks. The full moon was nearly as bright as day—and what it revealed had Kevin's jaw dropping.

It was a mixed herd of horses, mules and donkeys—all bone-weary and covered with froth and sweat, heads hanging as they walked. And something slumped over the back of one in the center that gradually revealed itself to be two near-comatose

people, seated one before the other and clinging to
each other to keep from falling of the horse's saddle.
The clan chief recognized the one in front, and slid
from his horses's back with a shout. The herd
approaching them stopped coming, the beasts moving only enough to part and let him through.

Then Kevin recognized the other, and tumbled off
his horse's back, all injuries forgotten. While the clan
chief and another took the semi-conscious boy from
the front of the saddle, cursing at the sight of the
chains on his wrists and ankles, it was into Kevin's arms
that Chali slumped, and *he* cursed to see the three
feathered shafts protruding from her leg and arm.

Chali wanted to stay down in the soft darkness,
where she could forget—but They wouldn't let her
stay there. Against her own will she swam slowly up
to wakefulness, and to full and aching knowledge of
how completely alone she was.

The *kumpania* was gone, and no amount of vengeance would bring it back. She was left with nowhere
to go and nothing to do with her life—and no one
who wanted her.

No-Voice is a fool, came the sharp voice in her
head.

She opened her eyes, slowly. There was Brighttooth, lying beside her, carefully grooming her paw.
The cat was stretched out along a beautifully tanned
fur of dark brown; fabric walls stretched above her,
and Chali recognized absently that they must be in
a tent.

How, a fool? asked a second mind-voice; Chali saw
the tent-wall move out of the corner of her eye—
the wall opened and became a door, and the young
man she had helped to rescue bent down to enter.
He sat himself down beside the cat, and began
scratching her ears; she closed her eyes in delight and
purred loudly enough to shake the walls of the tent.

Chali closed her eyes in a spasm of pain and loss; their brotherhood only reminded her of what she no longer had.

I asked you, lazy one, how a fool?

Chali longed to be able to turn her back on them, but the wounds in her side made that impossible. She could only turn her face away, while tears slid slowly down her cheeks—as always, soundlessly.

A firm, but gentle hand cupped her chin and turned her head back toward her visitors. She squeezed her eyes shut, not wanting these *Gaje* to see her loss and her shame at showing it.

"It's no shame to mourn," said the young man aloud, startling her into opening her eyes. She had been right about him—with his hurts neatly bandaged and cleaned up, he *was* quite handsome. And his gray eyes were very kind—and very sad.

I mourn, too, he reminded her.

Now she was even more ashamed, and bit her lip. How could she have forgotten what the cat had told her, that he had lost his twin—lost her in defending *her* people. *For the third time, how a fool?*

Brighttooth stretched, and moved over beside her, and began cleaning the tears from her cheeks with a raspy tongue. *Because No-Voice forgets what she herself told me.*

Which is?

The enemy of my enemy is my brother.

My friend. *I said, the enemy of my enemy is my friend,* Chali corrected hesitantly, entering the conversation at last. *Friend, brother, all the same,* the cat replied, finishing off her work with a last swipe of her tongue. *Friends are the family you choose, not so? I—*

"You're not gonna be alone, not unless you want to," the young man said, aloud. "Brighttooth is right. You can join us, join any family in the clan you want. There ain't a one of them that wouldn't reckon themselves proud to have you as a daughter and a sister."

There was a certain hesitation in the way he said "sister." Something about that hesitation broke Chali's bleak mood.

What of you? she asked. *Would you welcome me as a sister?*

Something— he sent, shyly, *—maybe—something closer than sister?*

She was so astonished that she could only stare at him. She saw that he was looking at her in a way that made her very conscious that she *was* sixteen winters old—in a way that no member of the *kumpania* had ever looked at her. She continued to stare as he gently took one of her hands in his good one. It took Brighttooth to break the spell.

Pah—two-legs! she sent in disgust. *Everything is complicated with you! You need clan; here is clan for the taking. What could be simpler?*

The young man dropped her hand as if it had burned him, then began to laugh. Chali smiled, shyly, not entirely certain she had truly seen that admiration in his eyes—

"Brighttooth has a pretty direct way of seein' things," he said, finally. "Look, let's just take this in easy steps, right? *One,* you get better. *Two,* we deal with when you're in shape t' think about."

Chali nodded.

Three—you'll never be alone again, he said in her mind, taking her hand in his again. *Not while I'm around to have a say in it. Friend, brother—whatever. I won't let you be lonely.*

Chali nodded again, feeling the aching void inside her filling. Yes, she would mourn her dead—

But she would rejoin the living to do so.

Bibliography

Arrows of the Queen *(DAW)*
Arrow's Flight *(DAW)*
Arrow's Fall *(DAW)*
Oathbound *(DAW)*
Oathbreakers *(DAW)*·
Magic's Pawn *(DAW)*
Magic's Promise *(DAW)*
Magic's Price *(DAW)*
Reap the Whirlwind, *with C. J. Cherryh (Baen)*
Knight of Ghosts and Shadows, *with Ellen Guon (Baen)*
By the Sword *(DAW)*
Summoned to Tourney, *with Ellen Guon, (Baen)*
Winds of Fate *(DAW)*
Winds of Change *(DAW)*
Winds of Fury *(DAW)*
The Elvenbane, *with Andre Norton (TOR)*
Bardic Voices One: The Lark and the Wren *(Baen)*
Bardic Voices Two: The Robin and the Kestrel *(Baen)*
The Eagle and the Nightingales *(Baen)*
Cast of Corbies, *with Josepha Sherman (Baen)*
Born to Run, *with Larry Dixon (Baen)*
Wheels of Fire, *with Mark Shepherd (Baen)*
When the Bough Breaks, *with Holly Lisle (Baen)*
Chrome Circle, *with Larry Dixon (Baen)*

The Ship Who Searched, *with Anne McCaffrey (Baen)*
Castle of Deception, *with Josepha Sherman (Baen)*
Fortress of Frost and Fire, *with Ru Emerson (Baen)*
Prison of Souls, *with Mark Shepherd (Baen)*
Wing Commander: Freedom Flight, *with Ellen Guon (Baen)*
If I Pay Thee Not In Gold, *with Piers Anthony (Baen)*
The Black Gryphon, *with Larry Dixon (DAW)*
The White Gryphon, *with Larry Dixon (DAW)*
The Silver Gryphon, *with Larry Dixon (DAW)*
Sacred Ground *(TOR)*
Burning Water *(TOR)*
Children of the Night *(TOR)*
Jinx High *(TOR)*
Darkover Rediscovery, *with Marion Zimmer Bradley (DAW)*
Storm Warning *(DAW)*
Storm Rising *(DAW)*
Storm Breaking *(DAW)*
Elvenblood, *with Andre Norton (TOR)*
Tiger Burning Bright, *with Marion Zimmer Bradley and Andre Norton (Avonova)*
The Fire Rose *(Baen)*
The Firebird *(TOR)*
Four and Twenty Blackbirds *(Baen)*

MERCEDES LACKEY

The Hottest Fantasy Writer Today!

URBAN FANTASY

Knight of Ghosts and Shadows with Ellen Guon
Elves in L.A.? It would explain a lot, wouldn't it? Eric Banyon really needed a good cause to get his life in gear—now he's got one. With an elven prince he must raise an army to fight against the evil elf lord who seeks to conquer all of California.

Summoned to Tourney with Ellen Guon
Elves in San Francisco? Where else would an elf go when L.A. got too hot? All is well there with our elf-lord, his human companion and the mage who brought them all together—until it turns out that San Francisco is doomed to fall off the face of the continent.

Born to Run with Larry Dixon
There are elves out there. And more are coming. But even elves need money to survive in the "real" world. The good elves in South Carolina, intrigued by the thrills of stock car racing, are manufacturing new, light-weight engines (with, incidentally, very little "cold" iron); the bad elves run a kiddie-porn and snuff-film ring, with occasional forays into drugs. *Children in Peril—Elves to the Rescue.* (Book I of the SERRAted Edge series.)

Wheels of Fire with Mark Shepherd
Book II of the SERRAted Edge series.

When the Bough Breaks with Holly Lisle
Book III of the SERRAted Edge series.

HIGH FANTASY

Bardic Voices: The Lark & The Wren

Rune could be one of the greatest bards of her world, but the daughter of a tavern wench can't get much in the way of formal training. So one night she goes up to play for the Ghost of Skull Hill. She'll either fiddle till dawn to prove her skill as a bard—or die trying. . . .

The Robin and the Kestrel: Bardic Voices II

After the affairs recounted in *The Lark and The Wren*, Robin, a gypsy lass and bard, and Kestrel, semi-fugitive heir to a throne he does not want, have married their fortunes together and travel the open road, seeking their happiness where they may find it. This is their story. It is also the story of the Ghost of Skull Hill. Together, the Robin, the Kestrel, and the Ghost will foil a plot to drive all music forever from the land. . . .

Bardic Choices: A Cast of Corbies with Josepha Sherman

If I Pay Thee Not in Gold with Piers Anthony

A new hardcover quest fantasy, co-written by the creator of the "Xanth" series. A marvelous adult fantasy that examines the war between the sexes and the ethics of desire! Watch out for bad puns!

BARD'S TALE

Based on the bestselling computer game, *The Bard's Tale*.℠

Castle of Deception with Josepha Sherman

Fortress of Frost and Fire with Ru Emerson

Prison of Souls with Mark Shepherd

Also by Mercedes Lackey:

Reap the Whirlwind with C.J. Cherryh

Part of the Sword of Knowledge series.

The Ship Who Searched with Anne McCaffrey

The Ship Who Sang is not alone!

Wing Commander: Freedom Flight with Ellen Guon
Based on the bestselling computer game, *Wing Commander:*℗

Join the Mercedes Lackey national fan club! For information send an SASE (business-size) to Queen's Own, P.O. Box 43143, Upper Montclair, NJ 07043.

Paksenarrion, a simple sheepfarmer's daughter, yearns for a life of adventure and glory, such as the heroes in songs and story. At age seventeen she runs away from home to join a mercenary company, and begins her epic life . . .

ELIZABETH MOON

THE DEED OF PAKSENARRION

"This is the first work of high heroic fantasy I've seen, that has taken the work of Tolkien, assimilated it totally and deeply and absolutely, and produced something altogether new and yet incontestably based on the master. . . . This is the real thing. Worldbuilding in the grand tradition, background thought out to the last detail, by someone who knows absolutely whereof she speaks. . . . Her military knowledge is impressive, her picture of life in a mercenary company most convincing."—**Judith Tarr**

About the author: Elizabeth Moon joined the U.S. Marine Corps in 1968 and completed both Officers Candidate School and Basic School, reaching the rank of 1st Lieutenant during active duty. Her background in military training and discipline imbue The Deed of Paksenarrion *with a gritty realism that is all too rare in most current fantasy.*

"I thoroughly enjoyed *Deed of Paksenarrion*. A most engrossing highly readable work."
—Anne McCaffrey

"For once the promises are borne out. *Sheepfarmer's Daughter* is an advance in realism. . . . I can only say that I eagerly await whatever Elizabeth Moon chooses to write next."
—Taras Wolansky, *Lan's Lantern*

*   *   *   *   *

Volume One: Sheepfarmer's Daughter—Paks is trained as a mercenary, blooded, and introduced to the life of a soldier . . . and to the followers of Gird, the soldier's god.

Volume Two: Divided Allegiance—Paks leaves the Duke's company to follow the path of Gird alone—and on her lonely quests encounters the other sentient races of her world.

Volume Three: Oath of Gold—Paks the warrior must learn to live with Paks the human. She undertakes a holy quest for a lost elven prince that brings the gods' wrath down on her and tests her very limits.

*   *   *   *   *

These books are available at your local bookstore, or you can fill out the coupon and return it to Baen Books, at the address below.